'It's been a while since I rea[...] an achievement. It is SO atm[...] [...] Daisy has captured west Ireland perfectly. Legend of the Selkie truly belongs in the literary category. Grainne's internal battles really drive the narrative forward. Chapter one is brilliant, such an exciting ending, and amazing imagery. I love the way this chapter seeds so much, the many differences in their personalities unfolding as the book progresses. Daisy beautifully elucidates the concept of Irish farms trapping generation after generation. There were quite a few times it gave me goosebumps – from a sense of building suspense and also wonderful descriptions.'

'Selkie is a great story in which to lose oneself. I fell in love with the stark beauty of the coasts. I very much enjoyed revisiting the area through the descriptions of the land and sea and their effects on the characters. The use of the so very sad Selkie legend as the bones of the story is wonderful. The mournful music of the folk song comes through when reading about the seals lingering longer than usual during Grainne's pregnancy. There was a wisp of fey which was just right.'

'Extremely emotional and heart-touching, I found myself crying several times. The characters were great and the setting couldn't be more perfect.'

'Wow, I'm speechless. This book was beautiful. The description of the land set the mood perfectly. It matched Grainne's cold, painful grief. What I found the most compelling was her insight. She had a few realizations that blew me away, and I had to stop and reflect on what I'd just read. An amazing book! I really enjoyed the Irish names, so I feel like I'm connecting a little bit with my heritage.'

'I really felt West Cork in my bones as I read; the atmosphere, characterisation and turn of phrase, well, they were all brilliant. The writing is so polished, I'm actually in awe. It's such a wonderful book.'

'I loved the setting, the atmosphere and the brilliantly claustrophobic lives created in Legend of the Selkie. This is a well-plotted, beautifully characterised and cleverly executed novel. I can see it sitting very successfully on a literary list. The author is obviously an extremely competent and talented writer. I'll be waiting to see it in print in Waterstones!'

'Set against the wild and rocky backdrop of the Atlantic shores on the southern tip of Ireland, this contemporary tale encompasses a deep feeling for the local environment and its people.'

Legend of the Selkie

Daisy O'Shea

Published in 2023 by Drombeg Press
Drombeg, West Cork, Ireland

DROMBEG
PRESS

Copyright © Daisy O'Shea
Second Edition December 2023
First Edition January 2022

The author has asserted her moral right under the Copyright, Designs and Patents Action, 1988, to be identified as the author of this work.

All rights reserved. No part of this publication may be reproduced, copied, stored in a retrieval system, or transmitted, in any form or by any means, without the prior written consent of the copyright holder, nor be otherwise circulated in any form of binding or cover other than that in which it is published, and without a similar condition being imposed on the subsequent purchases.

Note: all views expressed in this fiction are those of the characters, not the author. The names, characters, and incidents are products of the author's imagination. Place names are not always reflected by physical accuracy. Any similarity to events or individuals is entirely coincidental.

Cover by Daisy O'Shea,: original artwork by Dana Winder

Pronunciation & Explanation

Aidan	Ae-dan
Aisling	Ash-lee
Aoife	Ee-fa
Caitlin	Cath-leen
Colm	Coll-um
Deirdre	Deer-dra
Eilis	Eye-leesh
Eoghan	Oh-wen
Grainne	Gron-yah
Lén	Layne
Liam	Lee-um
Niall Mulcahy	Neel Mull-kee
O'Mahony	Oh-mah-nee
Rónán	Row-nan
Rón	Rone
Roisin	Rosh-een
Siobhan	Shee-vawn
Fionn Mac Cumhaill	Finn Mac Cool
Cailleach Bheara	Coll-yock bare-uh
Manannán mac Lir	Man-aan Mack-leer
Bere Island	Bear Island
Ballabuidhe	Bal-uh-bwee
Goulalough	Gool-uh-luff
Kilcrohane	Kill-cro-han
Boyeen	-een being a diminutive; boyeen = small boy.
Raths	Circular archaeological mounds, sometimes called ringforts, more likely the sites of clan or farm homesteads.
Fulachta Fia	(Full-akta-Fee-ah) Archaeological structures.
Ruaille buaille	(Roola boola). Uproar and commotion, associated with children or parties.
Selkie (or Silkie)	*a legendary creature who can transform at will between human and seal*

The Selkie

An earthly maiden sits and sighs
And, aye, she sings to a little wean
Little ken I my bairn's father
Nor less the land that he dwells in

Then a man arose all by her side
So comely fey, no mortal he
Saying give to me my only son
I'll teach him how to swim the sea

I am a man upon the land
and I'm a selkie in the sea
And when I'm far from every strand
My home it is in Suleskerrie

Traditional ballad

Writing as Daisy O'Shea

The Irish Key
The Irish Child
The Irish Family Secret
Her Irish Home (short)

Writing as Chris Lewando

Suffer the Little Children Crime Thriller Series
The Silence of Children
The Price of Children
The Loyalty of Children
The Recovery of Children

Stations of the Soul
Jessie Running
Night Shadows
Death of a Dream (Compilation)
Daemon Spawn
Dark Seer
Mendip Moon

Non-Fiction
Waymarks for Authors

Contents

Legend of the Selkie 3
   Chapter 1 11
   Chapter 2 22
   Chapter 3 34
   Chapter 4 43
   Chapter 5 67
   Chapter 6 79
   Chapter 7 96
   Chapter 8 114
   Chapter 9 122
   Chapter 10 143
   Chapter 11 166
   Chapter 12 179
   Chapter 13 191
   Chapter 14 204
   Chapter 15 214
   Chapter 16 228
   Chapter 17 240
   Chapter 18 248
   Chapter 19 260
   Chapter 20 267
   Chapter 21 275
   Chapter 22 280
   Chapter 23 287
   Epilogue 299
Writing as Daisy O'Shea 305
Writing as Chris Lewando 306

Chapter 1

'The forecast is good,' Aidan says. 'Cold easterlies, blowing in at force four, bringing a bit of a chop to the skin of the water. That's no bad thing; it brings the fish closer to the surface. We'll be out and back in no time, you'll see.'

Aidan is built strongly, his frame shaped by hard living, but he has a placid temperament and a soft way of speaking, which sets Colm, never at his best on water, at his ease. 'Best get to it, then,' Colm says, rubbing the sleep from his eyes.

They cast off the lines at Deepwater Quay, beneath the moon's cold light. The trawler pulls away from Bantry harbour, motoring gently past the towering burial grounds, where a clutter of leaning gravestones crawl up the steep slope like penitents. Colm doesn't like the graveyard, with its cold holes filled with the bones of those whose souls have apparently gone to a better place. He's not sure there is a better place, in truth.

Here, where religion is fused inextricably to myth, his birth had been attended by whispers of the fey, and somehow those distant possibilities, tales murmured over the dense smoulder of peat fires, have seeped into his soul. It's easy to believe in legend, here, in the west of Ireland, where the landscape still rings with the feats of Fionn Mac Cumhaill, and the hag Cailleach Bheara, who dropped stones from her apron onto the landscape to use as her bed.

Christ's miracles, in some distant land, in a different culture, seeped between the cracks in these ancient tales when they trickled onto the rocky shores of druidic Ireland. There, in grey monasteries on grey spits of land, men of the cloth gathered the ancient stories to their bosoms and preserved them, like jewels, binding these disparate legends into discordant union with the new religion.

Colm hasn't read all of them, but Grainne, the love of his life, has. She uses them in her stories, melding the old with the new, and they end up on TV. He's never quite managed to get involved in her series; fiction slides past him, somehow. There's too much to do in real life, what with the farm and everything. But he's so proud of her, it's hard to find the words.

Colm glances up as they slide past the shadow of Whiddy Island on slow revs, then Aidan opens the throttle, driving hard past Bere Island through the yawning jaws of Bantry Bay, and into the Celtic Sea. The diesel's growl stretches over the early-morning silence as the indistinct outline of the Beara Peninsula slips away behind them.

Colm's gaze is on the open black water, where iced tips of spume fluoresce in the white glow of a turning moon. This is the moment he loves and fears. He is a reluctant explorer, thrust by forces he doesn't understand into a hostile environment both terrifying and strangely beautiful. He glances back over the twin trail of their wake. His old farmhouse nestles out of sight beyond the cut of the Sheep's Head ridge, sitting on the edge of its scrubby acres, where Grainne will be sleeping, snuggled in their warm bed, thinking of him out here on the cold sea. He'd like to be with her right now. Instead, he's crewing on the *Faery Queen* for Aidan, along with Niall Mulcahy, a joint friend through the long school years, and Aidan's cousin, Eoghan, over from Kerry for the learning of it all.

They skirt the Mizen Head lighthouse, sleepily blinking the night away behind them. The lights on shore twinkle like stars, then are gone, leaving just the ghostly red and green steering lights of the other boats flickering in and out through a soft swell as they take a southwesterly bearing into the Atlantic. Dawn bleeds into the water as they head towards the curving horizon, followed swiftly by a full sun.

Aidan is a fisherman by trade, and Colm a farmer by inheritance, though in truth neither is a good living these days. Here, where the rocky fingers of West Cork claw towards America, he has seventy-five acres of marginal land; good for little, but they're his. Hefted firmly to the land of his birth, rather than emigrate like his forebears, he turns his hand to whatever brings in the coin. He's helped Lén shoe horses at the Ballabuidhe Races in Dunmanway, served pints at the Harbour in Baltimore, dug land drains, roofed houses, and fixed cars. Fishing is what he does occasionally, reluctantly, when his sheep, bawling into the dense air of the barns, are swelling with lambs and the grass is waiting for spring.

And in the long summer evenings, he drinks with his mates when work is done. Being sociable, *belonging*, is second only to being alive, which is why he's on the cold sea in the early morning, not his favourite occupation at any time of day. When a deckhand calls in sick, and a lifetime friend asks the question, how can a man refuse?

Aidan, up at the wheel in his yellow storm gear, whistles down and points. Colm gives a thumbs-up, slides the offending fish crates to the hatch and throws them down. He, too, is thickly layered with fleece and gumboots and waterproofs, for the wind more than anything. It can be a cold old job, out on the Atlantic, hauling in. Fishing isn't his calling, but is simply part of West Cork life, like coming home to a warm fire, a hot supper, and the loving arms of a wife; the latter still somewhat a novelty to him.

He is the luckiest man, really.

As the day rises, cold and clear, they seek the silver flicker of shoals, and finally loose the ratchets on the powerful winches, letting the nets fly. This is the quiet time before the frenzy of flapping, dying fish, and the cutting and gutting and boxing. It's now that the gossip falls and tall tales weave, as eyes focus on home or the past.

Colm and Aidan slouch companionably in the lee of the wheelhouse. Aidan is the same age as Colm, but the years on the sea make him seem ten years older, his skin toughened and ridged by the salt winds. He's picking absently at a broken nail with his knife as he asks, 'Anything new or strange?'

'Not yet,' Colm replies. 'It's early days.'

'That the seed hasn't set isn't for the want of sowing?'

Aidan casts a sidelong glance and Colm echoes his slow smile. 'You got that right.'

They've been friends since childhood, and it's no secret that Colm wants children. He's a little concerned that it hasn't happened yet, and questions whether there's something wrong with himself. He'd discovered Grainne at a time when he was wondering if he'd ever find a girl that suited, and his contentment will surely be complete when she falls into the family way. He'd love to give those local naysayers something positive to flap on about. They all said it wouldn't work: *What, her from the city, to live on a farm in the middle of nowhere? She'll be leaving as soon as she gets mud on her shoes*, they said.

But she had proved them wrong.

She's his wife of just two years and he still loves the scent of her when his eyes are closed, the warmth of her in the darkness as she responds to his caresses. He's realistic enough to know that this flurry of passion will fade to something softer, but young enough to hope it won't happen too soon.

She'll never make a farmer. Doesn't want to be one, her being an artist and all, but she's a good wife. She keeps a clean house and makes fancy London dinners, the likes of which he's never eaten before. She'll make a good mother, too. He saw it in her eyes when she'd held his cousin's baby, Morgan, on their honeymoon in Canada. And what a blast that was; the diaspora of his own ancestors arriving in droves to wish them well, gifts flying like snow. *And, oh my God, the generosity.*

Colm and Aidan fall into comfortable silence, listening to the soft chatter of the other hands.

'Mind the time when Old Liam fell overboard? But we didn't dare laugh, he was that mad...'

'Fishing's not so good now, not like it was once, for sure...'

'I heard your Julie's walking out with Chris O'Mahony, from Ballydehob?'

'Back along, we'd be finished and home in time for breakfast...'

'Jim-Joe got done for drinking and driving last week...'

'The days were when the fish would be jumping on board, there were that many...'

Rolling broadside on a deep swell, something lurches in Colm's belly, but he fights it back. He's glad it's a calm day. He has a love–hate relationship with the sea; it both fascinates him with its wild power, yet repels him with those miles of darkness under his feet. He prefers watching the sea from a distance, with good, solid rock underfoot. He's never brought himself to learn how to swim, for what good it would do if he went overboard out here. The heavy-weather gear has an incorporated life jacket with some little gadget on it which sends out a signal to say where you are, so the rescue boats can find you, even in the dark. Nifty, to be sure, but the best thing is to not be in the water at all.

For one born to a farm surrounded on three sides by salt, his fear of water is strange. He can stand on the point and revel in the storm, watching that huge expanse of water rise and beat itself to death on the barnacle-encrusted rocks, but can never as much as get his feet wet, not like the other lads who, as children, had thrown themselves off the quayside, risking their lives and the wrath of their mothers. The sea has freaked him out for as long as he can remember, and his da gave up trying to get him to swim, shaking his head, wondering where he found the courage to get washed in the mornings.

Hours later, when the sun has ridden low across the winter sky, and shadows are falling far out on the water, Colm's fingers are sore from the twine and stinking from the gutting. Although they can't see the shore, the seagulls have found them, following the trail of guts with screaming delight.

'We should head for home, lads, or the weight of it will surely turn us turtle,' Aidan says. His brief smile betrays satisfaction. It isn't always this way. The Irish waters are overfished these days, the distant fishermen in their huge boats having no concern for boundaries, or the fringe living made by individuals.

Then Johnny yells over from the *Callybird*, 'Stay on 'til tomorrow, lads? Give us a hand, and we'll share the bonus in Annie's bar.'

'Greedy fecker, John-boy. We'll hang on, but you owe us, okay?'

Aidan's response is disheartening. The *Faery Queen* is the smallest and oldest of the boats, loaded to the gunwales, ready to turn and head shoreward, but there's a code on the water, stronger than law: out together, in together. And when the fish are flying into the nets, you gather the harvest. There are many days when the lockers stay as empty as famine bellies.

Colm, looking towards home, a hot shower, and a hot dinner, resigns himself to a cold night. The comforts of home are strange to him. Having been brought up by Da alone, the novelty of having a woman in the house is still keen. It had been a man's house before, with pockets of dust, working clothes hanging in the kitchen, and dishes left at the sink. Now it's neat and clean, filled with the sunshine of Grainne's presence. She's slotted into their lives easy as a cotter pin, holding everything together, and it's the time before her that seems unreal. He doesn't know quite how it happened, but she's now central to every aspect of his life.

He spends cold hours below, huddled in his wet-weather gear, the only way to keep even a smidgen of warmth in a body, and drifts into a shallow sleep, waking abruptly to the knowledge that there's a shift in the sea's mood. She's scratching at the side of the boat, lifting and dropping it petulantly.

Aidan's head angles through the hatch. 'Sea's rising,' he says. 'Shame we didn't go back earlier. I doubt they'll get a strike now, for all John-boy's wishes.'

Colm clambers up into the chill air. The seagulls have fled, leaving a massive silence over the sullen water. Sure enough, the radio crackles. He hears Johnny's voice, distant and tinny.

'Ahoy, *Faery*!'

'Ahoy, *Callybird*,' Aidan yells back, hanging on to the wheel for support.

'Heavy-weather warning just came through. Old Tom's up for making a run for home.'

'I heard it. I'm with you there, John-boy.'

Colm assesses the peevish spit on the swell. It isn't serious enough for him to panic, and the imminent heavy weather hasn't been given a storm-name, but if there's a storm brewing in the wild depths of the Atlantic, he'll be happy to turn tail ahead of it. Theirs isn't a big commercial boat that could sit out a full-on gale; no, they'd be rattled like pennies in a beggar's bowl, him spewing his guts up, no doubt.

They double-check that everything is shipshape,

numb hands tightening the netted tarpaulins and battening the hatches firmly, then set a course to follow the *Callybird* and *Lively Lad*. He's pleased they feel more inclined to spend the night with their families than battle on in the hope of a bonus catch.

The wind is fitful now, the whitecaps slapping the boat with annoyance. There's still no gale warning, but this is the Atlantic, and she has her tempers. The engines pulse as they head nor-nor-east, the dawn obscured by the blanket of clouds now hanging low over the water.

Colm is looking towards home when Eoghan asks, 'What the feck is that?'

They look behind to see a grey curtain closing the gap between sky and sea.

'Squall!' Aidan yells. 'Hook on!'

Colm clips his safety line to a bolt on the wheelhouse and feels the boat leap forward as Aidan piles on the gas. The water ahead flattens to a menace of undulating black glass, marked only by the wake of the other two boats speeding before them. But the calm is deceptive, and as they run for home the sea rises under them as if pushed up by a giant hand. Then there's a machine-gun spatter of sharp raindrops, followed by a downpour so heavy it seems as if they are battling through the weight of the Atlantic itself.

Colm braces himself into a corner below the wheelhouse, clutching a stanchion with one hand, the hatch handle with the other, and prays to the fates, or a God he doesn't believe in. Niall leaps to help Aidan hang on to the wheel, and for a while they desperately hold course, but the sea is running faster than the propellers. Aidan screams a curse as the boat loses way. There's a mighty snap and the boat catapults around, broadsiding the following sea. Colm stares up at the slope of water; like a wall of black ice, it culminates in a hand of foam which begins to curl over them.

'Jesus Christ,' he whispers, clutching his seat tightly. Distantly, he thinks this is like that moment on a big dipper, when your carriage has chugged to the top and is just tipping over the arch, ready to fall at full speed without brakes, when you clutch your seat and try to contain the absolute heart-stopping terror of the moment, because there's nothing else you can do.

The boat shunts around again and the bow hits the dense black wall and ploughs through. Colm's hands are torn from their grip, and he flails at the end of the lifeline into the freezing shock of water.

Chapter 2

Grainne is at the harbour with Da when the boats limp in the day after the squall. Their eyes are strained from watching. It had been more than a squall, in fact. The mini tsunami had caused havoc all along the coast. A couple of deaths, loss of livestock, and severe damage to many waterfront properties came on the back of a flood no one had forecast.

As the *Callybird* and the *Lively Lad* tie up, the gathered crowd exhale soft sighs of relief. The motors cut out, and silence hangs, leaving just the gentle slap of a soft sea against the pilings. The boats are splintered, taking on water, the catch and half the gear gone. The fishermen who slump heavily to the quay are exhausted and traumatised. She stares past them, at the empty water, confused. They wouldn't have left the *Faery Queen* behind?

Old Tom, white with salt, limps up to them slowly and breaks the news. 'I'm sorry,' he says.

Then they know.

'The squall was like nothing I've seen in all my years.

We were chugging along in a stiff breeze when we saw it driving out of the west. We were fighting to get the hatches in, trying to run before it, when it hit us like a sledgehammer, bringing night on us, rain like razors, and a wall of black water. It seemed as if hell itself was rising up under us. It was all we could do to just clip on the lifelines and pray. Holy Mary, mother of God, did we ever just hang on and pray.'

He pauses, the memory riding across his face. 'Through the storm we saw the *Faery* lose way. She turned broadside then dived into the swell. I don't know what happened. Maybe her engine failed. Last I saw was her stern flagging the sky like a whale tail, then we were swept apart.'

He shakes his head, tears seeping down his weathered face, and his voice breaks. 'There's nothing could have survived that. Nothing.'

He means no one, of course.

The next day, and for many days after, Grainne watches and waits as Old Tom and a motley fleet of leisure craft go searching. He leads them towards the fishing grounds, where they trawl back and forth. She waits in a daze of disbelief as they scan for the bleep of the crew's personal location beacons. They search for bits of boat, bodies, anything at all from the *Faery Queen* to show they're in the right area, but their headphones echo with hollow white noise, and the final suspicion is that she was pushed under pretty much intact. Even now, she's probably sitting in the depths, her crew floating gently at the ends of the lifelines like bait for fishes.

It's now that memories of childhood rise to taunt Grainne, memories she had firmly buried while carving out her chosen career. Traumas had seemed so huge back then, impossible to change or solve. When her mother said her sister, Aisling, was the good one. When her father told her she'd never amount to anything, when she was expelled, briefly, from school. She'd had no notion of a future, couldn't conceive of one, but this present is so far from anything she could ever have imagined; it was like the fairy tale that had terrified her, with its witch's hut on a single chicken leg in the woods.

Aisling had been her friend, back then, her foil, the glue that held her together. She'd run to Aisling and cried when they tore up her pictures. Aisling had cried with empathy, sharing her raw frustration. At the time Grainne had thought herself abused, violated, that the tears had been grief, but now she knows they'd been tears of anger. She'd learned that grief itself brings no onslaught of tears; rather, it dredges an empty well, dragging the soul out by the roots, exposing it to daylight where it hangs, watching life unfold around it.

Time now has no meaning. Chores are performed perfunctorily, with forced dedication, every small thing reminding her with cruel precision that Colm is gone: his side of the bed unrumpled; the missing plate on the table; the shoes by the wall, still bearing the imprint of his feet; the coat hanging in the hall. There are no songs on the tip of her tongue, now, as she cooks, no moments of laughter and glorious self-congratulation as a tangled storyline suddenly unwinds into sharp clarity. Even her art, a lifeline in a strangely dislocated world, becomes static, her figures wooden; not that Nigel, the producer of her series, would even notice.

Colm's dad, Darragh - though everyone calls him Da – goes about his chores in a long silence, scarcely eating, the weight falling off him as she watches. These are strange days, filled with the unreal knowledge that Colm is dead. That is a fact as hard as facts can be, and yet there's no body, and somewhere in the realms of fantasy lies the hope that he has somehow survived – knocked on the head, maybe, not knowing who he is, picked up by a passing container ship. Stranger things have happened.

Three weeks after the disaster, the boat has still not been found, nor any part of it, and the search is abandoned, the heartless sea reluctant to give up its secrets.

Grainne stands above Goulalough, the evening buffeted by a hard, northerly wind, her dead gaze on the dark water with its distant chop of white horses. She imagines leaning into the wind's fickle arms, drifting like a blown leaf to the dark music of the swelling Atlantic, before sinking wraith-like beneath the chill waters. Is death that simple? No more thoughts of what has passed, no fear of what might be, no empty future, just the long foreverness of nothing? But the image is gone as soon as it emerges, a fantasy sucked away into the void of her mind. Even if she survived the rocks to end up in the swell, death wouldn't come easy as she clawed for air.

Was that how it had been for Colm?

By now Colm will know if there's anything beyond our world, whereas she's still floundering in the godless dark. If he were here now, he'd tell her to stop moping, get on with life. She imagines that little quirk of amusement hovering on his lips. He'd always been so sure of himself in a way she had never been, despite her façade of confidence.

Grief is selfish, Colm had told her, something for the living to indulge in. He's right about that, but she wishes now that she could believe in Heaven. It would provide some comfort. And her grief is, without a doubt, selfish. Colm is gone, but her future is an empty stretch of time, hardly bearing contemplation. A spark of anger burns behind her eyes. *How could he leave me? Did he not want me in his future?*

Maybe she should go back to London. The concept had already sneaked into her head a few times, as she went about her daily business, wondering quite what magic Colm had exerted to make her throw caution to the wind and accept his proposal.

She hugs herself against the chill, sea spume dusting her hair, the insistent Atlantic wind raising goosebumps on her arms. She shivers. She'd been born in Ireland, but had moved away, reaching for another life in

England, not realising, then, that the call across the water would be so insistent. The south of Ireland, where her mother's extended family still lives, is a place of untamed bog, howling gales and fairy mounds; a magic laced with the darker reality of oppression, emigration, and famine. In the ever-present hum of London, how had she ever imagined she could actually live here, in an ancient cottage surrounded by scrubby fields dotted with sheep? She's lonely here, on this strangely derelict patch of land, and yet, somehow, it has become home. But will it still be home with Colm gone?

Deep inside, she doubts it.

Her dreams had never included inheriting seventy-five acres of almost unfarmable land, on which in winter even the sheep decline to graze. Yet without her blue-eyed Colm, with his charm and childlike enjoyment of life, what is there to keep her here?

A hand touches her arm and she glances at her sister. They are alike enough in looks, but different in so many ways. Her sister, growing more like their mother as the years pass, is out of place and time in her city coat and inadequate shoes. Was that how people had seen her, when she first arrived?

'Grainne, come on in. You must be frozen. I've got dinner nearly on the table.'

'Go on back, keep Da company. Give me a minute. I need to be alone.'

Aisling hesitates, her brow furrowed, then steps away, as bidden.

What happened to you, Grainne? Where did you go? From the moment you met him you were different, somehow removed from me. Even when I married Brendan and had kids, you were still my big sister. When you visited us, it was as if time reversed itself. We were kids again, sisters, despite everything. You'd barge into the house with expensive, stupid presents for the kids, but since you met him you've gone away altogether, somewhere I can't follow. And now I don't know you at all. Colm took you away from us, changed you. I never liked him. He was brash and so daft. What did you see in him? You should never have come to this backwater. It's not where you belong. I think you would have realised that in the end. It couldn't have lasted, this fantasy romance of yours. Am I selfish to hope that now he's gone I'll get my sister back?

Grainne knows her sister wants to help, to do something, anything, but there's nothing she can do. Nothing can take away her grief, or the impossibly absurd guilt of being still alive.

At the mass, Da's older sister, Mary, had kindly told Grainne she was young yet, she'd get over it, she had time enough on her to find another husband, rear his children – as if that's the only reason she's on the planet! She had shivered with white rage. The only thing that stopped the fury from boiling over was compassion.

Mary, a childless daughter of the church, was as grief-stricken as Grainne at Colm's death, trying to believe God had a plan.

Grainne has heard all the well-meaning platitudes ten times over, but in all honesty, it doesn't help to know that she's not the first to lose a husband, or that there are other wives in other homes grieving right now from this same tragedy. She can't grieve for all the people she doesn't know. It's there in the news, day after day, a tide of human misery. Death steals where he will: the rich, the poor, the greedy, the saintly.

They say death is impartial, but maybe there's a hint of malicious sentience lurking there, as though his choices are not so random. Had she somehow been *too* happy? Is this a punishment? Why else would he steal her husband of two short, enchanted years? He has also stolen the dreams she had not been aware of dreaming; they crash into her mind like ghosts: her babes-in-waiting, her future, her grandchildren, her contented old age – all gone. Part of her now regrets not conceiving the child Colm had wanted so badly. But she hadn't been sure she wanted a child at all. She hadn't wanted to tie herself down until she was convinced it was right.

The wind drops into a sudden silence as the weight of night falls. In the encroaching darkness Grainne squeezes her arms around her pain; the sound she makes is inarticulate, raw. It echoes out over the bay, and in the dying light she catches the silver reflection of bobbing heads on the deceitfully still sea. Have the seals somehow connected with her primordial grief? She watches a while, then the heads slide beneath the waves and are lost. Imagining Colm's body under that oily, black mass, she can't breathe for a moment and clutches her stomach, fighting rising bile. Her vivid imagination is sometimes a curse. She knows, really, that the lonely barking cries simply signal the dying of a day as the seals wind their way to wherever seals go to rest: some wind-scoured shore or half-swamped ledge of rock, swaddled in seaweed.

When the rawness in her throat eases, she goes in to dinner, knowing it will please Aisling, and possibly Da. She's all he has left now. Not his son, but the girl his son unexpectedly discovered and brought home to brighten their lives.

And she's thinking of leaving.

They'd met at a wedding in Cork city, a distant cousin of hers marrying one of Colm's friends. They had been so instantly smitten with each other it was almost embarrassing to think back on. The vibrant, exuberant, beautiful Colm had picked her up in his capable hands and brought new meaning to an existence she hadn't realised was empty. They hadn't been able to keep their hands off each other. Now, two years later, that life sits heavy on her. Colm is gone forever, as is the whole reason for her being here. What woman anticipates widowhood when the flush of love is still warm?

*

At dinner, she sips the chilled wine and pushes the food around her plate. She's remembering Colm in those early days when they'd lain in bed, limbs tightly knitted, deliberating about their beliefs, the possibility of an afterlife, about religion and myth and ghosts and the strange science of the universe. They'd pledged then that whoever went first would somehow make contact with the one left behind. She sees now that this was a childish promise, one that transcends logic. When you're dead, you're dead. And even if there is an afterlife, wouldn't mortal promises, maybe love itself, seem insignificant and insubstantial in the realms of the angels?

She feels old, considering this youthful folly. They had meant later, some time in a distant future. Not right now, when their union was fresh and innocent, when their joint lives had scarcely begun. Had they truly believed passion could transcend the barriers of death? And had she truly considered the possibility of life after death, having always believed that faith is a crutch propagated by greedy individuals, to keep the weak in thrall.

Grainne muses that it's strange how you can be on two planes at the same time: the one where you're sitting in the kitchen talking, eating; the other where you're secretly envisaging your own demise.

The next morning, Lén waits at the head of the pitted road to take Aisling back to Cork to meet the Dublin train. He's a big man, a blacksmith and welder, dark-haired and bearded, though she doesn't know him beyond a passing hello. *The gentle giant,* Colm dubbed him. They had been buddies of a sort, by virtue of time and place. Lén was a decade older than Colm and his friends, but as he had neither married nor moved away, he'd been drawn into their circle almost by accident. It's lucky for him, Grainne thinks, that he hadn't doubled as a fishing hand that day, but it's no secret that Lén has no love for the deep sea. She recalls him joking, on the back of a huge, deep laugh: *iron is so end in my pores, it would drown me down before I could swim long enough to wash it off. No, fishing's for the brave or the foolish, and I'm neither.*

'Grainne? Did you hear me?'

She's jolted back to the present. Aisling has been with her for two weeks now, and her own family's needs beckon.

'Come with me,' Aisling cajoles. 'Brendan wants you to. He said to tell you. You mustn't be alone.'

'I want to be here,' Grainne says. 'Just in case... And right now, Da needs me.'

Before, her sister would have smacked a passing kiss on her cheek and waved a cheery hand, saying, *see you soon, I want to hear some good news!* Her sister has put on weight, become slightly matronly under that dark-haired, white-skinned colleen beauty of hers, and Grainne wonders if she's pregnant again. But now, they hug, trying to rediscover the closeness of their childhood, but it's out of reach. She presses the faint swell of her middle. For herself, good news is unlikely, now and forever.

'Well, any time, you know that, when you're up to it. Email or text or something, or I'll worry.'

'I will. And I'll visit soon, I promise. I haven't seen the kids in an age, anyway. Give my love to Brendan and the girls.'

Grainne gives a weak smile to show she's coping, but Aisling's eyes are bright with tears as she turns away abruptly and grabs her overnight case. Lén picks up the rest. His shadowed eyes rest on Grainne for a moment, but his expression betrays nothing of his thoughts. He hands Aisling up into the cab of his old truck, and Grainne watches until they fade into the haze of a soft day.

Chapter 3

Grainne is alone with Da and Colm's dog, Rusty, in the old house. It has never seemed so empty, so dark, dank, and miserable. It had belonged to Da's father, and his before him, an unexpected inheritance after all the older boys emigrated. Da, and then Colm, had been born and reared there, and it was here Colm's grandma had breathed her last.

It seemed that the O'Sullivan men were destined to outlive their wives, until Colm came home, bringing his young towny wife with him, and broke the tradition, damn him. There are times she wished she had never met him, then there would be no grief. But there would have been no magic, either.

But she's not alone, here.

Da had recently moved into the new bungalow in Bantry, but when the *Faery Queen* went missing, he moved back into the old house with no by-your-leave, saying someone had to mind the sheep. He's a dark shadow in the house, silently coming and going, trying not to interfere with her life. She wishes he'd go now, but she knows nothing of farming, and realises she's the one who should go, though she's not ready yet.

The dog Colm rescued for rounding sheep stays close by her heels, upstairs and downstairs, with patient determination, never following Da out to the fields or sheds. When they walk out, he avoids the scary sheep, sidling around the ditches, and bolting for cover when the sheep get curious. *As much use as a duck in a snowstorm.* She can hear Colm saying it now; see him bend to give the shaggy coat a hug, the image strong and clear as a painting. She still doesn't understand what he meant, but it makes her smile through her anguish. And now Rusty seems to have attached himself to her, as if sensing that his master is a long time coming home from the sea.

Long, empty days later, from the bedroom window, Grainne watches the post van lurch its way up to the cottage. The road had been metalled twenty years gone, but water erupts through it winter by winter, fighting to bring it back to the stony streambed it wants to be. There are streams both sides of the road now, flooding down from the dark backbone of the peninsula, past the tiny wreck below, which had once housed three families, and now loses a few more slates every time the wind blows. Colm had big plans to do the place up, maybe rent it out, but that's not going to happen now.

It's a harsh landscape, all right.

Keelan climbs out of the van to greet Da with a

handshake, then the two men turn as one towards Bantry Bay and grow still. Breath catching, Grainne makes her way downstairs. She doesn't want to know what news he has brought with him, but as Da says, bad news doesn't disappear for want of an airing.

Da's fathomless eyes are on her, and he doesn't procrastinate. 'They found Niall. Down the coast, by Rosscarbery.'

There's an unspoken understanding here: where one body was found, others might be soon in the finding. She wants to ask for details, but can't.

'He had his life jacket on,' Keelan says. 'That's all I know.'

She hopes Niall died in the storm, and had not lingered on, bobbing alone on the waves, dying while people were out searching.

'The funeral's to be organised once the autopsy's been done. They'll understand if you don't go,' Da says.

'I have to go.'

He nods, then adds bitterly, 'At least the Mulcahys have a body to bury.'

And no hope left, Grainne thinks. But is it hope or desperation that makes a person clutch the impossible dream?

No more bodies turn up, that week or any other week, and the inquest determined that Niall had drowned soon after going in the water, if not immediately. It appeared that his personal location device had malfunctioned, but as it turned out, that wouldn't have saved him. A joint funeral was organised for Niall and the missing boys in absentia. It was fitting, Niall's mother said, that all be mourned at the same time, and she hoped the physical presence of her son's remains would somehow help everyone to say goodbye to their own missing loved ones. She means it, too. Grainne is struck by the inbuilt decency of this small community.

The church is an unwelcoming grey building, the plain glass in its tall, leaded windows coldly impersonal, unlike the tiny English churches she has visited in her search for inspiration, with their colourful, medieval pageantry of saints and mythology.

Inside, sunlight shatters through the diamond panes onto row upon row of plain benches facing an ornate altar. Grainne feels slightly awkward, isolated by her lack of belief as the rest of the congregation moves as a single entity, standing, sitting, kneeling, murmuring mesmeric responses to the priest's words. It's like an ancient druidic ritual, she thinks. There's a pervading, hypnotic introspection to the rites that she assumes must be comforting to the initiated; to Da, too, who is going through the motions, though this is the first time since her arrival, to her knowledge, that he's entered the church.

The litany of dirges isn't relieved by hymns, for which she's grateful. How can one sing when the throat is choked with grief? But she wonders, seeing the grim faces around her, how the priest can call this a closure for the families when this is just the beginning. Their boys are gone, disappeared into the night without a farewell, and they have to carry on with a hollow space in their lives where there had once lurked the shadowy hint of a family fanning out into the future.

When the service is over, people file to the front to take the sacrament. Then, as if lightened by that valediction, they migrate between the nattering groups outside, catching up on news from relatives they haven't seen since the last funeral.

A local hall had been commandeered for a wake, and within minutes it's filled to overflowing. Voices grow loud, bursts of laughter ring out, and the gathering takes on the air of a celebration rather than the funeral of four young men'. These are people she's known by face and name for a short while, but most were closer to Colm, by kith if not kin. Some come and commiserate with her, but she's distanced, as if she's missing something, some secret code that hasn't been shared with her.

She seeks out Da. 'I'd like to go home now.'

He stares at her, and she knows he's churning it all over. Colm's strange choice of a wife, one who still works for someone in London, someone who draws cartoons for a living. She thinks sometimes that he doesn't like her, though he's never been less than welcoming. It's at times like this she wishes she knew what Da was secretly thinking.

She's out of her depth, poor girl. Damn, that's a bad comparison. But how could she be living here for two years and not know people? What's wrong with her? Didn't she want to belong, or was it Colm who kept her apart, like some precious trinket he didn't want to share? Perhaps it's my fault for not seeing, for assuming Colm knew what he was doing; as if the boy ever did. But her sitting there like a statue, the auld ones giving her the eye for not bending her knee, and smiling at her snooty mam and dad for doing what's right when their daughter can't, isn't right.

'Come on, then, let's get home. I think we've had enough, don't you?'

She's grateful that he understands.

The priest is by the door. He holds her hand a fraction too long as they leave, and she knows he means well. 'I'm sorry for your loss, Grainne,' he says quietly.

'He's not dead.'

She doesn't know where the harsh words come from, but in that instant believes them, absolutely.

The priest glances sharply at Da. 'It takes time...'

'He's not dead. I'd know it in here.' Her open hand presses her chest.

The priest falls back on platitude. 'If he's still alive in your heart, he'll always be there for you.'

'Come on, now,' Da says, drawing her away before she explodes.

*

Grainne's mum and dad follow them back to the farm, but leave within a few hours, back to Cork for the night, then back to Spain. They had flown over especially for the mass, and she understands that they did it for her, not Colm, who they didn't really know. Maybe they're trying to make up for past disagreements. If so, it's too late. Her infatuation with Colm had certainly confused them, although they seemed glad that she'd chosen a nice Irish lad, rather than one of the weird English set she'd taken up with in London, even if he was a bit young. They're no doubt wondering if she'll uproot herself again and go back to the city. She wishes she could, but the place is holding her fast in a grip she can't break.

They try, once again, to persuade her to go back with them to Spain, for a break, where some time in the sun would surely do her good, but she waves them goodbye, glad, in a way, to see them leave. They don't belong here, loud against the dark backdrop, in their expensive clothes and wafts of perfume. She feels more comfortable with Da's earthy presence than that of her own parents, who had forsaken their own culture to slowly bake their lives away under a foreign sun. As they leave, she feels they've faded to shadows of a past reality. She no longer knows them, but no longer knows herself, either.

A few weeks later, Da comes into the kitchen, stamping mud from his boots in the doorway. She's standing with her back to the fire, Rusty leaning against her leg. Da stands, facing the weather, as he asks, 'Are you going to leave, girl? I'd like to know.'

She's shocked. 'Do you want me to go?'

He strides over in stockinged feet to hug her close, pressing her face into his shoulder with his big, raw-boned hand. He smells of sheep and soap and coffee. 'Girl, I want you to stay. But you're young. Why would you want to be out here with just an old man for company?'

'I don't want to leave, Da. I need to be here. Near Colm. Near where—'

'Good girl,' he says softly. She realises he'd dreaded being left alone in the old house, permeated as it is with the past. His own wife had died when Colm was small, and now their son had followed her. Without Grainne, he has nothing.

He nods his understanding. 'But you're young, yet. If you change your mind, I'll understand. The farm can be sold. It's seen its day for this family, and I can't be keeping it up for no reason.'

No living heir, he means.

It's a strange time, living in the old house with just Da, watching winter give way to the hint of spring, accepting the slow, shocking knowledge that things are going to change again. It's as the young lambs drop into the world at Easter that she tells Da what he'd soon see for himself. They're at the big shed Colm had built with Da and Lén, just before she came to live at the farm: a huge frame of sturdy steel beams covered in green corrugated iron. The handmade wooden hurdles inside are pinned into birthing pens, the floor padded with straw. The whole place is scented thick with lanolin and blood and sheep droppings. There's a chill wind blowing from the Atlantic, but the shed is warm with bodies and the nasal bleating of lambs born hungry. Nature brings them to the teat where they tear into their mother's milk with desperate need.

Grainne feels her body ache in response.

'Da, I'm pregnant,' she tells him.

He's on his knees behind a hogget, hooking a gnarled finger behind the armpit of a hung lamb. He pauses for a second, then the sheep heaves, and the still lamb gushes out in a slither of liquid. He lifts it by its back legs, stands and swings it in an arc, once, twice. It breathes with shock, and gives a small wail. He hugs it close for a moment, thanking it for living, before putting it where the anxious mother can lick it into a ball of cotton fluff. When he turns, he has tears in his eyes. He hugs Grainne tightly, smearing her with sheep's afterbirth.

Chapter 4

'Grainne, we should go.'

Da's soft voice wafts up the narrow stairs, pulling her back into the real world. He's far more anxious about her pregnancy than she is. He thinks of it as a natural physical state, albeit a shock, but to Grainne it's a malignant tumour, like cancer, that is stealing her away, bit by bit.

She drags herself away from her drawing.

It's always been that way; when she's creating, her mind is somewhere else entirely, the self-seeded storylines breaking through the crust of her consciousness almost fully grown. Her eyes gradually draw back from the page and focus on the room. Where did it come from, this ability to envisage fantasy? An image slips sideways into her mind: herself barely six years old, listening with wide-eyed wonder as her mother reads bedtime tales of mermaids, pirates, dragons, and witches. Is the memory real? It was so long ago she isn't sure.

'Grainne?'

'Coming,' she yells.

Da wouldn't invade her work space, but she turns the half-finished image to face the desk. She's not sure what he thinks of her work, and sometimes sees him looking at her strangely. He'd probably feel more comfortable if she painted mediocre watercolours of the local scenery and sold them to American tourists, than produce storyboards for whole episodes of an ongoing TV series. It was like having a celebrity come to tea, and not knowing whether to act normally, or be discreetly sycophantic.

Comic-type illustrations are a mystery to him, like the fairy folk under the hills, avoided rather than questioned. Had he read comics as a child? Had they stirred his imagination? Or had he always been pragmatic, his feet planted firmly on the soil?

She clatters down the stairs into the real world and grabs her bag. The summer is thick and heady on the early morning breeze as he drives the old pickup down the narrow winding way towards Bantry hospital. The verges are jewelled with dew, waiting for the sun to claw the dampness from the air, but Grainne's eyes skate over the surrounding beauty as she broods over the child quickening inside her. She never told Colm's da that when she discovered herself to be pregnant, her first instinct had been to get rid of it, but she thinks he knows. He's full of care, treating her as if there was never a woman pregnant before, as if she might bend and break under the strain.

Sometimes she feels she might.

This isn't the life she'd envisaged for herself, living as

daughter to another man's father, a world away from what she had once considered the centre of civilisation.

When she'd moved from London, she'd supposed she'd still be in the loop, that friends would contact her to ask *how's it going?* from time to time, but no one did. No one does, even now. Maybe the news of a small trawler lost off the Irish coast was a newsflash, here today, gone tomorrow. They certainly wouldn't have tied the incident to Grainne, who had peculiarly upped and relocated to the back of beyond. The moment she had moved away, she'd moved out of their sphere, becoming a once-was. She recalls others now, rolling in and out of their lives, people she'd never thought to contact, as if they had chosen to move out of the loop, so it was their own fault. Now she wonders how many people had waited for her call that never came.

The people she had thought of as friends have faded to strangers who air their follies on Facebook. It's only from a distance that she's able to see how directionless that life was, how shallow. The realisation that there had been no two-way communication was sobering; everyone shouting about what they were doing, no one listening, just clicking *like* to confirm their own presence. Like a voyeur, she watches their lives spinning on without her, as they fall from one party to the next, always seeking, never finding.

Colm did that much for her – finding her so that she could find herself. Like stars from opposite ends of the galaxy, their orbits had collided, and afterwards neither of them could elucidate on exactly what had occurred. They were simply in love, instantly, without reason. To her it had been a magical awakening, like Sleeping Beauty, the kiss of a stranger transporting her into a different world, sometimes enchanted, sometimes bewildering. It didn't need to be rationalised or explained, though; just experienced. But as suddenly as their worlds collided, so they parted again, irrevocably, like celestial bodies in an ever-changing universe.

Is he still traversing his different universe, she wonders, or is death truly one long, dark night of nothingness? Whichever, she's left travelling a solitary path to a future she had never envisaged, with lonely responsibilities that scare the hell out of her, and right now, she's angry at him for leaving.

He was the one who wanted this damned child, not her. And in a way, she kept the child for him, not her.

The wail of a horn startles her as Da squeezes past an oncoming car without slowing. He knows the narrow road well, but she's unnerved and clutches the seat. Loss and pregnancy have made her more aware of her own mortality and the whole unplannedness of life.

She once thought she was in control of her destiny, but reflection unfolds a catalogue of decisions based on whims, accidents, and coincidences.

As a teenager she'd steered towards a sensible future in business; she even went for the interview at Oxford University dressed in a suit, sharply cut for a woman who meant to go places, and was offered a place. Her father was thrilled. Finally, the black sheep had done something right. He made it clear that she had a bright future in the bank, he being in a position to give her the jump-start so many others would have slit throats to get. Maybe that was the reason she opted out.

She wanted to carve her own life.

She didn't want to start her career in the passenger seat of her father's car; besides which, she wanted to study art. Her parents had been appalled. The arguments had been ferocious. No one makes a living in art, what was she thinking, throwing her career down the pan? She was being ungrateful for everything she'd been given.

She had been just eighteen when she walked out. Slamming the door behind her had been briefly satisfying, but had caused a rift in her relationship and a severe downturn in her finances. Her father had refused to support her in something so stupid, probably thinking she'd come crawling back for the luxury she was used to. This rejection merely fuelled the determination with which she smashed her way through closed doors towards the kind of success most artists only dream of. Her success, financial and otherwise, scabbed over the rift in their relationship, but never quite healed it.

Over the years, the childish fairy tale of romance became submerged beneath a rubble of broken relationships, and it was Colm who saved her, with his pure enjoyment of life and his casual dismissal of the material things she had deemed so necessary. These concepts he'd brought to her, like treasures, and she'd loved him for it. She would have followed him to the ends of the earth. Instead, she followed him to a small farm in West Cork and married him. And then he died, leaving her in an alien world, her bearings shot to pieces.

Some days she thinks of running, putting these recent years behind her, pretend they never happened. She could pick up her old life in London – the same crowd would still be there, working, shopping, drinking, and exchanging partners like used coins. She could slot back into that scene easily enough. There would be some who would never even realise she'd been absent. But those days are like old movies that churn on in the background; they belong to someone else. She's moved on in more ways than just physical distance, and there's no going back. Only forward, but where that might be, she has no idea.

Her phone beeps, and she grimaces, seeing Nigel's name on the screen. Even here and now, London intrudes.

'Sorry, Da, I have to take this.'

She puts the phone on speaker. The signal out here is tired, as though it loses impetus on the long haul to West Cork.

'Grainney, love, is that you?'

Perhaps one day he'd get her name right. 'Nige, how're you doing?'

His voice has that slight whine that means he's getting stressed. 'I'm still waiting for those outlines for next season, you know.'

'I told you you'd have them by Friday, and you'll have them by Friday. Have I ever let you down?'

There's a slight pause. His tension buzzes in her ear. 'No, but things are difficult for you right now, and we have this new kid who's pretty hot, and I just want to be sure—'

'Nige, don't you *dare* bloody give it to someone else! It's my work, my ideas, my storylines. If you renege on my contract, I promise I'll sue.'

He gives a hearty, false laugh. 'Ah, now, Grainney, darling, I was just making sure; you know how it is.'

'Everything's fine. The baby's fine. I'm fine. You'll have the roughs by Friday.'

She cuts him off abruptly, still fuming, but satisfied to have had the last word.

Everything's fine? Who's she kidding? Certainly not Da, who casts her a sidelong glance which speaks volumes. She's sorry he overhead that, he has enough to worry about.

That Nigel sounds like a proper langer. He doesn't give a toss about what she's going through. He just wants her to keep producing. And now, more than anything she needs those people to believe in her, but how long will they believe she's up to it, and how will she ever cope if they take that lifeline away? But the girl has a temper on her, and a spark. I like the way she stands her ground. It was strange, that attraction between her and my Colm. Polar opposites, I thought, but you can't second-guess where the penny's going to fall, and who am I to criticise? Sense doesn't control the heart. I should know.

At the hospital Grainne lies on the couch listening with indifference to the chatter that's supposed to make her feel at ease. Colm should be here with her, but there's a space by her side where his ghost walks. The nurse knows the story – she can see it on her face. She's heard how three fishing boats went out and only two came back. Her smile is too bright as she fusses with slime on Grainne's exposed belly and discusses progress and a future.

'It's developing well. Look, see the arms here, the heart beating, and oh, look! Do you want to know the sex, Grainne? I can—'

'No.'

Her flat denial silences the nurse, but against her own inclination, Grainne's eyes gravitate to the screen. The reptilian creature from the previous scan has morphed into a humanlike form, its limbs wrapped around a folded body under an unnaturally large head. It's a fine, healthy monster, she's assured.

Pregnant women are supposed to be happy; glowing with rosy, impending motherhood, but she hates the baby for being there, for growing steadily, weighing her down with its greedy presence. It's a cancer, an obscene joke. Cold rage washes through her, and she wishes she'd aborted it. A baby is no substitute for what she's lost.

As the nurse takes her bloods, checks her blood pressure, her heart, the baby's heart, the smell of the hospital takes Grainne back to her honeymoon in Alberta.

They had stayed with Marianne, one of Colm's many cousins. He called them all his cousins, but they were a catalogue of distant relatives who passionately clung to the legend of West Cork as their link to a lost heritage.

Marianne's husband, Wayne, had brought old wealth from a New England logging enterprise into their marriage, and the rustic and quaint log cabin Grainne had been expecting turned out to be a three-storey lodge with triple glazing, en-suite bathrooms, and a hothouse pool. Wayne had three cars, a snowmobile, and an aeroplane. Colm had roared with laughter at her amazement, and she realised he had deliberately fostered the idea that they were going to rough it.

Marianne told her that if the *family farm* in Ireland was ever sold, they would feel cut adrift, as if the diasporic ribbon, abraded to lace by time, had finally parted. But when Grainne stood on the opulent decking, leaning into Colm's encircling arms beneath the raw magnificence of the Rocky Mountains, she understood why the cousins had never visited Ireland. The place she now calls home, a grubby little cottage cobbled together out of field stones and soil on marginal land, battered daily by raging squalls off the Atlantic, would have punched a hole in their dreams. Better to leave it safely on the other side of the pond, in the idyllic past.

Those halcyon days had compressed into a roller coaster of a party, distancing her from anything that could be construed as normal. She'd had an enviable childhood, by most standards, but their time in Canada had been immersed in luxury, exotic surroundings, and an influx of visitors who could be mistaken for film stars; it was a suitable honeymoon by anyone's standards.

She had revelled in the unbridled fiction of the moment, and had sent boastful postcards back to her old buddies, but after a while the euphoria wore thin. She found herself an observer watching from the outside. Who were these people? In fact, who was this Colm she had married; this loud man-child with his youthful confidence and blarney?

He exuberantly introduced her to everyone as *My amazingly talented wife who I stole from London...* And off he'd go, shouting her praises, when he knew nothing of her work, didn't *see* it, and cared to know nothing of the life in London she had left behind to follow him. There were times she felt he did not know her at all.

More worrying, she did not know him.

At times during that strangely unsettling honeymoon, she had longed for London, where she could hide behind her vast antique draughting easel in the solitude of her flat. She'd been tempted to cut and run once more. She'd gone as far as marriage this time, but that wouldn't stop her from bolting if her sense of self were to become compromised; not after she'd fought so hard to dredge it up from beneath the layers of conventional silt that had once stifled her imagination.

Her work would sustain her as it had on those other times when relationships collapsed. When she tried to share this concept with Colm, the shadow of confusion drew itself upon his face. When he asked, would she choose her drawing over him, she realised he didn't get it at all. It wasn't a matter of choice. Drawing was a part of her, and couldn't simply be wished away.

But the most disturbing aspect of her honeymoon had been Morgan. They had gone with Wayne to collect Marianne and her latest baby from hospital. Grainne found the newborn's presence invasive. She was demanding, noisy, scented with sour milk and excrement. She screamed every time Grainne was pressed into holding her, then Colm would take her and rock her back into good humour with an instinctive touch Grainne could not – did not want to – discover in herself. She had never hankered after children, wasn't cut out to be a mother, but seeing Colm rocking Morgan in his arms, staring down at the child with an intensity that was frightening, she realised that when he had said he wasn't bothered about a family, he'd lied. Maybe he even believed it, but how long would his love last if she didn't produce a child?

In that last screaming argument with her previous

boyfriend, Andy, he had yelled that she was a stupid bitch, terrified of responsibility, that she'd end her years as a shrivelled spinster with nothing but her stupid comics to keep her company. Had he been right? She wondered now whether Colm's exuberant infatuation had caught her on the rebound, whether she had just leaped at the chance to have a different life. She's never asked herself that question before, and is scared of the answer.

A door slams, jolting Grainne back to the maternity clinic. It's a moot question now. She, who doesn't want a child, is pregnant, and Colm, who did, is dead. What a joke. The nurse has gone, and Grainne's eyes rove. The room is a fresh apple green. It's small and functional with its hospital bed, its sink and monitors and wheeled, bleeping gadgets. There's a faint hum of machinery and air conditioning. There are images on the wall of a healthy baby in its various terms within the womb, its mother's skin carved away in a neat slice like orange peel.

Grainne's imagination spikes into comic-book mode. She imagines the druid reaching his hands through the woman's belly and physically tearing the child out of her womb. The room splatters with blood, the onlookers gasp with horror, the mother gurgles horribly and dies... But why is the child so important? What does the druid want it for, to what end?

She mentally stores it for later use.

The doctor arrives, wearing his stethoscope like a

necklace. He has the sharply defined features of a man not yet padded by maturity. His dusting of stubble is for effect, but his curly hair is already receding, and his mouth stretches into a smile that doesn't reach the pale blue of his eyes. He's seen too many pregnant women already, she thinks. She wonders why men become gynaecologists, daily observing a woman's secret anatomy with clinical disinterest, monitoring the cumbersome fruits of other men's labours.

'Everything's looking good,' he says, his eyes lowered, skimming the chart.

'Define good,' she snaps.

Confusion ripples across his face at the sarcasm.

'This is Grainne O'Sullivan,' the nurse reminds him.

Grainne sees that moment of recognition; the point at which he is mentally kicking himself.

Oh, God, yes; it's the woman whose husband went down with that trawler, what was it? The Fairy Girl *or something. It was unsound, I read. Should never have been in service at all. Good job that Aidan guy died too, or he would have been up for the death of those other lads, more than likely. She doesn't seem to be too pleased about being pregnant, which seems strange. I can't work this one out. You'd have thought she'd see it as something wonderful, a new life in the wake of tragedy, but you can never second-guess how people think. I've seen it all: girls not old enough to be mothers, women who should never be mothers. Sometimes you take one look and know you're bringing some child into the world to be abused or neglected, and you can't do anything to halt the inevitable. And the fathers I see – don't talk to me about fathers. Last year I had to jump through hoops to rehome a dog from the rescue centre for my boys because I work full-time. But you don't have to be vetted to have a child. You just do what nature intends, and months later discover the cost is twenty years of aggro and blame.*

He puts gentle hands on her stomach to determine the baby's position and size, then turns to rinse the gel from his hands. The nurse hands Grainne some paper towel to clean herself, then Grainne heaves herself up and slithers off the couch. She tidies her shirt over the elasticated trousers. It's getting difficult to move. The tumour of life, something her eyes gloss over on other women, feels much bigger on herself. She hates it. It's a massive statement attached to her front: Yes, guys, we had sex.

'How are you coping, Grainne?' The doctor turns, newly composed.

'How do you think?'

There's a subtle pause. The nurse freezes, the doctor searches for words.

'Sorry,' Grainne says. 'It's not your fault. I'm just lashing out.'

Now his face betrays true compassion. 'Are you

seeing anyone?'

'In this state?'

'I meant a counsellor.'

'I know. I was attempting humour. No, I'm not seeing anyone.'

'You don't have to cope with this alone, there are—'

Her voice hardens. 'I do have to cope with this alone! No one can do it for me, can they? My husband is dead – drowned. I'm pregnant with his child, and nothing is going to change the facts. I'm getting on with things. I'm okay.'

He scribbles something on a piece of paper and hands it to her. 'Here's my mobile. If you need to speak to me, day or night...'

Chastened by her outburst, caught off-guard, knowing he really means it, she feels slightly guilty. She navigates back through the windowless corridors with their squares of tasteless happy art, past a man hovering over a rotary floor polisher and a couple of young orderlies wheeling a bed. From under the hump of a sheet a wrinkled, grey face with expressionless eyes stares at nothing.

Outside, she finds Da anxiously pacing the broken concrete path beneath a few sad lime trees. He looks older, these days, his jeans hanging loosely on the braces. When she first met him, she'd been amused by the checked shirt and flat cap. He was the relic of another era, a character from a black-and-white movie. He's younger than her own father, though maybe only fifteen years or so older than her. It's as though the outdoor life has hardened his skin, sucked the juice out of him. It occurs to her in a fleeting revelation that the locals would think it less strange if she'd married the father rather than the son. They probably called her a baby-snatcher behind her back.

'All's well, I'm told,' she says brightly. 'The baby is progressing as it should.'

'Good, good.' He takes her arm with old-fashioned courtesy. 'Will we go for a coffee, up at that organic place?'

She'd rather go on home, but smiles and nods.

Da obviously cares that she's well, but she guesses he cares more that his son's child is swelling inside her; his grandchild, his blood. An unexpected hand reaching out to drag him into a future he'd given up on. She feels as though she's an unwilling incubator to Colm's seed. Perhaps when the child is born, Da will take it from her, and be relieved when she drifts out of his life.

They drive down into town, and not for the first time, Grainne thinks she should learn to drive. It was never necessary in the city, but here she sometimes feels trapped by the wide landscape with its crags and unexpected bogs, not to mention Da's driving being so erratic. His eyes are aren't so good, and he says it's difficult for him to see edges on anything, but he won't wear glasses; he says they just get in the way when he's working. He parks the old pickup halfway across a pavement, pulls on the brake and climbs out; whether he hasn't twigged, or is beyond caring about parking fines, she doesn't know.

I know she's thinking that one of these days they're going to take my licence from me, and then what will we do? Of course, I'd expected Colm would be here; that he would outlive me. That's what was supposed to happen. I was supposed to live in the bungalow over the other side of Bantry, and I could walk along the estuary path, past the harbour, and into the bar where I could natter with the old ones over a glass and watch the seagulls squabbling. And he'd visit, sometimes, with a brood of young, and I'd brew tea. I don't know what's going to happen now. All my years of caring and... Poor Grainne. She's more vulnerable than she lets on. I did wonder why Colm didn't take to that local girl, Deirdre. It was obvious she was infatuated with him, and this one is different enough to be foreign, but I get it now. For all Grainne's sophistication, she's an innocent, and for all Deirdre's lack of worldliness, she isn't. I wonder why Grainne's carrying the child to term? I know she doesn't want it. There was a time I was afraid she wouldn't, now I'm afraid she is. When it's born, what then? Who's going to love it, if she doesn't? I'm so tired. Tired of death, tired of life.

From a window seat in the café, Grainne watches people pass by, wondering what those expressionless faces could be hiding. She wonders what their day is like, how they feel when they get up in the morning, whether they're bored with their lives, or whether there's some trauma dogging their footsteps. Because the one thing she's learned, over the last few months, is that loss is an insidious stalker which consumes every moment of every day. She wonders whether it ever gives up.

'What do you want?' Da asks.

'An espresso, thanks. And one of those home-made scones with a pile of butter.'

He's pleased. 'Good, good. You need to keep your strength up; you're eating for two now.'

She finds herself clutching at little things, trying to keep herself from falling, but what she used to enjoy when Colm brought her here on shopping trips provides little comfort now.

When the *Faery Queen* went missing, it had been impossible to believe Colm could be dead. She'd been holding onto the dream that he would miraculously be found alive. The slow realisation that he would not had gradually formed a knotted fist in her gut. And during all the searching, the scouring of storm-wrecked beaches for the boat, for bodies, for anything at all, after all the hoping and waiting, glued to the news channel and the telephone, she discovered fate had already played its wild card.

She'd initially supposed her missed period was the result of trauma, just her body rebelling from something it couldn't cope with. She'd read about that in one of the pamphlets about coping with bereavement. Then it all fell into place. The morning sickness had nothing, after all, to do with death or bad dreams. It was quite simple: she was carrying a dead man's child.

People say she's lucky, that her baby is a miracle, a new life to cherish in the face of tragedy, but what do they know? She doesn't want to be a single mother, she wants her life back, as it was before.

She's going through the motions in a haze of doubt, sometimes even fooling herself that she's sane, that she's coping. It's at night, when she surfaces, panting, from barely recalled nightmares, that she thinks she's going out of her mind.

Sitting in a café with Da, watching the world go by, she's almost amused. What would those passers-by think if they could see into her mind, those whirling images of Colm's body, bloated, nibbled at by fish, rotting, falling apart, his white bones sinking to litter the deep ocean floor. What would they think if they knew she was outlining them onto a storyboard for the next season of *Maeve, Queen of the Celts*? It's what she does, after all: turns interesting snippets of real life into storylines. She had fallen on her feet, really, starting as an artist who make other people's storylines visible, and ending up, somewhat uniquely, as a storyline creator, too, through the creative power of her imagination.

Never before have her characters intruded into her waking day, hinting at future adventures. As the episodes fling themselves out of dark corners in her mind, she wonders if this is just her way of coping, of processing this previously unimaginable situation.

She can't recall a time, however, when she hadn't been awed by comics and sequential art. Becoming a TV storyboard artist had epitomised her wildest dreams. As a child she hadn't just devoured comic-book storylines, but had challenged each image, gauging the perspective, the overtly portrayed characterisation, the action, the whole impact. And she had drawn her own cartoon images.

She still had some of the drawings that had nearly got her expelled, ones which depicted her headmaster and teachers as zombies, becoming desiccated caricatures feeding gruesomely off the children in their care. The images had spread round the school faster than a virus, causing a riot of giggles in all the classrooms before one teacher snatched a copy from a pupil and marched it, with indignant wrath, to the headmaster. Why had none of them stepped back to wonder how a child could create such believable caricatures?

Grainne received a final warning, and the paper copies in her desk were confiscated and ceremoniously ripped, during a massive lecture on respect. She had come home from school that day to find her father had raided her room and destroyed the rest of her scribbles, as he called them. To be embarrassed so by his own daughter, and him a pillar of society!

He had no idea how hurtful that callous act had been,

or that he had planted the seed of her later rebellion. It had only been luck that a small portfolio had been in her sister's room at the time, to be rescued and hidden away.

Only now does she allow herself to see how like her father Colm was. He had expected her to 'grow out' of her art. In those last months before his death, he had hinted it was time for her to give up the drawing. He wanted her to show that last bit of commitment to him, to their marriage, and throw her past entirely to the wind. If only she would stop drawing and start a family, everything would be as it should be.

How had he not understood?

She sighs. It's only in the cold aftermath of his death that she understands they were both living a lie, or perhaps a dream. It was a time out for both of them, but she wonders now whether the marriage would have survived.

Every time she picks up her pen these days, the stark, comic-book images that emerge are of boats and waves and seaweed and storms, and things that float on the back of nightmares, as though Colm had died specifically to provide fodder for her imagination. Nigel likes her new thread and doesn't care what prompted it as long as she keeps producing, and the ratings fly.

But her head is thick with indecision.

She's always kept her options open – choosing to cut and run whenever she needs to move on. But she can't cut and run from a child. And there it is: the acceptance that this bump is something other than a tumour. It's a baby, a child, a small person that's going to grow into a teenager, an adult. She winces. The sense of responsibility terrifies her. She hadn't lacked love as a child, but it had been distant, not the hugging and kissing kind of love other families shared. Will she neglect her child, as her parents had unwittingly done in so many tiny ways? Was that why she had been so afraid of falling pregnant?

On the one hand, she had been afraid of losing Colm. She'd imagined the misty veil of their mutual passion gradually solidifying into a barrier. Maybe he'd start to wonder why he'd married an older woman, one who didn't want children, one who had maybe even reached the age where children were no longer possible. She'd envisaged the dreamy lust fading, his eyes turning to younger women, herself back on her own again, living that bright existence, pretending not to care too much about anything. But the desperate conceiving of a child to consolidate their relationship is a world away from finding herself pregnant and Colm nowhere to be found. The smell of the scones makes Grainne nauseous. She nibbles and swallows and the crumbs stick in her throat. The place is filling up, families and couples immersed in themselves. They laugh and eat as though death is far away, not realising that he sits by their shoulders, listening to their plans with a knowing smirk on his face.

All we had were two years, she thinks. Not long enough even for the marriage to settle, for euphoria to sink into complacency. He was here one day, gone the next, leaving me behind to carry his child, whose presence he hadn't even suspected. The child that's now mine alone. Da gazes out of the window. Grainne sees his mind is elsewhere.

Ah, Colm, my boy... A windy day, the two of us kicking a ball around, do you recall? The sand flew in your face, and you wiped your eyes, laughing. Then the sea crept in, closing off our small patch of beach. Your face went white. It's just a short paddle, I say. No harm done. But you screamed and screamed. Nine or ten years old, I forget now, but I had to leave the ball behind and carry you. I've never known a child be so scared of the sea. But perhaps you knew. Perhaps in some dark place in your soul you knew that the sea would one day take you as it took your mother.

Da says, 'Shall we go into town? Is there anything you want? Anything you need?'

He's hoping she'll show an interest in buying baby things, but it's early days yet. Who knows what will happen? Maybe it will be born dead. Maybe she will give it up for adoption.

'No, nothing, thanks. I'd like to go home.'

Back at Goulalough, Da goes out to check the sheep, and Grainne sits at her tiny pine desk for a while, but can't find the space her creative mind needs. She gathers up the unformed scribblings of something alien growing inside her heroine's womb, screws them up and lobs them at the bin. She misses the light in her London apartment, and her big easel with its sloping face, where she would clip the various story strands as they evolved.

Colm thought she'd got rid of everything, cleared her past life. He had little time for 'stuff', as he called her amassed treasures. Two chairs alone came with her; they had been her grandmother's, inherited when her parents left Ireland to seek the sun. The rest was an accumulation of a lifetime of trawling through antique shops with money to spare. He thought she'd put her old life out for sale, and had been thrilled at the few thousand she'd brought into the farm, like an old-fashioned dowry. Somehow the time had never been right to admit that her treasures, her *stuff*, was in storage, that she owned her apartment and had rented it out. The income was accumulating, providing the secret comfort that she could leave this life and go back to the old one in an instant. Well, except for the child.

Chapter 5

These are long, lonely days for Grainne, waiting for the baby to mature. The farmhouse is small, confining, but she's reluctant to move out into the wider world, knowing that if she ran, she wouldn't stop running until Ireland was dust on her heels. And what would Da do then?

An old song her mother used to sing comes to mind:

> *Cold the wind is blowing,*
> *angry is the sea,*
> *guard ye saints his going,*
> *and bring him safe to me...*

Only the saints didn't listen, did they?

Her mother had a fine voice and a good recollection of the songs from her childhood, but that was as far as nostalgia went. Marrying money, she'd gladly left her humble roots behind, and gathered a social life around herself like a mantle, shutting out the cold past.

Grainne and her sister had been pampered.

Their mother had taken them here, there, and

everywhere. It had been fun: the shops in Paris, the clocks in Prague, the museums, swimming pools, health spas. And so many weekends away she can't recall where or when, just a long blur of different hotels in different countries. And always they sent postcards home to their distant father. *Dear Dad, I hope you are well. We are having a lovely time...*

Aisling and Grainne had thought they were lucky. All their friends thought so, too. They were certainly privileged. Only when it all stopped, she by walking away and Aisling by getting married, did Grainne realise that the travelling hadn't been for them. They'd been trawled around in their mother's wake like matching baggage, their white skin and Irish lilt providing a key to conversation, opening social doors. Her mother had been bored with her own pampered life.

When their father took early retirement, he and their mother simply sold up and left. Then there was no big house to congregate in at Christmas, no place to run to when you needed sanctuary. The family was no more. Some other family was living there, obliterating all those childhood memories, uprooting them and hurling them on the muck heap with the unwanted garden ornaments.

And yet Grainne knows the huge sense of loss that belts her from time to time isn't for the house or the past or her parents, but for the childhood she might have had. The one where Mam bakes cakes and Dad brings belly laughs home from work. They never speak of it, but

Aisling's overbearing attention to her own children's needs suggests that she feels the same.

Grainne struggles up the hill to stare out over the water. It sleeps, tranquil, under the sun, its surface a polished mirror of the sky. When she first came here the sea amazed her; she loved its moods and tempers, but she sees it now as the wolf of fable that lures the unwary onto its back with the promise of sanctuary, only to snatch them into its jaws when it quickens to hunger. The surf is no longer evocative of pretty white horses, or unicorns, but of white teeth exposed through the stretched lips of an evil smile.

The nurse said the baby would save her, but she knows otherwise. It's a burden on top of grief. She's a reluctant mother, and has secretly wished for a spontaneous abortion, but wishes are fickle breezes, and she's fast reaching term. Even if the baby comes early now, it would no doubt survive.

With Colm gone there's little to keep her in this tiny community where she doesn't belong and never felt truly welcomed. Only Colm's dad. And that's the problem.

When she'd arrived, he'd half moved out to the bungalow he'd been building, existing on the periphery of their marriage: a stranger, culturally removed from everything she'd ever known, driving up to the farm on a daily basis, like some paid hand. Yet now, sharing the same grief and the same house binds them closer. She feels more affection towards Da than she ever felt for her own father, who had been a distant figure, always at work. She had been a little jealous of Colm's closeness with Da, and had more than once wished he would get out of their lives, but she feels guilty for that now, with this new tragedy on top of the old. He'd known grief enough, with his own wife dying young, leaving him to bring up Colm on his own. He seems to be diminishing every day, as though he's reaching towards death deliberately to be with his wife and child.

She hears him coming up behind her, his breath laboured against the steep climb. Perhaps he has some illness he isn't admitting to.

'Grainne, are you all right, girl?'

'I'm fine,' she says, knowing he's not fooled.

Loss, she realises, has finely tuned his radar. He knows, more than any other, that she's not all right, and he's afraid she will do something awful, like kill herself, and the baby. But if she'd been going to do that it would have been when the seed had been no more than a whisper, when the claws of grief had ripped her heart.

Now, she is simply waiting. They walk back together and she feels a flood of compassion for this man who is not her father. He lost his wife, then his son, and will eventually lose his daughter-in-law, for this lonely isolation will destroy her.

And what of the child?

Will it stay here with Da, or go with her? And if she leaves, where will she go? Keeping the apartment in

London had been a safety net, a secret comfort, but she has gradually come to realise that going back would be a mistake. The old life had been a different time, not one she wants to go back to. Where she is now is another stepping stone on a journey into the unknown. Maybe that's the point, that the destination isn't as important as the journey, and her leap of faith with Colm had been no more than a desire to get on the next flight to who-knows-where. She could go anywhere in the world, except that there's something holding her to Ireland. A tie she can't quite grasp, an umbilical cord that refuses to be severed.

Her father was born in Dublin of parents who had already clawed their way to a better income, but her mother had come from West Cork farming stock and could trace her ancestors back into the era of famine. The echo of hardship resonates through generations. Though her mother knew the old songs, and had once played a bit of a tune on the tin whistle, she'd looked resolutely towards the future. A strong woman, she had deliberately turned her back on the old ways, entwined as they were with tragedy, peopled with lost loves and lost lives. She thinks her choice to retire to the south of Spain, where rain is sparse and the sun burns the land daily, was a deliberate and final separation from their Irish past.

But maybe it's the past that Grainne is seeking. Here, in the wildest corner of Ireland, she feels as though the twilight world of legend has taken her by the hand to join an endless line of long-dead women forever wailing their grief. And yet, somehow, they are her past, too.

Marie arrives from the shop in Kilcrohane, bringing Da's bread and milk, as she has since Colm died, and gifts for the baby from the wider community; people Grainne doesn't know. Some small part of her resents the attention. If she hadn't been Colm's wife, if this were not his baby, would they care? Yet another part of her understands that there's compassion in people that isn't obvious until tragedy strikes. She shouldn't be knocking Marie's kindness.

'Grainne. You're looking well, love.'

'I'm okay.'

Marie's smile is motherly. 'You're showing just fine, now. It won't be long, then you'll be so busy you won't have time to mope, you'll see.'

Mope? What an inadequate word for what she's experiencing. But Marie means well.

Well, she got her comeuppance, the auld slag. Spent her time whoring in London, then snares young Colm, that my own Deirdre was hankering after, and brings him round her thumb. And she ten years older than him, almost past her child-bearing days. Married him for the farm, no doubt. Deirdre told me Da had already made it over to Colm, to avoid the inheritance tax. She'll probably just sell up now. Maybe won't even wait till Darragh's in his grave,

God help him. Artist, he calls her. Artist, my arse. There are artists aplenty in Cork, their work scattered through the pubs and restaurants. But did ye ever see the girl so much as lift a paintbrush?

'I brought a cake up from Sara, and Lén is going to bring up a cot, later. He made it. Out of respect.'
Respect for the dead, not the living, no doubt.
'Will you stop for a cup and cake?' she asks Marie. 'There's no way Da and I can eat all that on our own.'
'No, love, I'm doing a delivery round. I just popped in to see if you're wanting for anything.'
'We're fine, thanks.'
'Well, if there's anything you need, Grainne, love, just give us a call. Either meself or Jerry will bring it out. Darragh's looking weary these days, to be sure, and that's not a wonder. You look after Colm's little one, mind. Well, I'll be going, now, so.'
'Well, thanks again.'
Grainne watches her little van bump down the muddy track and disappear from sight. People are kinder than they had been before. They visit with cakes, invitations, and good intentions, pulling her fractionally closer towards their community. As Colm's wife, she'd been tolerated, not quite treated as a blow-in, but not altogether *belonging*, but even now, she hasn't truly been accepted. Marie said it herself without realising: Colm's child will belong, but she never will.

Later, Lén's truck growls up the rutted driveway. He'd been one of Colm's drinking buddies, but she doesn't know him any more than she knew the rest of the crowd. To her, he seems a bit of a loner, not quite in with the old ones, nor fitting in with the crowd of youths who strut their stuff for the tourists, hoping to get lucky. She's seen him observe their posturing, amusement on his dark, bearded face. She's never seen him with a woman, and wonders if he's gay.

They had been unlikely drinking buddies: Colm, slender and fair, and quick with the banter; Lén, ten years his senior, a big bull of a man, dark and taciturn. She's always been intimidated by big, hairy men, as though there's a remnant of primal aggression lurking there, ready to explode at any moment. But she knows he's not stupid. He has a degree in something-or-other, and from what Colm said, he's pretty switched on about all sorts of issues, particularly those which concern the earth and its troubled prospects.

There's a hesitant rap at the open back door, and Lén bends his head to peer in. 'I brought the crib,' he says. 'Did Marie mention it? Where do you want it put?'

'Marie said you'd be along. You're very kind. Would you mind carrying it upstairs? I'd rather Da didn't have to.'

Rusty follows them upstairs, sniffing the scented wood, giving it a seal of approval. Lén pats him absently on the head. It's only when he's put it in her room that she sees its beauty: the clean joints, the polished wood rails, the mechanism that allows it to rock gently within the frame, as he demonstrates.

'You made this?'

Her eyes hit his in astonishment, and he holds her gaze. 'Colm told me you liked things that were handmade. It's a bit rough and ready. You've done this room up nice, sort of summery and bright. That's good for a child to grow up with.'

She feels uncomfortable showing this man into what had been their bedroom, where they had indulged in sleepy sex, where their child had been conceived. But there's no hint of innuendo in his voice, and his eyes rove with innocent interest. 'He'll be in here with me for a bit,' she explains, 'but I'm doing up the little bedroom for him.'

'Him?'

'Scans are good these days. I couldn't help noticing, even when I didn't want to know.'

He's amused. 'And proportionally speaking, a boy has to grow to fit those bits, like puppies born with big feet.'

She lifts one brow in query.

'I've got two sisters and half a dozen nieces and nephews. I've changed a few nappies in my time.'

She's entranced by the image of his dark hands powdering soft baby skin. 'And here's me with no experience at all. It was Colm who was the authority on babies.'

Colm, an authority on babies? Good God, girl, he was a child himself who never grew up. Every day was Christmas. God only knows how he managed to snare himself a girl with a head on her shoulders, him with his pranks and his daydreaming. Sure, it was a sad day for us all when he drowned, but perhaps you'll never have to learn that it wasn't going to last. Oh, he wasn't unfaithful, but he would have been, sooner or later, when the fancy took him, when the novelty of his London prize wore off. What a pickle you've left behind for others to cope with, Colm, eh? Her with your child, and you gone. Will she stay, or will she leave, I wonder? If she takes the child away, that will be the death of Darragh, for sure.

Grainne follows him back down the narrow stairs. 'Will you stay for coffee? Marie brought over a massive cake earlier.'

'Well, I can't refuse cake, now, can I?'

He's silent for a moment while she clatters around, putting the kettle on the range and pulling mugs from the rack. The sun is high, lighting the kitchen briefly, highlighting the dirt on the floor. She feels embarrassed, as though she should have been a more diligent housewife.

'You're doing well, girl, coping. It's lonely enough out here.'

'I didn't mind that before, but now...'

She stops as Da comes in, stamping his boots on the step. The men reach out and clasp hands briefly.

'Saw the truck outside,' Da says.

'Yep, she's still going. More welds than original metal, these days. How're you managing?'

'Getting by, boy, getting by.'

Da cracks open the door on the stove, and they bask in the flickering heat, hands wrapped around mugs. Summer or winter, the range takes the chill off the room. There's talk of sheep and weather, then Lén leans the chair back on two legs, just as Colm used to. It creaks alarmingly as he stretches and yawns before thumping it back down and heaving himself to his feet.

'I should be going. Ben O'Leary wants his ponies shod for the trotting.'

Grainne is surprised. 'You still shoe horses?'

He gives a slow smile. 'Not so often, these days, but I keep my hand in. I started out with smithing. My father was a blacksmith, God rest him, and his father before him. I still have the old forge, but these days I mostly work out of the back of the van. There's not so much call for it, though. Now, I'd best be on my way.' He stands, and slides the chair under the table. Colm had never learned that trick. 'Darragh, see you later.'

Lén puts a heavy hand briefly on her shoulder. 'That was grand cake, thanks. You're doing all right, girl. Colm would be proud.'

She's startled, but though it's the first time they've exchanged more than a few words, somehow the familiarity doesn't annoy her.

Da stands up to see him out, and their voices recede.

'There's a couple of gates need the bolts fixing, if you have a spare minute.'

'Sure, Darragh. Can it wait a couple of days?'

'Of course. What's baler twine for, anyway?'

'Sure, I mind the time Colm said that, and do ye recall the ruction when the sheep went east?'

Their retreating laughter lifted the moment.

Chapter 6

Grainne decides to have the child at home, in defiance of her sister, who, being a mother twice over, thinks she knows everything. Aisling had been perceived as a sensitive child, taking hard the verbal knocks that other children barely noticed. But frustration had hidden an inherent strength of character. She had simply wanted to be liked, which had been more important to her than academic qualifications. She'd achieved only average marks, and was favoured by their father as the good and obedient daughter. Unlike Grainne, a high achiever who had always been in some trouble or other. Grainne had been a good big sister throughout the school years, protecting Aisling with words and even fists where necessary, but no one thought to see beyond the aggression to the needy child inside who had wanted someone to help her understand why she didn't fit in.

At nineteen years of age, Aisling had surprised her parents by announcing she had been seeing an older man, and was going to marry him. Even Grainne had been taken aback, thinking that she and her sister had always shared everything, gossiping under the bedcovers into the night well into their teens.

In the end their parents had been brought around by the fact that Brendan, firmly ensconced in Dublin's world of international finance, could support his intended wife and children in some style. Which, Grainne thinks, on the back of an internal sneer, had impressed their father no end.

But her relationship with Aisling had changed in that moment. Free of parental control and provided with all the social status she could handle; Aisling had blossomed into a veritable harridan. And now she's given herself the right to talk down to Grainne, who, for goodness' sake, is still her older sister, and has carved a career path for herself using her own talent rather than marrying it. But perhaps that's an unfair reflection of her sister.

When Aisling phones again, conversation turns quickly to the same argument.

'But, Grainne, you *have* to be in hospital. What if something goes wrong?'

'What can go wrong in this day and age?'

'Lots of things! Did you even have a test for Rh disease You were an undiagnosed Rh baby, after all, and you always said it was probably what made you a bit wacky. Was Colm's blood positive or negative?'

'I don't know. And if I said that, I was joking. But I've been prodded and tested for everything under the sun, so probably.'

'Well, I still think you'd be better off in hospital. You're not young to be a first-time mother, anyway.'

'Thank you,' she says politely.

But it's what the staff at the hospital say, too.

She's tempted to say that if things go wrong, it would solve her problem, and she could walk away from everything, give up the struggle of analysing, caring about Da. But she can't be so insensitive, especially as Aisling miscarried her third a few months after Colm's death and is now pregnant again. She tries to explain, and finds herself saying out loud things that have never been verbalised before. 'It's Colm's baby. I want to have him where Colm was born, and his dad, and his grandpa. This is his home, where he belongs. If I get into difficulties, there's always the air ambulance.'

'But—'

'No buts, Aisling, it's my decision.'

'I'll come down, then. Brendan won't mind. You'll need a hand around...'

'No!' Grainne takes a deep breath and softens her voice. 'Aisling, I don't need a hand. It's my choice. I know what I'm doing.'

'Well, forgive me if I think otherwise.'

Aisling's words are sarcastic, but she's probably right. Grainne hasn't a clue about babies, never wanted to. In these last few years, she's happily seen herself as the maiden aunt, checking in with her nieces every so often, handing them back gratefully when they become too heavy to handle. But she doesn't need Aisling busying herself in the middle of her own mess at this time

Grainne tries to smooth the waters. 'Don't be snippy, love. I know you've got all the experience, but I want to be in my own place, with just Da.'

There's a moment's silence.

'Grainne, you're worrying me.'

'I worry me, too, Aisling. I'm still thick with the unfairness of it, God only knows.'

'But it's not right to—'

'No, stop. You listen to me, now. I love you very much, but I just want the midwife here for the birth. I'm told she's got loads of experience, and will have me in hospital in a second if she thinks something isn't right. I want to be alone with my memories, and share this with Da. Don't get cross. I love you, but try to understand.'

'Well, then.' She doesn't sound mollified at all. 'Just let me know when I can come, or when you feel up to visiting us.'

'Aisling. Please. How things might have been, I don't know. But this is outside of normal. I'll call you, okay?'

Grainne puts the phone down gently and rests her hand on her taut belly as the baby shifts. She hadn't known she was going to say any of that, but it's true; the baby belongs to her and Da and, somewhere in the thick of it all, Colm's ghost.

No one seems to think her capable of making her own decisions. Her father suggested she might be more comfortable moving back to Dublin, to be near Aisling; and her mother, tentatively wondering whether she should join them in Spain – God forbid, that would end in disaster! – had sounded inordinately relieved when Grainne said it probably wasn't the best idea.

She guesses her parents would even understand her heading back to London, something Nigel had been pressing for since Colm's death. She knows they all find it exceedingly strange that she chooses to remain in an isolated corner of Cork, sharing a home with her dead husband's father, not even her own kin. She isn't sure why herself. It's not altogether because of the compassion she feels for Da, but something more elusive, a sense of betrayal, perhaps, as though by leaving she'd be abandoning Colm, and she simply hasn't made that decision yet. She tells herself it's too soon for logic, and that one day the right decision will make itself known.

She immerses herself in her work, to forget and get ahead of schedule, because the one thing she's sure of is that the baby's arrival will knock her plans sideways. The stories that tumble out of her head into glorious splashes of colour – to provide working perspectives for the director – will subsequently become 'the book that accompanies the major TV series'. Glossy, full-colour books are expensive to produce, and never make serious money, but the marketing gurus are quick to capitalise on the fans' craving for associated paraphernalia and collectables. She doesn't really care about all that stuff, though it's nice to have the books stacked on a shelf with her name blazoned on the cover. It's a reminder that her success is real, not a figment of her own imagination.

At school her flair for maths had been perceived as her key attribute, the one which would launch her into the high-powered world of finance. The moment in which that changed had been an epiphany prompted by a mild-mannered substitute art teacher who had looked at her work with a kind of wonder, and asked, *And with all this talent you're going to go into business studies?* She can't recall his words exactly, but it ended with the phrase: *Who knows what the future holds, but if you don't try, you'll never know.*

These words had resonated in her mind for a long time before erupting when her family least expected it, the repercussions rising from ripples of consternation to full-blown warfare. She can't now recall the art teacher's name, but sometimes wonders if he's still around, and whether he would derive pleasure in the realisation that his words had changed the direction of her whole life several years after he had uttered them.

A couple of weeks later there's a knock at the door, and she opens it to a sturdy woman with sallow features and greying hair, wearing flat lace-up shoes, and a faded-green Barbour coat. The frames of her glasses are an unhealthy jaundiced yellow. Why would anyone choose that colour?

'You must be Grainne, dear? I'm Katie, the midwife. You were expecting me, weren't you?'

Grainne plasters a welcoming smile on her face. 'Yes. I got a call from the hospital to say you'd be visiting.'

The woman gives Grainne an awkward hug over her bump. 'I can see you're nearly ready to pop, dear. I sometimes get places and find I'm not expected at all. You know, one time I knocked on the wrong door, gave the poor woman a real fright, her daughter being only sixteen and not married. Now, let me show you what I brought.'

She dumps a huge bag onto the kitchen table, and pulls things out with the air of a magician. 'Onesies with poppers, great for keeping nappies on. A couple of sleepsuits, blankets, disposable nappies...'

Grainne is taken aback. 'But I didn't...'

Katie lays her hand on her arm. 'Grainne, dear. Darragh asked me to bring some essentials. He said you hadn't felt able to do any shopping yet.'

He'd been right, she hadn't felt able, or interested. 'Thank you,' she manages to say. 'That's very kind.'

'And I take it you're going to feed the baby yourself?'

'I hadn't thought—'

'It will be better for baby, if we can. Those first few weeks are so important for the immune system, you know? Some women can't, but we'll give it a shot, will we? It's what breasts are for, after all.'

Katie's eyes rove the kitchen. Grainne's pleased she cleaned the windows, even though it earned a reprimand from Da. Apparently, that's one of the things a pregnant woman shouldn't do, along with hanging curtains. He couldn't say why.

'Now, just you sit down, dear,' Katie says. Her voice holds the relentless drive of someone on a mission. 'I'll make us a brew. You're from London, Darragh said, but you don't sound English at all?'

'Dublin originally, then Leeds university, then I followed opportunities to London. I'm an artist. I mainly do graphic novels, cartoons, like in comics, and storyboards for a TV series.'

'Oh. Well. It's a nice hobby, I suppose.'

She can't help the irritation that slides into her words. 'It's not a hobby. It's work. It's a pretty good income, actually.'

From drawing comics? So, what was Colm doing working on the trawler, to go and get himself drowned? And you being from London, and older than him, and not so pretty at that; though you seem nice enough. Marie's Deirdre was pretty cut up when he came back with a woman in tow, but I guess that wasn't your fault. Must be more to you than I can see, girl, but love is surely blind. And being eight months pregnant doesn't do any woman any favours, whatever they say about the bloom. It just makes a woman's ankles thick and her face go red with the effort. I should know, I've seen plenty enough.

'So, will you be after returning to London, now? After

what's happened, and all?'

Grainne briefly thinks of a job she was once offered in New York, and rejected. She could go there. Or anywhere, rally. A million miles from Ireland and Colm and everything she doesn't want to cope with. She's tempted. 'I don't know. There's Da to think of. How would he be if I took his grandson away from him? He'd have no one.'

'Well, now, I did wonder that myself. But, young Colm, did you meet him in London? What would he have been doing there, I wonder?'

Grainne likes that she can say his name so easily, many can't, and becomes amused at the inquisition. 'No, he never went to London till after we met. A relative of mine got married in Cork, to one of Colm's friends. I came over for the wedding. That's where we met. Colm was dancing when I noticed him. He loved dancing. He had all the old figures, and the stepping. I honestly don't know what he saw in me.'

She's quiet for a moment, remembering, but that time is a wine-fuelled haze, him pulling her around the dance floor, her treading on his toes. She can't recall how she ended up in a hotel room with him, but she remembers waking up in amazement the next morning because whatever had happened hadn't worn off in the night. She can't remember how they had decided he should drive back to London with her to collect her things, or why on earth she thought it was a sensible thing to do.

It just happened.

'I remember thinking it was time I had some luck,' she says softly. 'I'd never met a man before that I wanted to marry. And all we had was two years.'

She *had* felt that way, once. But it's only now he's gone that she allows herself to see the underlying truth: that their relationship never had a chance of standing the test of time.

There's a long silence, the old black kettle steaming gently on the range behind them.

'Well, then. You have to think on the good times,' Katie says, dabbing at her eyes. 'You have to thank the Lord for those two years, because you might still be in London on your own, having never had them. And you wouldn't be having this child – that's going to be the saving of you.'

'Maybe one day I can think that. Right now, it's too hard.' She deliberately changes the subject. 'Tell me, how did you come to be a midwife?'

'Oh, I've always loved babies, and that's the truth. Don't ask me why, I haven't a clue. I started off as a nursing assistant at Bon Secours Hospital in Cork, and ended up on a maternity ward in Belfast General. I loved that job so much, but it wasn't to be.' Her voice wobbled with fleeting self-pity. 'Dad died several years back, and when Mammy started to get frail I came back and took up peripatetic midwifery in the local community so I could look after her. I was born in Ahakista, you know, just down the road.'

'Your mother's a lucky woman. Did you never want your own children?'

'Well, yes, dear, of course. But I never found the right man, and, you see, it just wasn't done, to be having a child without being wed. I know some girls don't mind, but the community, you know, and the priest? My parents would have been mortified. Anyway, isn't it better this way? To be bringing newborns into the world time after time, and never having to cope with teenagers!'

She bursts out laughing, but Grainne is saddened. How many people truly get what they want out of life? She eases into a daydream as Katie talks without pausing for breath.

'... and then there was little Meg, now she had twins a month ago, and a hard time she had of it, I can tell ye. From the size of her, it was amazing she didn't end up getting a C-section, but the babies were only just over six pounds, neat as kittens. You always suppose there's a bond, what with the baby being inside the mother all that time, but it's not always so. It's sad, so it is, the stories I could tell, and poor Colm would know, what with his mother disappearing and all. No wonder he went off the rails for a while. Darragh did a fantastic job, though, and him with no more idea about children than the next man, though he's brought enough lambs into the world maybe he has a better idea than some...'

Half hearing the monologue, which doesn't seem to need more than the odd interjection, Grainne is jolted back into awareness. She never actually learned what

Colm's mum died of and hadn't wanted to ask. She'd just assumed something like cancer.

'Colm's Mam disappeared? What do you mean? I thought she died.'

Katie flinches. She slaps her hand over her mouth and whispers, 'Oh, I have the mouth on me. I wasn't to say anything.'

'Well, you might as well say the rest now,' Grainne suggests dryly. She pushes aside all the baby paraphernalia, leans her elbows on the scrubbed pine table and rests her chin on her hands.

Katie brushes her hands nervously down the housecoat that seems to be her adopted uniform. 'Da would sack me on the spot.'

'He can't sack you. I need you.'

'Well, you never heard it from me, then.' Her eyes drift into the past. 'It was all the talk, Heaven only knows. Alyssa was a rare one, foreign, but they never found out from where. She turned up in Ahakista one day like something out of a story. She was a beauty all right, with somewhere around sixteen years on her, and fey, if you know what I mean. She was just a child, but I thought she was the witch out of Snow White, all white skin and black hair and eyes that were like, oh, coals with fire in them. Colm had the look of her about him, that cheeky grin of his. Anyway, she was found walking up the road from the shore, wet and confused, like she'd fallen off a boat or something. And she couldn't speak...'

'You mean couldn't speak English?'

'I don't know. I just know she didn't say anything *real*. She was wrapped in a tarpaulin they reckon she found on the beach, and didn't have a stitch on underneath. That's why they thought she'd come off a boat – a refugee or something. At first, they thought she'd had some accident, damaged her head, but they couldn't find anything wrong. I'm telling it as Mam told me. They put her on TV and everything, but no one knew her.'

'Poor girl.'

'Maybe. Anyway, old Chrissie in the shop, Marie's mother, God bless her, took her in while people were trying to decide what to do with her, and the girl wasn't above making herself useful. Chrissie said she learned quick enough, even started to talk – not proper, but so as you could understand what she wanted. They'd been calling her Mary, but she called herself *Alleessa*, foreign-like, with a kind of hiss, but aside from that it was like she had no past at all. Never a word did they get out of her about where she came from, but she could move to music all right. Soon enough she had the boys queuing up to ask her up for a dance, and it was Colm's dad, young Darragh as he was then, who won her. He was that chuffed, but it was a sad day for him, though, as it turned out.'

Grainne recalls Colm's instinctive ability to dance, and is fascinated. 'What happened?'

'Well, they got married, and she was the apple of Darragh's eye. He couldn't stop looking at her, everyone said, as though he'd been touched. They were the happiest couple, always together, always smiling, holding hands. She produced Colm but never fell again. She was fine until Colm was about six, then went a bit strange. Started sort of pining away, crying all over the shop, going thin. Darragh was out of his head, not knowing what to do. Anyway, they couldn't find anything wrong with her. Then one day she just upped and disappeared.'

'What, *poof*, into thin air?'

'Not quite. Darragh got worried when they didn't come home after her picking up the boy from school, and there was a big search. Eventually they found Colm, along with her clothes, down by the shore. Hysterical, he was, but her body never turned up. Darragh wasn't himself at all for a long time, but he had to keep it together for Colm. There was talk that Darragh had done away with her. The authorities were even talking of taking the child away. If it hadn't been for everyone here making a roola boola about what a sound man he was... Anyway, they decided she must have drowned, but whether she'd just gone swimming or had intended to kill herself' – she crosses herself swiftly – 'no one could say. Colm went kind of quiet for a bit, but children, you know, they survive. It was Darragh who suffered. Then and now.'

'So, Da never walked out with another woman?'

'Never. Not even to give the boy a mother. Some reckon he's been burning the candle for her from that day to this. Maybe he thought she'd come walking back in one day. It's romantic, but sad, all right.'

'Tragic, I'd call it. Is that why Colm would never swim, do you think? He was terrified of going in the water.'

'He was? I didn't know that. Well, why would he go fishing?' Genuine confusion lit her face.

'I've asked myself the same question. I couldn't stop him. I said we didn't need the money. But they were short of a hand, and he wouldn't let his mates down.'

There's a pause as the weight of Colm's death, and the death of the other lads on the boat, hits them anew.

Then Katie takes up the story again. 'Poor Colm. He was waiting a long time for his ma to turn up. He was convinced she wasn't dead, and there are those who think she was a selkie—'

'That's nonsense.'

'Well, I'm just saying what others said. She came out of the sea, and went back into it, so you can see why.'

'People really believe that?'

'Sure, they do.'

Grainne stands and paces the small kitchen, easing her back. 'Why didn't someone tell me? Colm's mother died in the sea and now Colm's gone the same way. I should have known. It's not right to have left me ignorant!'

'Darragh wanted it that way. He won't believe Alyssa killed herself, which is what everyone says, because that would mean she didn't love him or the child enough to stay. Besides, suicide is a mortal sin, isn't it?'

Grainne shakes her head. What a vicious piece of nonsense. If there were a God, would he really be so cruel as to bring eternal damnation upon those desperate enough to escape their troubles in this way? She wonders if that's why Da doesn't go to mass. He still crosses himself sometimes, hardly aware of doing it, so his religion is still smouldering in him, somewhere. She wonders, too, is there such a thing as fate, or is this just one unlucky family?

There's a knock at the door. Da breaks the tension, peering nervously around the jamb. 'Katie, hello, now, how are ye? Is it safe to come in?'

Grainne laughs, and realises it's probably the first time since Colm's death. 'Did you see what Katie brought?' She wafts her hand over the pile of baby clothes, and it hits her suddenly that the baby is real, that she will soon be easing tiny limbs into these doll-like clothes.

Her face must betray panic, for Da walks over and pulls her head onto his shoulder. He smells of straw and earth. 'Ah, girl, now then, now then.'

Her voice is muffled in his jacket, and she's honest with him. 'I don't know how to do it, Da. Be a mother, and all. It was Colm wanted the child, not me. What if I can't?'

'Sure, and you'll be fine. It's easy as riding a bike.'

She hiccups, pushes away, and wipes her eyes. 'I've never ridden a bike.'

'Never ridden a bike? Girl, you need some educating!'

Katie chips in, 'Well, there's a challenge for the future, but not now, eh?'

'I've never felt so useless,' Grainne admits. 'Like a stranded whale. How do women do this time and time again? Why do they?'

'Didn't have a choice, one time,' Katie says. 'Babies did ever have a habit of coming out where men did go in.'

Da raises a brow, and Katie flushes a deep red as she bustles to the door.

'Look, now,' she says, 'I'll leave you to it, and be up in a week or so. If you need me for anything, just call the mobile, leave a message. Next time I come up we'll go through some things and make sure you have everything ready, but there's no rush. Now, take care of yourself, Grainne, d'ye hear?'

Chapter 7

As the baby swells to term, Katie instructs Grainne not to be lazy, to walk lots and keep herself healthy and fit for the birth and, God willing, a quick recovery. It's the ones who mooch around feeling sorry for themselves that have the trouble after, she says pointedly. Grainne, who had been spending a lot of time at her desk, burying the present beneath the pressing demands of the media, wonders if she's been talking to Da.

But she obediently pushes her work aside every afternoon, heaving her increasing bulk out of the stifling gloom of the old house, and up on to the wild, untamed landscape rimmed by the Atlantic. She stares at the sea, wondering exactly where Colm's body lies. Niall's was the only body that ever turned up. Niall had been wearing a life jacket, so it was likely the others had been, too, but the lifeline was still attached to a cleat that had ripped from the wheelhouse, so the consensus of opinion was that they had all simply gone down with the *Faery*, still attached by the lines. She had once hoped that the huge, emotionless expanse of water before her might, in a moment of benevolence, give up its secrets, provide a sense of closure, but it's unlikely, now.

Grainne finds herself avoiding people towards the end of her pregnancy. When people ask how the baby is doing, when is he due, won't he be an absolute treasure, and hasn't God sent the baby to save her in her hour of need, she wants to scream at them. Don't they get it, that their precious God killed Colm in the first place, and she's stuck here in the middle of nowhere with his child?

Sometimes she walks high on the wild goat path, along the ridge of rocks limned with bog, and watches the seals bobbing off the headland. She imagines one of them as the fey Alyssa, the selkie, watching the place that used to be her home, waiting for her grandchild to be born. She laughs at herself, but later incorporates that image into her storyline: Alyssa walking down to the water, throwing off her human guise and slipping into the water as a sleek grey seal, leaving her hysterical child on the shore.

Sometimes she struggles down to the beaches that nestle between the rocks, to scramble around the rubble shores where small fishing smacks have been drawn out of the water, where seaweed and salt-bleached plastic trays and buoys rim the tideline. She listens to the whisper of the waves and collects the small treasures they deposit: broken shells and bits of coloured glass worn into jewels by the constant churning. But her mind is elsewhere.

*

'Grainne, are you listening to me?' Katie snaps.

She had been miles away, lost in some fictional conundrum. Shocked into the present, only the resonance of a thought echoes. She blinks and pulls herself back towards the scrubbed pine kitchen table on which she's placed a cut-glass vase filled with brilliant orange montbretia. She thinks it would be nice to get more than potatoes and cabbages from the tiny garden, but wonders whether any flowers suitable for cutting could flourish under the scouring wind.

'You need to stop walking on your own. You're worrying the life out of Da,' Katie says.

It's funny hearing her talk of Da as her dad, not Colm's. But it isn't the first time. She has a strange image of herself slipping inexorably into Colm's space, as though there are only so many places, and someone had to move out for her to move in. 'But you told me to walk! I've told Da not to worry, I'm fine, and I have a mobile.'

'That was before. You're nearly full term, now. You know there's not always signal, and he comes out looking for you most days.'

'I've told him not to.'

'As if he wouldn't! Do you want to be the death of your baby and Da?' The words explode out of Katie. 'You know he's doing a job that used to take the both of them, and on top of that you're making him walk miles looking for you! Think of others for a moment. You're not the first to lose a husband and won't be the last. Do you think Colm would be happy to see you doing this? And what of the baby? You don't want to be out on your own when labour starts.'

Grainne recoils. She's never seen Katie angry before, her plump cheeks splodged with red, making her quite ugly. Da never complains, and it hasn't occurred to her that she's adding to his burdens.

Katie reaches over and pats her on the arm. 'You spend too much time on your own, love. I've told you to come down to the toddler group, get to know some of the other mums. I really don't know why you won't do that. You need to stop moping around and find something to keep your fingers busy and your mind occupied.'

'I don't want to speak to other mums. We have nothing in common.'

Quite honestly, the thought appals her: all those younger women, discussing her behind her back, pretending to be interested in her and her imminent child. She's overheard snippets of dialogue in the last month, that she's never mentioned to Da or Katie: *And did you hear that Da's signed the farm over to Colm so she owns it now? And her coming here with nothing but the clothes she stood up in... Yes, fell on her feet, for sure... And did you know, she's ten years older than him? She looks it don't you think? Skinny, too, you'd think she'd put some weight on... And still into those London fashions, she doesn't dress right, you know... What was he thinking bringing her here? And*

Deirdre after wearing her heart on her arm for him to see. But neither of them have him now, do they? Who'd have guessed he'd die young, though?

Later, Katie's words echo around Grainne's mind, and she wonders if she will ever feel at ease here, find a niche for herself, a group of people to belong with. Is this what it's like for all those immigrants who arrived in swathes on the back of the European Union? She's heard the mothers chattering away in their own unidentifiable languages on the street corners, gathering like birds into discrete flocks, sorted by tongue and plumage. But where does she fit in this community? Everyone speaks her language, yet she's isolated by more than miles.

Da comes back from the shop with groceries and a box with knitting needles, patterns, white baby wool, books, and magazines. She lifts a brow at this manifestation of Katie's good intentions, and they share a smile. She has no interest in knitting baby clothes, and the magazines, plastered with photographs of ridiculous clothes and money-pit homes, just irritate her.

She's hit by a pang of nostalgia for her tall-ceilinged flat in London, and her slim alter ego who lived there. She'd rather be getting on with her work, but the imminent birth consumes her, and it's difficult to breathe, bent over the small table upstairs. Her huge bulk gives her no pleasure, making her feel ugly and wanting to pee all the time.

But after Katie's diatribe, she walks closer to home,

and a few days later, when Da asks kindly if she'd like to go with him to the point to watch the seals basking in the sun, she feels like a prisoner let out for good behaviour. He drives her up the winding narrow road between islands of exposed rock to the wind-scoured ridge. The goat path is dry, presently bounded by verdant grass and sheep droppings. Here and there are patches of heather draped with dusty pink bells, and the scrubby tangle of gorse bursting with coffee-scented flowers. And, way down, the twinkling sea clutches the seal-dotted headland in its ever-present grip.

'It's strange, them being here so long,' Da says as they stand, arm in arm, watching the seals. 'They usually follow the shoals north.'

'Marie says there's more than usual. They're good for trade, though, bringing in sightseers. And Old Tom doesn't fish any more, after the incident; just takes out tourists to see the seals.'

'The shop and bar are doing very nicely, too.'

He goes silent.

She wonders if he's thinking of his wife of just a few short years, the beautiful Alyssa who appeared one day from the sea, then just as mysteriously disappeared back into it. 'Katie says the old ones aren't so happy,' she says finally, her eyes on the dark headland over the water, a faint breeze lifting her hair. 'The boys want to go in swimming to see if they can touch the seals, but the old folks won't let them in case the seals drown them, or turn them into selkies.'

'The seals wouldn't let them anywhere near. And the silly auld biddies know full well the selkies are a folk tale. Well, they should, anyway.'

'Katie says they're also whispering that the seals are waiting for Colm's baby to be born. Da, why didn't you tell me about Colm's mother?'

He freezes momentarily, then sighs. 'Katie's got a mouth on her, all right.'

'But, Da, I should have known about Colm's mother. Why didn't you tell me? Everyone knew, except me.'

'Maybe I should have, but what would it have changed? I did the best I could for Colm, after.'

'But—'

'She died. That's all we know. Listen, the seals are singing.'

The seals are making long, guttural barks that echo over the water, reverberating from the rocks; an eerie sound that lends itself utterly to the realms of fantasy. The resonance verbalises her sense of isolation from the real world. She remembers the tales of sailors believing they were hearing mermaids calling, when what they were hearing was whale song.

Gradually, the fantastical chorus peters into silence.

They turn and walk arm in arm back to the truck as the sun spreads blood-red stains across the sea, turning the clouds into pink candyfloss. She wants to ask more about Alyssa, but Da has firmly closed the door.

Then he pulls her to a halt, pointing. 'Look. Isn't that something? A crown made by nature itself,' he says quietly.

Ahead, the ring of trees which circle the rath have been tipped with golden light. She takes a breath and wishes she had her camera to hand, but the image is imprinted on her mind. Now she knows where Shay, the fairy girl she's introducing into her story, lives. It amuses her that her fantasy world is looking more like West Cork every day.

Da rarely exposes his thoughts, and she tightens her hand on his arm as the gold fades to shadow. She wonders how it must feel to still be living in the place owned by your father and your father's father, your roots still firmly embedded in the same soil.

'Katie says it's bad luck to go into a rath,' Grainne says, as they start to walk.

'That woman doesn't know *how* to stop talking.'

She smiles at the tetchy comment. 'True, she's a mine of useless information. She says the raths are fairy mounds, doors to the fairy kingdoms under the hill. I wondered why you'd never cleared the gorse.'

He rolls his eyes. 'It's called respect. It was once home to a whole clan of people, a homestead. They used to stand here and look at the sea just as we do. It's been there for a thousand years or maybe more, and should be allowed to just sit and remember. Maybe it's the gateway to the fairy world, too, who knows.'

She casts a sly smile. 'Katie says...' But he doesn't rise to the bait. 'Well, it seems to be a local tale, that you're not supposed to step inside the circle. What's meant to happen if you do?'

Da laughs, pushing his flat cap to the back of his head. 'What doesn't happen? Milk goes sour, crops don't grow, cattle don't flourish. And if it's All Hallows' Eve, the fairy folk ride, and they don't like being spied on. And if a woman is young, she'll get seduced by a handsome fairy warrior, who would then disappear back into the mound to never be seen again.'

Just for a moment she sees a hint of Colm in the amused exasperation, and gives a faint echoing smile. 'It's one way for a girl to explain how she got pregnant. What about when men go in there, then?'

'Ah, well, if a one is young and beautiful, the fairy queen might take him for her lover for a year and a day, then when she's had her way, she thrusts him back out into the world, where he finds a hundred years have passed, and his family is long dead and in the grave.'

'That's horrid.'

'It is, but the fairies aren't like folk, for all they look like us. They can be like children, innocent, but wicked and harmful by the by.'

'I thought you said you didn't believe any of it?'

'It might be nonsense, girl, but it's our nonsense. Are you all right, love?'

She's startled by the unexpected casual endearment, and realises they have walked a long road since she first arrived. He'd seemed distant and cold to start with, but perhaps she'd been awkward with him, too. Now, she has more empathy with Da than she ever felt for her own father, and wonders whether this would have happened if Colm had lived.

'Truthfully, my back's aching.'

It's a struggle to walk back to the vehicle, even leaning on his arm, the weight of Colm's child heavy in more ways than one. She wants it to be born, to rid her of these endless days of waiting, and find out one way or another whether she has it in her to love this unexpected legacy from her dead husband. And, then, perhaps, to decide what to do with her life.

Katie comes more often, checking, probing, and chattering; then soldiers up with her overnight bag when Da phones in a panic to say the baby is coming and there's no woman of the house to help.

Katie talks her through the long hours of labour with tales and stories, including her own wistful statement that she's now too old to bear a child. Reading between the lines, she'd never met a man who wanted to marry her, but then, maybe she'd had a lucky escape.

In the same room in which Da and then Colm were born, freshly papered with a cheerful tangle of wild flowers, Grainne's labour ends with the surprisingly quick and easy birth of a healthy eight-pound boy. Amazement at this blue-eyed scrap of humanity floods into some of the dead places in her soul and she finds she can't keep life at arm's length any more. It has reached out and pulled her back from the abyss.

'You're a fine strapping one, aren't you?' Katie tells the baby later, after he's cleaned and nursed, rocking him as if he were her own. 'What will your name be called, I wonder?'

'I hadn't thought,' Grainne lies. Da had never argued with her about anything, but wanted the child to be called Colm. She wanted to call her son anything but. *Colm is never coming back. I can't be calling his name day in day out and having his son come to me*, she'd said.

'How about Duirmid?' Katie volunteers. 'I've a cousin called Duirmid. It's a grand old name.'

Grainne murmurs a non-committal 'hmm' as her mind wanders to the seals that had lingered off the headland since the *Faery Queen* was lost. Lost, she thinks, as if it's misplaced and they're still looking. The seals had remained while she'd been half-mad, stalking the lonely path day after day, thinking Lord knows what, then coming home to make Da's dinner in a routine which had become her anchor to reality.

'Rónán,' she says finally, holding her hands out for her son. She looks down at his face, so tiny it's hardly real. She seeks signs of herself or Colm, but the perfect, sleeping face is the baby's own, innocent and strange. 'Rónán,' she whispers to him, trying it out. 'That's who you are. Rónán Colm O'Sullivan, my little seal baby.'

Katie throws a startled glance and crosses herself.

'What?' Grainne asks, amused. 'Isn't that a good name?'

'Well, it's not for me to say.'

Grainne lifts a brow at the tight, snipped voice. 'Out with it,' she says, and settles back to nurse Rónán.

'Well,' Katie's voice hushes. 'Alyssa being a selkie and all...'

She can see how the name Rónán, Gaelic for little seal would spook Katie's superstitious bones. 'Whoever Alyssa was, she wasn't a selkie. There's no such thing.'

'Maybe,' she says, somewhat tetchily, 'but there are things in the world we don't know.'

Like God, Grainne thinks. There's no proof, but belief overrides logic. And how can Katie believe in the Christian God, and also in the fey, like the fairies, and mermaids and selkies? But then, the Christian religion had engulfed the pagan one so subtly that the old beliefs still showed through the cracks. She'd known about selkies since childhood, from the song her mother used to sing:

He is a man upon the land,
and he's a selkie in the sea,
and when he's far from every strand,
his dwelling is in Suleskerrie.

A selkie! Grainne has an epiphany. In her storyboard, the crown of eternal youth coveted by Queen Maeve is sitting on the bottom of the sea, as the boat that was carrying it sank during a storm. She hadn't been quite sure how to get her plot out of that hole, but the answer had been there, all along.

But even as her mind wanders briefly back to her work, she realises that Katie isn't joking. Despite her pragmatism and firm grounding, she has a great capacity to believe in the unbelievable. And if Alyssa was a selkie, did that make Colm one, and Rónán also

'In the old Scottish ballad,' Grainne muses, 'the selkie was male. He came out of the sea and made a woman pregnant. Whether she was raped or beguiled isn't quite clear. Anyway, he came back a year and a day later, to claim his child, leaving the mother a bag of gold for her bother. I never heard a story of a female selkie.'

Katie shakes her head. 'I don't know that one. The story I know is that one day the selkie, who was a girl, saw a fisherman out on the water and fell in love with him. She followed him back and shed her sealskin in a cave by the shore. He was smitten by her beauty, and guessed she was a selkie because she couldn't speak. So he searched until he found the cave where she had left her sealskin, and hid it from her so she couldn't leave him. They married, and had a child. He thought she was happy and she loved him well enough, but she was sad sometimes, staring out at the sea.'

Like me, Grainne thinks. But what had the fey Alyssa been thinking of? A home, perhaps, over the water, that she had never been able to forget? Parents who had never known what happened to their beautiful daughter?

'Well, one day,' Katie carried on, 'the selkie and the child were playing on the shore, and the child found the sealskin where the fisherman had hidden it and showed it to his mother. The selkie put the skin on, threw herself into the water and was never seen again.'

It's no wonder the locals thought Alyssa was a selkie, if that's the story going around. 'That's sad.'

'Sad for the child, so.'

'And the fisherman.' Grainne stares towards the window where the tired curtains hang listlessly. She leans her head back and closes her eyes. She had thought of folk tales as superficial plots in which idealistic love or greed drove handsome princes or wicked goblins to do their deeds. They were tales which didn't delve very deeply into motivation or emotion. Now, however, the sadness reaches out to touch her: the mortal husband, like Da, who waited fruitlessly by the shore for his selkie wife to come home, and the child, Colm, who grew up motherless. The stories once whispered about Alyssa have come back to haunt them with Colm's death, and his unexpected legacy.

Grainne wants to rewrite the tale, give it a happy ending, but can't see how it would be possible. Folk tales are riddled with such crossovers between human and non-human entities, but somehow Katie's story holds a deeper tragedy than the one in the song. A love that destroys both parties, and a child who can never be wholly of one race or the other. Three people made miserable by emotions over which they had no control. It would be easy to fall into the trap that lurks between reality and belief, and wonder whether, after all, Colm had been of the other world. He had certainly enthralled her, utterly and hopelessly, and had left her with child before departing.

She doesn't know now whether she had ever truly loved Colm, not that she would voice that out loud. She had been smitten by his passion for life, his humour, his wayward lack of respect for society. She had come to realise, since his death, that it had been her own dissatisfaction with a life gone stale that had sent her headlong into his arms, and his world. And West Cork is as far from London in both miles and social structure as Suleskerrie might be.

She finds Rónán's hand and wraps his tiny, almost translucent fingers around her own finger, dwelling with wonder on the fingernails, so perfect and dainty. It is hard to believe this scrap of life could possibly grow into the big strong lad his father had been. She wonders why she's so consumed by fantasy, when real life can produce this child from a couple of microscopic cells.

It's magic of a kind.

Staring at Rónán, she tries to recall the features of Colm's face, but they've become indistinct, unreal. Even the few photographs of him seem to have become a little fuzzy around the edges, as if he might fade out of them entirely one of these days, leaving a gap in the image. Tears push through her closed eyelids and she brushes them away. He would have loved this moment, and she's forgetting what he looked like.

Katie bustles over, tidying the bedclothes, her face

crumpled in empathy. 'Ah now, ah now, we mustn't get tearful. I didn't mean to upset you with my silly tales. Sure, and the boyeen's father would have been pleased. He's a gift from God himself is this one. To make up for the losses this family have suffered.'

Grainne tightens her arms around Rónán. His eyes are closed, the delicate lashes fanned over his cheeks; he's at peace with the world, knowing nothing yet, save warmth and a mother's breast. Contentment seems to be catching; she feels herself droop.

Katie gently takes Rónán from her arms. 'Well, now, you have a nice rest, girl, you're looking fierce tired. I'll put the boyeen in the cot, and go and put some dinner on for Da. If the babe cries, don't you get up, now. I'll be here sooner than you can say Saint Patrick.'

Da is in the room when Grainne awakes to the first sound of Rónán's whimpering hunger. He's staring down at the baby so intently, with such personal confusion, she makes waking-up noises to allow him time to recover his equilibrium.

'A fine lad,' he says huskily, turning to face her; then manages a real, if watery, smile. 'Rónán Colm O'Sullivan. Grainne, love, thank you. You've made an old man very proud. It's not as if he takes Colm's place, you know, nothing could ever do that, but—'

She asks softly, 'Katie told you? You're happy with that name?'

'It's a good choice, girl. I shouldn't have been after

hassling you to call him Colm, with himself drowned and all.'

'Will you hand him to me, do you think?'

'I've the big clumsy hands on me.'

'You've got the same hands that picked up Colm when he was that age. You won't break him. He's strong, like his dad.'

As if taking a precious teapot from the press, Da reaches into the cot and lifts his grandson, bundled warmly into a blue sleep-sack, and hands him to Grainne, then leaves hurriedly as she slips aside her top to put Rónán to the breast.

Grainne winces as Rónán latches on ferociously and guzzles for a few moments before settling to feed with more decorum. It brings to mind Colm's way of devouring her home cooking. He would try to eat slowly, but couldn't stop himself from shovelling the food in. He invariably finished before she was halfway through. He'd then lean her grandmother's old chair back on two legs and clasp his hands over his full stomach. *I tried*, he'd say, with a big, satisfied grin. *You need to make it taste bad if you want me to slow down.* And she'd remember he'd been brought up on boiled bacon, cabbage and potatoes, all Da knew how to cook.

Katie pops in and out for two more days, then moves on to her next mother-in-waiting, leaving Grainne alone with Rónán. Da is out working the farm most days, and Grainne wonders whether he's secretly keeping the farm together for Colm to come home to, or so it won't be gone to ruin when Rónán is old enough to take over. Or maybe Da is thinking she's still young and might one day bring another man into the home, to be father to his son's child, to take on the work of the farm? Would he mind that? she wonders.

She thrusts the thought away. At the moment, she can't at all picture herself with another man, although, despite Da's distant presence, and Rónán's constant needs, she's desperately lonely. No, she's made one mistake that dumped her in a strange place, and isn't about to make another that will keep her here. Besides, she rationalises, Da would find it strange, the farm owned by someone not his own kin, not to mention it is far too soon to even consider such a possibility.

It hadn't occurred to her until Katie said it, that Da is struggling to keep up with the work on his own, so something has to be done, and whatever he says, she won't suggest Da sell up.

Chapter 8

Grainne wonders where the last few months have gone. Winter has the land in thrall once again, but West Cork rarely knows the cold beauty of snow. More often the days are overcast, chilled by unrelenting rain. The roads have become streambeds, and new potholes burst open with each passing week.

It's a year to the week the *Faery Queen* was lost. Grainne dresses well, and Da drives them down to the memorial service in Kilcrohane, an event which is moving, but not as traumatic as she had feared. The loss being too raw to be consigned to the past, the village turns out en masse to lend moral support. There are kisses and hugs between the bereaved families, and a fair smattering of brightness in the eye as together they mark this shared tragedy.

Rónán is, of course, the centre of attention. He's four months old, and even in this short time has grown from the exquisite fragility of a newborn to a sturdy baby, chubby around the elbows and knees. Cooed over and chucked under the chin, he's quiet for the most part, drinking in everything with wide-eyed solemnity.

He's a good child, almost too good, Grainne thinks. She'd been told that babies cry and wail, keep you awake at night, take away your humanity and your sense of self. Yet Rónán is a placid and unfussy baby, and sometimes gives the impression of understanding the stories she reads out loud.

The women gather around.

'Isn't he the one?'

'Well, doesn't he look like his father?'

Grainne drinks in the compliments as if they are personal. It isn't quite so hard to smile, these days.

The service is emotionally draining, yet she also feels strangely detached, as though it hadn't been her Colm who died, but someone else's loved one. He is fast becoming a dream, something that had happened in another life.

Grainne's hands are busy enough now. Rónán fills a larger space in the household than his size might suggest, yet when he's asleep, or nursing, her mind still wanders the cold space in the house where a vibrant life once held court. The need to cut and run hits hardest at those times, pulling her towards a sense of inevitable tragedy, which rises to engulf her whenever she is tired or lonely. At these times, she distances herself with fiction.

It isn't Colm she fears, nor his ghost, but the fear of every mother who cares for her child. This scrap of humanity is now so much a part of her life, she cannot imagine living without him. And Colm's untimely death is a constant reminder that nothing is forever.

She lies Rónán on a nest of cushions on the living room floor and croons an old lullaby while putting together a casserole, sliding it into the oven of the old range, where it will spend long slow hours softening to perfection.

Tá gaotha an gheimhridh sgallta fuar,
Thart thimchioll an Drom'-mhóir,
Ach ann sna halla tá siothchán,
A pháiste gheal a stóir.
Ta gach sean-duilleog dul air crith,
ach is og an beannglan thú...

Da's voice startles her. '*Though autumn vines may droop and die, a bud of spring are you.* That's lovely, girl. I didn't hear you sing that before. My Alyssa used to sing that tune. She had a voice like an angel.'

Hadn't Katie said Alyssa couldn't speak? But she hides her puzzlement. Da looks tired, ill, and the busy time of lambing is still yet to come. 'It's one my mother used to sing to me,' she says. 'It's a bit out of season, though, with winter fair on us.' She hesitates. 'Da, I've been wondering—'

His brow rises. 'That sounds serious?'

She smiles. 'Nothing bad. It's just than Young Liam wants to rent the farm for a few years. He said he thinks he can make a bit of money even if he has to pay us rent, and I'm thinking that might be a good idea. He said he would make an offer for the sheep we have now, after we have the lambs sold.'

'You don't think I'm up to the job any more?'

'Da, you're not, not on your own, and you know it. You can't keep this up till Rónán's big enough to farm, and even then, he might not want to. He might want to go to the city and become an accountant.'

'Jaysus, girl! I hope that's not what you're whispering in his ear?'

She hides a grin; he rarely swears. 'Of course not. But I'll see that he gets an education so he has the choice.'

He catches the note of defensiveness in her tone. 'And you think I didn't do that for Colm?'

'I know you didn't.'

'That's harsh, girl.'

He sits at the table, and she senses him watching her bustle about, boiling the tea and setting the mugs and milk, even though she studiously looks away. 'Colm knew you needed him on the farm. It was a choice he made.'

'And what did he want to learn, then, that I kept him from?'

'The modern ways of farming, up at the college. The science of it all, he said.'

Da drags a hand through the fine grey hairs which are thinning every day. 'He never told me that.'

'You had no one but him. He knew you wouldn't

make it alone. But he read a lot, when he could. He said he didn't need a bit of paper to let other people know what he knew, but it did matter, to him

'He read it in books?' Da looks fair gobsmacked.

Grainne laughs. 'He wasn't stupid, your Colm, for all he acted it sometimes.'

It might have been the anniversary mass rather than the present talk, but without warning he breaks into heavy sobs, two or three, then buries his face in his cupped hand and shakes silently. Grainne pours the tea, waiting his grief out. He isn't a man who'd want her to put a hand around his shoulder. She guesses he's never been one to let his feelings show.

'If I'd let him go,' he says finally, 'he could have got a good job, and not have to go after all the ways to make money. It's my fault he's dead. It's my fault altogether.'

Tears beget tears, and Grainne finds herself wiping her eyes, while arguing. 'Sure, and that's daft, Da. You haven't been thinking that all this long year, have you? No one made Colm go out fishing. I tried to stop him, but he wouldn't be told anything. And no one made him stay on the farm except himself. He was a grown man. And if he did something for love of his family, that made him a good man, so. He cared about the land, about keeping his family. And he cared about helping his friends. And who was to know there'd be a freak squall, a tsunami, pretty much? It was an accident of nature. The man on TV said it was probably caused by some sort of underwater landslide. You know when that wave hit the land, it flooded places that had never seen salt before. The *Faery Queen* wasn't the only tragedy in West Cork that day.'

He regains control, clears his throat, and asks, 'So, what's Young Liam offering to rent the farm? Does Old Liam know?'

'They've fallen out and that's the truth. Young Liam was always set to inherit the farm, but when the time came to tie it over to him, Old Liam told him he's selling up to go to America to visit his other children, so Young Liam's pretty upset.'

It wasn't an unfamiliar story. In the past, a farm had stayed in the family, handed down, father to son, yet times had changed. With new money flying around, the farm could be easily sold. Even if it generated less than the land's worth, money in the hand offered previously undreamed-of luxury and freedom for the one who sold it.

Except that money doesn't last like land.

Da muses, 'It was a strange one, though, for Liam to expect to inherit it all.'

'Young Liam says it's not like that. His brothers are upset, too, because the farm was their home, and if their father sells it, they'll have no home to come back to. And they all agree it's not as if a pile of money in Old Liam's bank is going to last long, or buy another farm, or even a house once he starts tipping away at it. No, it's Old Liam who's dreaming of a different life.'

Da shakes his head. 'It's a sorry day, all right.'

'So, anyway, Old Liam is determined to go and live with his other sons in America, and Young Liam is leaving him to it.'

Da gives a half-smile. 'I doubt his other three sons and their wives and families will be expecting him to live with them.'

'It's a disaster in the making,' Grainne agrees. 'The grass isn't always greener over the water. No doubt he'll discover his mistake when it's too late. Anyway, Young Liam knew you'd made the farm over to Colm, and asked me first, for fear of upsetting you.'

Pa says, 'Well, legally it's yours now.'

'Without a body to bury, I don't inherit for a few years.'

'Could you contest that?'

'I don't know, but why would I?'

'You would, if you intended to sell up, and move on.'

It was a concept that must have been plaguing him.

'I haven't made any plans, Da. I was thinking that if he rented the farm for a few years, we wouldn't need to leave the house, and you can help Young Liam out when it suits you. You'd have to sort the details between you.'

'Maybe I should sell the bungalow in Bantry?'

'No, don't do that. There will come a time you might want to retire there, and we don't need the money. I still have an income from my job.' He didn't have a clue how much she really earned, and she'd have to be careful when spending it, so as to not hurt Da's feelings. 'We could let Young Liam have the wreck down the road.

You could put some windows in, and a range. You always said it'd be grand to see the place recovered, and if it's done up, we can let it out for holidays one day. As to what's a reasonable rent for a farm, I haven't a clue. For now, we just need enough to live on and keep a car on the road. After that, we'll see.'

'I'll think on it.'

Chapter 9

Grainne walks out with Rónán in the pouch on her front. He's happy, snuggled against her breast, but soon enough he'll be too big for her to carry that way. She's seen baby carriers that go on the back, but is there any point? Soon enough he'll be too heavy for her to carry at all, and will find his own feet.

She still imagines that other life, the one where Colm is still around. In her mind she can hear Colm say, *here, love, pass him over, I'll take him from now on. Come to daddy.* She imagines Rónán reaching happily for his father's safe arms, and is surprised by an unexpected jolt of jealousy. She doesn't want Rónán to reach for anyone else, the way he does herself or Da. She doesn't want to share this deep and amazing gift with a husband she has difficulty recalling.

And all those cute family images Colm had once dwelled on now seem like the tail end of a sugar-coated film. There is no daddy to take Rónán on his shoulders to the meadow, to sit him on his knees in the tractor as they turn the cut grass, or teach him to bring the hay to the sheep in winter.

It's for her alone to mind him as he grows, to face the possibility of him falling down the stairs, falling off the cliff, even just falling over. Colm is gone, there's no coming back, so why does she keep getting this strange feeling that her life with him is somehow unfinished? Is it because he'd just gone out one day and not returned? It's as though the door is still ajar, as if one day he'll just breeze through it and take up where he left off. Only he won't find his wife waiting for him. He'll find a woman he doesn't know, any more than she knows him.

She finds Da in the sheepfold with Young Liam, checking the ewes' feet, dagging the dirty wool away from the rear readying them for birthing come the spring. It must be hard for Da, having another young man working alongside him where his own son once was, but she doubts he allows himself to dwell on what can never be. He's too pragmatic.

Even so, she feels Da's pain, knowing this isn't the first tragedy he's survived. How does someone survive that desperately unkind brush with fate: the loss of a young wife, then the loss of their only child who he'd brought up by himself? She's his family, for now, and maybe Rónán will be the salvation of both of them, as Katie suggested.

She watches them awhile, this old man who had become her family, and Young Liam who she scarcely knows. When he'd sought her out to speak to her about the farm, he'd chosen a time Da was away in town, buying Lamlac for orphaned lambs who would need to be bottle fed. He must have been watching, waiting for a chance to speak to her alone. She finds that slightly disturbing, but sees why he would have found it difficult to speak to Da. He was Colm's friend since school, and often worked at the farm with Colm before she'd arrived.

Presently, Da's the boss, with Young Liam taking on the heavy work. He's being paid a small living, but next year the roles will reverse, with Liam managing the farm, and Da helping as and when. Liam has the smooth appearance of a boy-band singer, but he holds a deep knowledge of livestock management.

In the meantime, Young Liam has been busy making a start on repairing the window surrounds for the old wreck down below. Da was lucky enough to source decent second-hand double-glazed windows which are, even now, propped up against the building, waiting to fill the gaps.

Liam's enthusasm is boundless; and he seems invigorated by this promise of a new future. He has reinvented himself from a disenchanted, moody youth into a dynamic force.

Weather permitting, he's up at the wreck all hours. He's removed the remains of the rotting roof timbers, and made the walls. Da helps him to line the rain-washed chimneys with ceramic pipes and give them new pots and concrete caps. Young Liam is deliberately throwing himself into this new project to drive away the frustration of his lost inheritance; he is determined to make it without his father's help. She feels sorry for him, in truth. She recalls her father pontificating that inheritance is not a right but a privilege, but the way Old Liam betrayed his son's trust is despicable. The boy had been told all his life the farm would be his, so he'd left school early, putting his energy into pulling the farm into better shape than his father had ever managed, only to see his future ripped out from under his feet. There has been no offer of compensation for his lost years, his lost education. Grainne wonder what kind of reception awaits him in America.

In April, the bleating of new lambs fills the steaming sheds, and for four weeks their lives are governed by the sheep as Da and Young Liam take turns to keep watch during the night.

The lambs will provide the year's income for the farm, and each and every one counts. Those not born easily give up and die in an instant if care is not to hand, and a ewe will give up on a lamb that doesn't suckle immediately, instinctively knowing it isn't strong enough to survive.

Grainne is faintly disturbed by the continual production of lambs, the close attention they're given at birth; then six months later the fields are quiet again, all the lambs gone to slaughter. It never occurred to her before, when buying lumps of meat in the butcher's, how little the lambs were, how short their lives. It bothers her when she sees them spronking in the field by their mothers, cute and fluffy, filled with the joy of life, their hind legs seeming too big for their bodies.

Then lambing is over, and work begins anew on the old house below. Lén comes up to measure the roof and order timbers, and Da lays a water pipe from the well above to feed the concrete mixer, in which the lime render thumps like dough. Lén digs new drains with a team of young men who labour for Young Liam with no expectation of reward, and the knowledge that he would do the same for them, if needed. Sometimes they wield picks into the wet turf; sometimes a mechanical rock breaker carves a channel through bedrock, the noise of it echoing rhythmically out over the whole peninsula. Grainne knows they're doing it not just for Liam, but for Colm's child, because Colm is not here to do it for himself.

Lén, whose experience has made him the unofficial site foreman, has also refused all offers of payment. He's probably got a fair idea she has money behind her. His eyes are always moving, assessing, and she senses acquired knowledge lurking behind his bland expression.

A concrete lorry finally trundles up the lane to cap the septic tank, and one blustery, dry day, a team of carpenters from Ahakista help Lén and Young Liam put up the new roof timbers. Roofing felt is laid, and battens begin to march up the roof in neat formation, keeping the rain out for the first time in generations. Finally, the slates arrive and a roofing party gets underway. Da seals the chimneys around the base with lead, and slates are handed up in a human chain. One lad, surely not old enough to shave, balances on the battens at the gable end, marking the end slates and passing them back down again for cutting.

At lunchtime Grainne lugs sandwiches and a cool box filled with cans down to the building site, and is surprised at the near-finished state of the roof, in just a few hours. Da said that was the way it had always been done, many hands to get the roof slated before the rain started, though today there's not a cloud in sight.

The lads pass Rónán, one to the other, between slurps, cooing and making faces that bring a smile to his face. She had thought she might find it painful, seeing these lithe bodies and fresh faces loud with life, but, strangely, doesn't, and she's glad that for a short while the long silence of the land is lifted by laughter.

One of them, Mark, had actually been on the *Lively Lad* on that fateful day, but no mention is made, and if his nights are sometimes dark with recollections, he doesn't speak of it. The tragedy of that day belongs to the past, and he has a future to live.

The old house will be even gloomier than theirs, she thinks. It had been built in a hollow, and the bare rock at its back that shelters it also overshadows it. On days when the wind blows, the house will be snug, but the sun will only hit the windows after it has climbed over its zenith.

'What we need,' Young Liam says, pointing with his can of lager, 'is to build a conservatory, there. You'd get the sunlight, and watch the sea, and not know the wind on cold days.'

'When you win the lottery,' one of the boys says.

'Or marry some rich go-getter.'

'No rich go-getter would want to live here.'

'Well, it wouldn't be so hard,' he insists, tipping his head to drain the can. 'A few concrete blocks and some old windows...'

'First get the place habitable, then you can think about conservatories, and maybe a heated swimming pool.'

'That would fetch the babes in, all right,' another comments.

Lén's smile is almost lost in the dark tangle of hair as the banter takes a turn towards male fantasy.

She drinks, too, and listens as they talk of the things young men talk of, forgetting to be mindful of her presence, naïve as children. It's balmy on the side of the hill, the green fields below scattered with sheep, and their own dialogue drifting lazily.

'...d'ye mind Annie May's Bar when we played darts against the Bantry lot? And didn't we beat the shit out of them?'

'And that party when the silage was in? Weren't we that langered we didn't make it home, and slept in a barn?'

'...that time your mam was that angry she was after ye with a broom?'

'...that game where Michael scored right across the field...'

'Oh, and those girls, by God, the redhead with the enormous...'

Grainne laughs into the sudden embarrassed silence, reaches for Rónán, who has snuggled into someone's mud-encrusted vest, and leaves them to it.

Colm had been lucky with these close-knit childhood friends. When she had uprooted herself, she left behind more than her own family.

'Will I walk you back up to the house?' Lén asks, helping to settle Rónán into the sling.

'I was going to take a walk first.'

'A walk is what I need, too,' he says, stretching. 'Do you mind the company?'

She really does, but is too polite to say so. 'That would be great, thanks.'

He turns to the lads. 'You can manage the capping slates without me. Wash out the mixer and leave the cans in the truck. I'll see you all later, down below.'

Grainne is sure she didn't imagine the look of annoyance that passes fleetingly over Young Liam's face. Things had gone from bad to worse with his own father, so Da said he could stop with them until the little house was ready. She wishes Da had asked her first, but even if he had, she probably would have said, yes, of course. How could she not? Yet his unasked-for presence must rub salt in the unhealed wound of Da's loss, and as for herself, she finds his presence intrusive.

What Liam and Da had agreed financially, Grainne doesn't know, but both seem happy with the arrangement. Young Liam had proved his worth when lambing started, taking the strain from Da's shoulders. This year's lambs weren't part of the deal, but Liam had a good reason for being on hand, overseeing the birthing, getting the benefit of Da's experience of the land, and making sure they didn't lose any ewes through inadequate hubandry.

She'll be glad to see him out of the house, though, and thinks Da probably feels the same. It's cruel having another young man under the roof, filling the space at the table where Colm used to sit, walking in through the door with a cheery howdy, and sitting down to dinner as though he owns the place.

Grainne doesn't dislike him, there's nothing about him to dislike, she just doesn't want him there for the times she turns around and thinks, for the briefest of moments, that he is Colm; that, she resents him for.

She does wonder, if Colm were to suddenly turn up, as if by magic, whether she would discover love again, whether the doubts would all fade, simply because he was there. But at this moment, she resents the way Young Liam holds Rónán in the air above his head while Rónán screams with laughter, for the way Rónán holds his hands out to him, for the way Rónán goes to Liam as easy as he goes to her or Da; so she's looking forward to him leaving. She concerned about Rónán latching on to him as a father-figure, so the sooner he leaves, the better.

Grainne is thinking this as they head up towards the rath, while feeling slightly uncomfortable with Lén's taciturn presence, but as they walk, the silence settles and the landscape wraps itself around them. It's strange to have another man walk beside her, quietly, allowing her the freedom to think. Colm could never be quiet or still. He would bounce over the rocks, pointing, talking, joking, as if he needed to break the silence to prove to himself that he existed. She wonders if the rocks beneath her feet retain the echo of his ebullient presence, or whether they have slumped gratefully into the peace of aeons.

As the path narrows, Lén leads them up the slope, his back dominating the small path. His jeans and work shirt are spattered with cement and slate dust. There's something inherently calm about him, as though he came to terms with himself a long time ago. As he turns to offer his hand on a steep slope, she notices it's scarred, and missing the tip of his middle finger.

She imagines him in the finely spun wool-weave of the iron-age, perhaps with a leather jerkin and leather protection on his arms and legs. He would have made a fearful warrior, with his size and sheer brawn. With a sword in his hand and a circlet around his neck, the promiscuous Queen Maeve would surely find him irresistible. He obviously lost the end of his finger in a sword fight.

As if reading her mind, he asks, 'What will Queen Maeve do now? Or is that a secret? She thought she had the crown of the underworld in her grasp, and now it lies in a broken ship under three fathoms of water. I don't think they'd invented diving suits in the Iron Age, unless I'm much mistaken.'

She gives a shocked hiccup of laughter. 'Are you following *Queen Maeve?*'

'Without fail.'

'Did you always?'

'To be honest, I looked it up when Colm brought you home. I only read non-fiction, myself, as a rule, and have a bit of an inkling about our past history, but after a couple of episodes I was hooked.'

'Truly?'

'Truly. And amazed. Here is this talented woman writing a TV series from a farmhouse in West Cork, and no one seems to have cottoned on. How did you manage that?'

'No one really cares who I am. I just get paid, and the actors and producers get the glory.' She stops talking for a moment to negotiate a step. Lén is there, his hand steadying her, as she carries on. 'If something happens to me, others will pick it up and run with it, but Nigel likes that even he can't second-guess where it's going to go. Also, he knows there are others out there who'd take me on in an instant if he drops me, so at the moment he's hanging on to his golden goose, even if he doesn't like it that I'm not in London.'

'Did you think of going back?'

'When Colm died? I thought seriously about it. But Da needed me more than anyone has ever needed me, so I couldn't. And then, of course, Rónán made his presence known. That was a bit of a curveball. I'm still in shock.'

They stop at a vantage point and look back towards Whiddy Island and down into the small cove where boats sometimes moor. She and Lén, strangers with the shadow of Colm between them.

The hedgerows, which had been thick with white blossom until a brief easterly squall had ripped them from the bushes, are now darkening with leaf. Though there's a chill in the air, still. The Atlantic is slumbering; a deceitful, passive sheen of glass mirroring small scudding clouds.

'Colm said he understood about my art,' she says finally, 'but he didn't. It took me a long while to realise that. He wanted me to stop.'

'So, things weren't all happiness and light between you?'

She shrugs hopelessly. 'As far as he knew, they were. He thought I was going to finish the series, and that would be the end of it. I never promised that.'

'He didn't understand that it was more than a job, that it was an integral part of your life.'

No one has ever got that before, she thinks. 'He didn't listen. I don't think he ever listened to me. He saw what he wanted to see. And maybe I did, too. To start with, anyway.'

'Do you need me to carry Rónán?'

'No, I can manage. Thanks.'

She turns to follow the path, taking a circular route back to the Goulalough farm, and Lén steps in behind her. It's strange having company up here after the last troubled, lonely year. Lén's a good listener, at ease with his own thoughts, whatever they are.

What an idiot Colm truly was. He found a rare orchid and ripped it from the soil, cherishing not the strength of the plant, just its blossom. The words of 'On Raglan Road' might have been written for him: 'That I had wooed not as I should, a creature made of clay...' Oh, I don't doubt he thought he loved her, that man-child, flitting from dream to dream without a thought for the consequences. That's why we all loved him, wanted to be him, sometimes. He was able to lift the care from our shoulders just by being. And now he doesn't exist any more, the orchid is blossoming. Poor Colm.

They carry on around the rath and down the goat path the other side. It has been a glorious day so far, but now dark clouds are gathering over the sea. Within moments a spit of rain hits her face.

'Four seasons in a day and never a winter,' Lén quotes as the rain starts.

'That's pretty much the truth of it,' she agrees. Except that recently it has seemed more like winter than ever, as snow briefly flurried around their sheltered corner of the world for the first time in years.

The squall hits, sending them scurrying.

It is a strange environment, though. She had never experienced squalls before, but here they sweep in from the Atlantic, flashing over the land like daemons, flattening the trees one moment, gone the next.

'We got that roof on just in time,' Lén comments, trying to shield her from the driving rain, protecting Rónán as they run the last few yards to the back door.

Rónán gasps with shock at the rude awakening and begins to howl.

Lén flashes a smile. 'That's my cue to leave. I'll see you tomorrow.'

Grainne nurses Rónán with Lén's amusement in her mind's eye. Fancy that! He'd been watching her series. Soon he'll be in it. She won't tell him, see if he guesses.

Rónán is nine months old, the bluebells have died back, and summer's in the air when Liam finally moves in to the renovated house. Grainne feels herself expand to fill the space once more. 'It's nice to have our house back again,' she says to Da.

'Don't you like Young Liam?'

'He's a nice person in just about every way. But he's not Colm.'

'I know. It was hard. I kept thinking it should be

Colm here, too. But if you like him, girl, I wouldn't be upset.'

'Like him? Oh. No, Da, not like that. I still...' she hesitates, then says it anyway. 'I still can't really believe he's dead. It's as if his ghost is haunting me. I keep expecting to turn around and find him there. Not seeing his body, the boat not turning up. It's as if there's a space still waiting to be filled, if you know what I mean.'

Da grimaces. 'He's dead, girl, and that's a fact, even if we didn't get to see his body. Don't be wasting your life, now, waiting for him to come back.'

Grainne wonders if he is talking of himself, thinking of Alyssa.

'Anyway, I'm not in a hurry to meet anyone else. Maybe one day, you never know, but not yet. Not for a long time. Now, sit and have your tea.'

She takes the big pot from the stove, heavy with the ham and potatoes, and serves it with the big chipped enamel spoon that's probably as old as the house. She can no longer envisage living in the London flat with her designer cookware.

When they're seated, she asks, 'Will you be moving to the bungalow in Bantry now Liam's taken on the farm?'

Da stops, the fork halfway to his mouth. 'Do you want me to?'

'No, then we'd both be lonely, wouldn't we? I've been wondering, that's all.'

'I'm thinking of letting it. I was going to run it by you.

It's doing no good sitting there empty. The cash would be useful, until Young Liam starts paying rent. He needed that break.'

She nods. 'He did, that was a decent thing to do, especially as he isn't family. And it's good you want to stay. Rónán needs a man about the place, and whatever happens, this is always your home.'

Even as she says it, she realises *she* needs a man about the place, and Da is easy to be with. There's been a subtle shift in their relationship since Colm died, and she's come to love Da as if he truly were family; more, maybe.

'Besides,' he adds, through a mouthful, 'you don't drive, and if I wasn't here, you'd be pretty much relying on Young Liam. I'm thinking that wouldn't be such a good idea, now.'

She nods. 'It would be sending him the wrong message. I don't want to make him think he's going to inherit Colm's wife and child and farm as a package.'

Da nods. 'If that's not your plan, then I'll stay.'

'I was wondering whether I could learn to drive. At my age, is it possible?'

Da snorts, making her smile, then says, 'Liam asked, now the well's bored, if we'd pop by the old house, see how he's doing. Shall we go now?'

'Now's as good as any.'

It's a soft evening as they walk down the lane, the fine dusting of mist sitting on their hair and shoulders. Da's carrying Rónán, who is enjoying the sensation of dampness on his skin, his face turned to the sky and a smile playing on his lips. He's alert to his surroundings, these days, gazing with interest, clutching at everything within reach.

Liam greets them with bouncing enthusiasm. He points proudly to an old range he and the boys have cobbled together from three old ones. 'Me and the lads got the stove going a couple of days ago. It works fine, altogether.'

'It's probably better than the one we're using,' Da comments, stroking the old cream enamel with admiration. 'They made things to last in those days.'

Liam was bursting with pleasure. 'I'm almost looking forward to winter!'

Grainne smiles. 'Don't be wishing the summer away. It's short enough.'

'No, but it'll be cosy all right, and look, here's my kitchen up and working.'

He's bought a Belfast sink and has propped it up on piles of concrete blocks and boards to make it serviceable. His table is of the same design. There are plans for the future, but it will be a tidy enough house for a single man, sound from the wind and rain, with a bed, a chair, a kitchen table, and a range. What more could a young man need?

'If you get some rails up, I'll sort you out some curtains,' she offers.

'You don't have to go to that bother, sure, and I don't

mind the dark.'

'It's not a bother, and it'll keep the fairies from the glass in the dark.'

He laughs. 'Then, thanks.'

'And it will make the place more homely, besides. If you're after courting, she'll want a bit of home comfort, and there's little enough of that, yet.'

Liam flushes. 'I wasn't thinking of bringing any woman to the place.'

'In good time, in good time,' Da says.

'Well, and with the work on the farm, there'll be no time to go on the razz.'

He casts Grainne a glance that makes her uncomfortable. She's pleased he's moved in here, no longer hanging around her kitchen asking if she needs anything doing. He'd made himself comfortable with her, helping out, looking after Rónán, fetching in wood for the stove. But now he's in his own place, maybe he wishes he hadn't sorted it so quickly.

While he'd been in her house, she had treated him with the familiar care of a close friend or brother, but suspects he'd read more into her attention, hoping, in the grand scheme of things, to fill Colm's shoes in more ways than one. Perhaps he had fooled himself into believing his desires were reciprocated.

She knew all too well. She'd done it herself.

In London, during those heavy years of the art degree, living in rough lodgings with too little cash, she'd become friendly with Paul, a young manager from the local store where she'd been doing some shelf-filling before she'd the idea of creating her own comic strip.

She got on really well with Paul, and the fact that there was no spark between them, or thought for the future, had made the relationship more comfortable. He owned a little house – nothing grand, a mid-terrace left to him by an aunt. It had three bedrooms, and was neat, still with dainty lace curtains at the front windows. She had been with him a couple of times when he stopped to collect his wallet on their way to the local for fish and chips and a pint, and she couldn't help thinking how nice it would be to live there – he certainly had the space to take in a lodger. She wouldn't have to share a filthy kitchen with three other girls who lived like sluts. She wouldn't have to put up with their loud music, or the raucous, late-night trysts, with those embarrassing noises bouncing through the walls.

Paul would be grateful, she knew, for someone else to keep the place for him, clean it, make dinners for him to come home to after his overlong hours at the shop, and also, he'd earn a little more money from the rent.

After stewing on it for some time, working out every tiny detail, she'd been pretty sure he would agree it was a good idea. One evening in the bar she broached the subject.

'No,' he said.

'Why not? It makes perfect sense.'

His eyes turned cold, as if an internal light had been flicked off. 'I like my own space. I don't want someone else there. I keep my own house clean. I don't need a housekeeper, and I don't need the money.'

'But it—'

He put his unfinished pint on the table, got up and walked out without looking back. She lost his friendship and also the job, as suddenly there was no requirement for a casual shelf-filler.

She wondered, later, whether there ever had been, whether he had just taken pity on her from the first, and she'd pushed the boundaries of his goodwill. Whichever, she had been enormously hurt at the time, but several years later, when she was able to rent her first flat in London, she understood. She didn't want anyone else living there with her, even if it would have helped with the finances.

Even the times when Andy stayed over, she'd felt her space invaded. And that last time, when he'd said, *okay, so how about we make this a permanent arrangement, then?* – not the most romantic of proposals – she'd said she didn't want his stuff in her space, his dirty washing in her laundry bin. The words just fell out of her mouth during the argument, and as they fell, she realised the truth of them.

She'd been happy with the relationship; sure, it wasn't going to last. But he'd been heading for marriage, and a comfortable life, supported by a wife with a good income.

'I think I should tell Liam,' she says to Da, on the way back up to the house. 'Make it clear.'

'Let things cool,' Da advises. 'Time usually sorts these things out well enough without us making a meal of it.'

Chapter 10

When the nights begin to lengthen, in the end, she has to tell Young Liam straight out, that there's no chance of their having a relationship. She simply doesn't feel for him that way. The look he gives her would curdle milk.

Well, the auld ones were right enough, that she's a hard case. She got Colm with her city ways, and made eyes at me for the last months, then says, no thanks, not having any of it. Well, it seems we're lumbered with each other for a while, what with me running Colm's farm, and her nursing his baby, so she can just sit back and live on the earnings of both of us. Just as well Colm hasn't a clue what kind of bitch he married. She says she didn't lead me on, but by God, I saw it in her eyes, and sure, wasn't she just stringing me along to manage the farm for Darragh and herself so that Colm's boy will inherit? Isn't it always the way? But what's a man to do? With my farm gone to the winds, my father off to the States, and I'm left here holding nothing, as before. Perhaps

I should have followed my brothers and made a new life over the water. Maybe I'll do that, anyway, and damn the lot of them, once I've got a bit of money behind me. At least Darragh's as honest as the day.

Though she hadn't made any promises, and doesn't believe she led him on in any way, she sees now that he sees her in the same light as his father – someone who made promises when it was convenient, and broke the promise when it was no longer wanted. She didn't remind him that he lived rent-free in a house she'd paid to have renovated, and wonders whether the chip on his shoulder will weigh him down. She hopes not; it had never been her intention. But she now wonders what promises his father had truly made, or whether Young Liam's expectations had been formed out of nothing but his own dreams and expectations.

Rónán is turning one year old. His eyes have changed from baby blue to the dark seductive hazel that had been Colm's. 'Sure, you'll break hearts with those eyes,' she tells him. He laughs, but everyone who sees him says the same thing.

Grainne is not looking forward to today, though. Katie had encouraged a few young mothers from the mother and toddler group to come up and see Rónán's first year out, to provide Rónán with company of his own age, she said, but Grainne knows it's also to try to get her involved with the community.

Three young mothers turn up, eying the place

curiously, carrying well-dressed babies, and up-to-the-minute baby bags. Katie introduces them: 'Grainne – Roisin, Ann, and Jeannie, and the babies,' she touched each one gently, possessively on the head, 'Mary, Caitlin, Jimmy, Rónán.'

Grainne sees them settled in the living room and excuses herself to go and fetch tea and biscuits. She leans for a moment on the kitchen table. Why on earth had she agreed? This is absolutely dreadful.

She'd bought some colourful throws to liven up the tired armchairs, and the women now sit in a circle, clutching mugs and muttering comments on the weather, and the various developments that the children, all profoundly advanced for their ages, are achieving. Between them, the children on the rugs play their solitary games, eyeing each other suspiciously, and stealing toys from each other with determined detachment. It seems that socialising needs to be taught.

Grainne doesn't know these women, and has the increasing sensation that it's all going horribly wrong, when she hears another vehicle pull up outside. She excuses herself with relief. 'I'd better just go and see who that is.'

To her surprise, Lén is struggling through the door with some carrier bags. 'Heard about the party. Thought you might need some moral support,' he whispers. And out of the bag comes six bottles of wine, a box of new wine glasses, chocolates, and various bags of nibbles and pots of dips.

'Wine?' she whispers, shocked. 'It's just after lunch, and they drove up, with babies!'

'These aren't for the weans.'

She giggles.

'And no doubt Katie will drive them back. She doesn't drink, and this was her idea. Have you got a tray? Good, there you go.' He shows her a bottle of Tullamore Dew whiskey, peeping from his inside pocket. 'I'll go and share a tot with Da, he's hiding in the sheep shed.'

When she walks in with the tray, the air feels brittle, but within a half-hour, Grainne finds herself relaying anecdotes of life in London to a group of wide-eyed, rather merry mothers; Katie, for once, is listening rather than talking.

'You didn't!' says one, agog with curiosity.

'Sure, I did,' Grainne says. 'She deserved it. The bitch was virtually hanging out of her dress, making a play for my bloke, and my job.'

'What, she was after Colm?'

'No, Andy. I'd already ditched him when I met Colm. at my cousin's wedding in Cork. He was lust at first sight.'

As the mothers screech with laughter, Grainne realises that her life is divided into *before Colm* and *after Colm*. But *after Colm* seems to be after his death, too. As if those short years of marriage had just simply evaporated.

After providing liberal doses of coffee, Katie drove the three young mums home, with a promise to bring them up the next day for their cars.

Grainne clears the dishes and tidies the kitchen, feeling light-headed and a little happy. The girls had been fun, after all. She'd surprised herself by agreeing to meet them at the mother and toddler group the following week, and isn't feeling too unhappy about the decision. At least she won't be walking in cold. The thought of that sudden silence, all eyes turned on her, was what had put her off before.

Rónán is stashed in his cot, hopefully for the night, and Grainne is heading upstairs to her drawing table when the phone rings. She waits on the stairs, looking back, as Da picks it up. It's unlikely to be Nigel, she thinks. He insists on using her mobile number, though she's told him a million times the signal is out here is so unreliable it's probably steam-powered.

'Oh, Karen, hello.' Da lifts his brow at Grainne. 'How are you? I'm well, thanks. I'll get her for you. Bye for now. It's your mother, Grainne,' he says, unnecessarily loudly.

Her mother calls rarely. Theirs isn't the kind of relationship that invokes an unloading of comfortable gossip, so thoughts of disasters, of Dad dying, of financial ruin or whatever, flash through her mind. God forbid she's asking to come over and stay!

'Mam?'

'Look, love, there's something you need to know. Good news. Amazing news... I think.'

There's a long pause after her hesitation, which isn't

like her mum at all. Grainne can't recall ever hearing her flustered, as if she can't quite find the words to express herself. 'Yes?' she prompts.

'It's Colm, love. We think he might be alive.'

The blood rushes from her head, and for the first time in her life she experiences the dizzy, light-headed sensation of being about to pass out. She sits on the stairs and takes several deep breaths, thinking it's some kind of bad joke, except that her mother doesn't have a malicious sense of humour. In fact, come to think of it, her mother doesn't have a sense of humour at all.

'I don't understand.'

Her mother's words gush out now, unstoppable. There's an echo on the line as if they're coming from a different universe. 'Dad and I were watching the TV last night, and we caught the tail end of a newsflash about a man who's got amnesia. Apparently, he was picked up out of the water by a trawler, and hasn't a clue who he is.'

'But it's been eighteen months, Mam,' Grainne whispers.

'I know, love. It seems they've put newsflashes out a couple of times, but I guess we just never saw them before. Anyway, they showed this man on TV. I couldn't swear to it, neither could your dad, but it looked like Colm.'

'Looked like, or is?' Her voice is strained.

'Well, that's what we wonder, of course, but how could it be him? The thing is, he's in Spain, so it seems unlikely, and we didn't know Colm so well, but I got online and found out a bit more. Look, check your email. I'm sending you over the links for what I found. I think it's best if you read it yourself, look at the pictures. It could be a dreadful mistake on my part, but I had to let you know, didn't I?'

Of course... I... um...' Grainne collects herself. 'I'll have a look. Thanks, Mam.' She puts the phone back on the charger, and remains sitting on the stairs in a daze.

Da is standing at the living room door, holding onto the frame, concern on his face. 'What's wrong? Is it your dad?'

'No, Da. Mam says...' She takes a breath. 'Mam says Colm might be alive.'

Da visibly winces. His face goes tight, the way it hadn't for a few months, now. 'No. That's impossible. Is she out of her senses? She shouldn't go saying things like that.'

'Da, listen. There's a man, in Spain—' She understands now how difficult it must have been for her mother to find the right words. 'He was pulled out of the water, with amnesia, and never recovered his memory. They put him on TV, and Mam and Dad saw him. She said he looks like Colm, but she didn't know him so well. It's probably a mistake.'

Da is silent for a long moment, and when he speaks his voice is small, tired. 'How can we know?'

'Mam sent me a link on email. Come on up to my room, we'll check it out. It's got to be wrong. There's no way he survived. And if he did, why would he be in Spain?'

'Well, best to make sure,' Da agrees. 'Then we can rest easy.'

Her computer has never taken so long to fire up. She finally finds her mother's email in the junk folder, and wonders if somehow the computer knew where it belonged. With a sense of detached disbelief, she clicks the link. A grainy image of a man's face pops into view, and she winces. Were it not for the tubes in his mouth and the mask over his nose, she'd have assumed this to be the image of a cadaver. The man's eyes are closed, and it would be hard to know if he was twenty years old, or fifty.

She has a smattering of Spanish, picked up along the way. 'I think this is just after they found him. They're asking if anyone recognises him. They call him Pedro.'

Da leans in closely, and says flatly, 'That's not my Colm.'

But Grainne isn't so sure, and follows a link to a more recent article. He's recovered enough to give a press conference, but the article says he recalls nothing except a vague thought that he might have been a fisherman. That fits with his being found in the water after a storm. Grainne can't make out all the words, but she gets the gist of the story, and translates roughly for Da.

'A Spanish trawler picked up a personal beacon signal on' – Grainne mentally backtracks on the dates – 'Oh, God, that would have been a day after the *Faery*

Queen was lost. They were heading home, *hacia al sur*, it says. I think that means south, from Icelandic waters. They hauled a man up out of the sea. They, ah, believed they were recovering a body. They were surprised to find he wasn't dead. He was barely breathing and in deep thermal shock, so gave him, ah, I think that means assistance or first aid. They called the French emergency services for evacuation from their boat, and the man was, um, airlifted, to a French hospital. He was unconscious all this time. The gendarmes traced his personal location tracker. It was registered to a ship, no, a trawler in Spain, which turned out to have been out of commission for a couple of years, and was due for scrapping. They're seeking the owner. Because of that, they decided the rescued man must be Spanish, so the French sent him – offloaded him more like – on to a Spanish hospital. That's the end of that article.'

Grainne scrolls down and another image appears on the screen. She recoils from the screen; the ground beneath her feet no long feels solid. For a second, she struggles to focus on the image. She shakes her head to clear her vision and forces herself to look at the pixelated face in front of her. This time there are no tubes, and the man's eyes are open. The expressionless face, skeletal and sunken, looks not like Colm, but Da.

Da stares at the image.

She says flatly, 'We have to go over there. We have to know, for sure.'

When the storm hit, when Colm's boat went down, Grainne had felt useless, her anger having no focus, that insubstantial thing called fate having decided the issue. She had thought nothing could ever be so bad as those long days of waiting; waiting to know if he had survived; then waiting to see if his body would be recovered; waiting for anything, long after the acceptance that nothing would ever be found of the *Faery Queen* or her crew. For weeks she had existed in a bubble of helpless confusion, knowing that nothing she did or said could make any difference. Then, finally, after Rónán was born, she'd come to terms with her widowed status, learned to live with it, and move on. And now, after all this time, she finds herself, far too late, with a specific job to do. Somehow this is worse. If it is Colm, what will she do?

The night passes without sleep. The words *what if it is him?* whirl in an endless cycle. She wills herself to sleep, because tomorrow will be difficult enough, but her brain refuses to shut down, endlessly scrolling through a mismatch of stored data.

In the morning, she's awake before Rónán and has his breakfast ready before he has a chance to yell for it. She's weaning him now, and only feeds him from the breast in the evening, to settle him down. Da looks as haggard as she feels. She hugs him silently as he comes in from the fields, sharing this new bewilderment, before going through the motions of brewing a pot of tea. In a daze, she makes toast, boils eggs, and puts butter and jam on the table, though neither of them is inclined to eat. It's a desperate effort to make the abnormal seem normal.

'I didn't sleep, either,' she says. 'After all this time, it's just not—'

She was going to say *fair*, but it seems childish.

Da seems to understand, and says, 'Sure, if it is Colm, this should have happened eighteen months ago, not now.'

'I have to go to Spain. Will you go with me?'

'I must, mustn't I? Colm was my son.'

The buttered toast sits between them, cold. 'Da, I'm afraid. I don't know how to handle this.'

'Nor do I, girl. Nor do I.'

Grainne's mother, never more efficient than when managing someone else's life, is in her element. She calls the authorities and the hospital, and checks out flights. As her emails come tumbling in, Grainne learns that her father is out golfing, keeping out of the way. Having seen her mother in full-on managing mode, she totally gets it, but is irritated all the same.

When Young Liam calls up to the house, Da tells him what's happened, and that they'll be away for a few days, in Spain. Grainne watches him churning it over. Although he makes a good show of being pleased for Da, for her, she can see sentiment warring with yet more disappointment. Colm's return isn't exactly good news for him. He's just renovated a house, taken on the farm, and if Colm returns, all that could be pulled from under him in an instant. It just wouldn't be fair. There was that phrase again. But life, as her father had often lectured, isn't fair.

And would it be good news, after all, to find Colm alive? She doesn't voice this to anyone. What's good news, anyway? There are so many shades between good and bad, and for each individual it's a different story. What if it is Colm and he never recalls his home, or his life with her? What if it's Colm and he does remember? Of one thing she's sure, even if it is him, life won't simply fall back into the comfortable pattern of *before*. Too much has changed.

She has changed, never mind anything else.

Her mum also, to Grainne's annoyance, passes the hot gossip to Aisling, who is straight on the phone wanting to come along.

'Don't be daft, Aisling,' Grainne snaps. 'We're going to check it out, no more. It's probably a false alarm. There's nothing you can do to help even if you did come.'

'I could help take care of Rónán, and that will leave you free to take care of Darragh. It's going to be difficult for him.'

It will be, not least because Da has never left Cork county, let alone the country. She wonders how he'll cope with flying. Anyway, he'll be used to driving on the wrong side of the road, she thinks, with a flash of humour. But she isn't going to be browbeaten. 'Da doesn't need taking care of. He's not senile. And Mam is going to take care of Rónán for a couple of hours while we visit this, ah, man.'

'But I could come to Cork and look after him for you there.'

'No, you can't, I'm still feeding him. Besides, Rónán would be frantic if Da and I went away for several days. He'll only be with Mam for a few hours in the hotel.'

'But—'

'For pity's sake, Aisling, back off. You're getting more like Mam than she is!'

Her voice rises. 'I'm only trying to help.'

'You're pushing in where it's not needed... Sorry, that was horrid. But true.' Grainne waits for the outburst, but it doesn't come. Instead, Aisling tries to muffle her sobs. 'Oh, shit, I'm turning into a harridan, too. I didn't mean to upset you.'

'It's okay, I understand. It's just that I'm so unhappy.'

What? She tells me this now? 'Look, when we come back, I'll come up and stay over, and we can talk, okay?'

'You've been saying that for the last year, and you wouldn't let me come to see you, either. It's not my fault Rónán doesn't know me.'

'I know. I'm sorry.'

Doesn't Aisling recall that Grainne has had her own problems, things she needed to work through, come to terms with?

The snivels have abated, but Aisling's irritation betrays something deep and festering, and Grainne is hit by a stab of guilt for being so self-involved. She's neglected her sister, and hopes her marriage isn't failing.

She likes Brendan, despite his inherent arrogance. And Aisling has a good life – on the surface at least – but who knows what goes on behind their closed doors.

'When I get back,' she promises, 'we'll get together. Whatever the outcome.'

Aisling sounds doubtful. 'Really?'

Grainne says, 'Cross my heart.' She no longer adds *and hope to die*. It seems to challenge fate, somehow. If hopes were prayers, someone might be listening, and she has Rónán to think of.

'Have a good trip. I hope—'

There's a long pause. Aisling isn't stupid, and has probably stewed over the implications. *What does she hope? That it's Colm we find? Or that it's not him, so that maybe I'll spend more time with her once the tragedy has receded further into the past.*

Grainne grimaces. 'If it's not Colm, we can all get on with our lives, and it if is...' She can't finish that sentence, either.

Da is in a panic as he doesn't have a passport, but a few quick calls set things in motion. For once, the authorities react without the usual officious obstructiveness; it seems even bureaucrats like being part of something bigger than themselves. He is told to drive up to Dublin tomorrow, and is given a list of documents to bring.

'I'll need to put some petrol in the truck,' he says.

'Da, you've never driven that far in your life.'

'I know, but—'

'I'll call Lén, see if he can drive you. In the meantime, see if you can find your birth certificate.'

Lén turns up an hour later. He'd been working on a building project. She'd given him the barest facts, but he'd dropped everything to help.

She hears his big vehicle growl up the drive, and goes out to meet him. The clouds are low, roiling in a stiff breeze, and there's a spit in the air. He jumps down, strides over and puts his arm around her shoulder, briefly, and she senses that he understands her utter bewilderment.

'Sorry about the short notice,' she says.

'It was a bolt out of the blue, I'd say. I guess you must be feeling a bit strange.'

She pushes away and wipes her eyes. 'I don't know what to think. But we have to go and see, don't we? Me and Da? Just in case.'

'Of course you do. Do you want me to come?'

She would; he'd be a rock in her emotional storm, but she imagines Aisling's indignant, wounded recriminations, and shakes her head. 'My mum and dad will be there. Mam's Spanish is pretty good, and if you come, I'll have to answer all sorts of questions about who you are, and...'

He smiles. 'It would get complicated. You're right. Look, you don't need to come to Dublin,' he says. 'You look fair done in. It's going to be tough enough coping with Rónán, with the flights and hotels and whatever.

You stay here and get your stuff sorted, so. I'll be back up for Darragh first thing in the morning. We'll stay over, and make sure he doesn't come back without a passport.'

'Thank you.'

His dark eyes are fixed on hers and she can't look away. There is a depth and a warmth to his gaze that betrays something more than friendship, and her heart gives a jolt. 'Is Da ready?' he asks, and the moment is gone.

She gives a damp smile. 'He's trying to find his birth certificate; he hasn't seen it since he got married.'

Lén shakes his head with a rueful grimace, but as they go into the kitchen, Da waves an envelope triumphantly. 'It was in the jug where it's always been. I just forgot.'

'Great,' she says. 'All the other stuff is on the kitchen table. Come on in while we go through it one more time. Then we can run into Bantry to get a photo, and get it signed.'

The next morning, everything checked three times over, Lén picks up all the paperwork, saying, 'We'll get on our way, then, Da, or Dublin will be closed when we get there. Ready?'

Da stuffs his wallet in his pocket and slaps the cap on his head. Dublin itself is an adventure, so goodness knows what he'll make of the airport, and Spain. But one step at a time. She can't think clearly. Her brain is whirling with what-if scenarios.

In Dublin, Da will be an anachronism, a figure of fun. She hopes no one is nasty to him; but they wouldn't dare, not with Lén watching over him like a giant guardian angel.

It's a dark day, the clouds low over the farm, and as they drive off, she watches the road long after the tail lights have disappeared into the mist.

She hasn't mulled over her feelings for Lén until now. Her growing interest had been vague, not fully acknowledged. He's comfortable to be with, and seems to know her thoughts before she does, but now that there is a possibility of Colm coming home, she finds herself in an emotional quandary, because it's not Colm she envisages sharing her future with, but Lén.

There's no keeping this quiet, of course. Her mother emails saying this has become big news in Spain. When the daily news comprises a sea of gloom, the odd miracle becomes a happiness pill that everyone wants to swallow.

The next day Lén calls saying they have Da's passport sorted and are on their way back. Grainne's stomach drops. Now there's nothing to stop them from going to Spain, to find out one way or the other. She has the disturbingly selfish wish that her mother had never seen the newsflash, then this present madness might never have raised its head. Though logic suggests it would have happened sooner or later, so perhaps it's best to get it over with

The phone rings again, and it's Katie.

'Oh, Grainne, darling,' she says, breathless. 'I just heard the amazing news! Colm's been found, alive! Praise be to God! It's a miracle, to be sure, so it is.'

'Katie, for goodness' sake, don't be telling everyone that. We don't even know yet if it *is* Colm. Da and I will make sure, one way or the other, before we get excited.'

Katie's voice softens. 'A year to the day since Rónán was born, just like the stories. It's Colm, you mark my words. He's coming back for his child.'

A chill rushes through Grainne's body, and she sits down abruptly on the stairs. Katie's voice rings with the authenticity of prophecy. Colm is coming back for his child, not her. Trust Katie to pick up on the local legend of Colm's mum being a selkie.

She pulls herself together, saying tiredly, 'Katie, we don't know it's Colm. And if it is, he doesn't even know he has a child, so don't go spreading fairy tales, now.'

But as she puts the phone down, she knows it's too late. By now, word that Colm has been found alive will have exploded through the community, and Katie will have added her own unique twist to the story: the only way Colm could have survived is that he truly is a selkie, like his mother.

She still has her hand on the phone when it rings once more, making her jump. She picks it up automatically.

'Hello?'

'Grainne, it's Cara Mulcahy.' She's confused for a moment, until the woman adds, 'Niall's mother?'

Of course, those who had lost family on the *Faery Queen* would be seeing this as a miracle. Or a further grief.

'Oh. Yes, I see.'

'Well, I heard the news, and I just wanted to say I'm pleased for you. And Da, of course. It's strange enough, to be sure, just when we'd all got used to the idea that our boys are gone.'

'But...' Grainne takes a breath. 'But the thing is, we don't know it is Colm. We're going tomorrow, Da and I, but till we know, it's best to assume it's not him, don't you see?'

'Oh, but I was told...'

'They found a man in the water, after the storm, but he has amnesia. He doesn't know who he is, how he ended up in the water, or where he came from or anything. It's a long shot, at best.'

'Well, dear, if it *is* Colm saved, it's a miracle, for sure. We're all praying for you.' Then she adds with conviction, 'If it is him, it will surely be the best news ever, God be praised.'

'The best,' Grainne agrees. She thanks Cara for the call, then pulls the plug from the wall. The last thing she needs is a string of calls from people wishing and praying, when she's not sure herself what she's wishing and praying for.

Grainne imagines the news hanging like a smog, the radio waves thick with exclamations of amazement. Gossip will be flying. Those who lost family will be imagining the joy of reunion, jealously living the magic of the event, wishing it was their son, father or brother who had been miraculously reborn; but she is, quite simply, overwhelmed.

She's moved on with her life, and no one seems to know that, except Da, and maybe Lén. The Colm she married is dead. She doubts he ever truly existed.

She recalls as a child picking the petals off a daisy, chanting: *will he, won't he?*; *can I, can't I?* Now her mind is chanting endlessly: *is it him, isn't it him?* Just how many petals does this imaginary daisy have to spare? But if it is Colm, the story won't have the happy ending everyone is assuming. And she'll be the outsider, once more, the stranger in the nest, the one Colm should not have brought back from London. And what of Rónán? There is absolutely no way on this earth she will allow Colm to take him from her.

A couple of vehicles turn up during the day, and leave again when there's no answer. Marie even opens the kitchen door and calls, but Grainne hides guiltily behind the door in the living room, willing Rónán not to wake and cry out. When Marie is gone, she bolts the door from the inside, for the first time since her arrival. Maybe the door has never been locked in all its hundred years of hanging. And now she's locked it, not against thieves, but against well-wishers.

Rónán, sensing his mother is uneasy, becomes fretful and whiney, unwilling to settle at anything. She's relieved, eventually, to hear Lén's vehicle crunching up the pitted drive.

At least Da and Lén share her reservations.

Somehow, it's those beyond the family who see this bizarre circumstance as a reason for hope. After all, as Da had hinted, before leaving for Dublin, it would almost be better if it were not Colm who had been picked up out of the water, so his bones could be left to rest, wherever they had drifted. But Colm was, or is, his son, so poor Da has yet another tragedy to live through.

If it is Colm, he probably believes Grainne will leave, taking his grandson from him, and if it's not, the trauma of this moment will sit on his shoulders for another decade.

If it *is* Colm, of course, he might be changed in ways it's impossible to guess. Things will never be as they were. A man can't rise from the dead and simply take up where he left off, despite what people think. He will be like a ghost, haunting their past and present and future.

And if his past has been sliced away, like the front half of a novel torn off and thrown onto the fire, how can he possibly step back into a role he has no idea he previously played? He'll be meeting a dad he doesn't remember, and a wife he doesn't recall courting and falling in love with and marrying. And he will find himself with a son he didn't even know he had conceived.

*

Da is tired, bewildered, as he climbs from the vehicle. 'Go and sit a while,' she tells him. 'I have the kettle on.'

Lén passes her a weary smile. 'It all went well,' he says, 'until they saw Darragh's birth certificate. It was so damaged, they didn't believe it was authentic, and had to get someone to check back through old ledgers. But we got there in the end.'

'It was good enough for the priest when I got married,' Da mutters. 'Even though it fell in the road on the way home and I didn't find it for two days. I dried it over the range. I never thought I'd need it again.'

Grainne feels the tension run out of her, and her smile is genuine. 'We'll get you a new one,' she says. 'For next time you want to get married.'

Even Da smiles. 'God forbid! Once is enough for any man.' But there's an expression of wonder on his face as he reverently places the shiny new passport on the table.

Lén raises a brow at her. 'My cousin's a security guard at Cork airport. He's says reporters are flying in from Dublin and London.'

She paces the kitchen. 'I hope he didn't tell them we'll be flying out of Shannon?'

'No, he'll lie well enough. And the manager at Shannon won't say anything. He's promised VIP service to get you to the plane, but maybe it would be a good idea to leave tonight, and stay overnight in some small B & B? It strikes me they'll all turn up here, trying to get you before you leave.'

'It's not the good news they're after, it's the sensationalism. If it's not Colm, it will all go away, but what if it is?' She pauses, mid-stride, turns, and says in a hushed whisper. 'What if it is Colm? How will we cope?'

Da shakes his head. 'I don't know, girl. It's difficult, is what it is.'

Chapter 11

Ready as they ever could be, they clamber into Lén's truck. Grainne finds an Airbnb while they're on the move, and pays with PayPal. 'Done,' she tells Lén. 'I booked it under my maiden name, so hopefully it won't get out.'

It's a drive of several hours to Shannon, but they're silent most of the way, each lost in their own reverie. It's a bizarre situation, almost unbelievable, except that here they are, on the way to Spain.

They find the accommodation easily enough. It's new and clean, and tagged on to an older property, like a granny flat.

'There's a loo in my bedroom,' Da says in wonder.

'There are en suites in all the rooms, and central heating,' the owner says proudly. 'I built it on, especially for Airbnb. What with the internet and all, it's easy these days to make a few quid, even if the tax man does get his share.'

'Thank you,' Grainne says, just as Rónán lets out a bellow. He was good for the journey, but is now frustrated and cranky. 'But we're pretty tired, what with the drive and all, and the baby needs feeding.'

'I'll let you to it,' the man says, heading for the door. 'I hope you find your lad, and all.'

It's strange to be a face that everyone recognises. It hadn't been possible to totally avoid the local reporters, and national media had pulled the stops out, finding images of her from London, their wedding, and local coverage of the tragedy. 'You won't say anything?' she asks anxiously. 'We were trying to miss the reporters.'

'I have a son lost to me these twenty years,' he says. 'I won't be putting the cart before the donkey. It might not be him, after all.'

She's grateful for the voice of reason. 'Thank you.'

'I'll nip out and get a takeaway,' Lén offers. 'No one knows me.'

By the time he comes back, Grainne has settled Rónán. He's never slept anywhere but in his own home, but doesn't seem to mind the change. They sit around a new pine table in the pristine kitchen, and pick at the food.

'Strange, this,' Da says, his eyes skipping with wonder. He's never stayed anywhere but his own home, either.

'That's an understatement.'

Grainne is exhausted. Unlike Da, she's not talking about their present location, but the whole unknown future.

Lén puts a hand over hers, where it lies fisted on the

table. 'Relax. It might be him; it might not. Take each day as it comes. We can't second-guess the future, Grainney. Let's cope with what happens when it happens, eh?'

She gives a snort of laughter as he deliberately uses Nigel's mispronunciation of her name. A tingle of warmth spreads in her chest as their eyes meet in a shared, private moment. Perhaps this isn't the right moment to recognise that he's a kindred spirit, that he makes her feel comfortable with herself in a way that she's never been comfortable before.

They're out early the next morning, and at the airport well before time. The place is strangely calm. There are no reporters in sight. 'He kept his word,' she says, surprised.

'Good man,' Lén agrees. 'I've booked that place for a couple of days. I'll be waiting here when you get back.'

'Are you sure you can spare the time?'

His eyes soften. 'It's not a bother, girl. Be in touch. Let me know, soonest.'

She nearly bursts into tears at the term of endearment. *Girl.* She wants to ask him to drop everything and come, but this is something she and Da have to do, and they both know it.

'So, I'll be off, now,' he says. 'Take care.'

He gives her a hug, clasps Da's hand, and as he turns away, she feels abandoned. She takes a deep breath. 'Come on, then, Da.'

Da simply does as he's told, like a child being taken on holiday. The manager is expecting them. His suit had been made for a smaller man, and his red face and hassled expression don't bode well for longevity. He hustles them into a small room with a coffee machine and a plate of biscuits. 'Wait here,' he says. 'VIP lounge. No one will bother you. I'll have your luggage taken through security, and there's a van to take you out to the plane. It'll be bad the other end, I'm thinking.'

'I'm thinking the same,' Grainne says. 'It's kind, what you're doing. Thank you.'

The hours pass slowly, but better here than fighting through a blockade of microphones. She allows herself a brief smile. The reporters are probably miffed, and there will be no missing them on the way back. This story is a legend come to life. If they come back without Colm, the whole country will be disappointed.

Time stands still on the flight from Shannon to Barcelona. Grainne hasn't bothered to pack a book, and Da is in some kind of a daze. She was worried he'd be nervous on the plane, but perhaps the fear of what is awaiting them in Spain has overridden any potential fear of flying.

Aside from the slight buzz in her loins at take-off and landing, Grainne is comfortable with flying. Statistics aside, if her time is up, whether by rail or road or plane, there would be little she could do about it. She isn't really fatalistic – sure she'd be as terrified as the next person if things went wrong, but she's never allowed fear to rule her. When Colm took her by the hand and brought her home, she had simply decided and acted, letting the future take care of itself. This is what she's doing now.

In Spain, they're met at the foot of the plane's steps by an electric passenger buggy. A tall man with a practised smile steps down and ushers them on, amidst a stream of incomprehensible patter aimed towards a film crew, while a heavily made-up lady interprets. 'Señor Garcia is alcade, that is, ah, Mayor. He is saying welcome, and please come along with us. There is to be a meeting of reporters. You will speak to them.'

'No,' Grainne states. 'We won't.'

There's a startled silence, followed by a noisy conflab between the interpreter and her boss. She turns back, her smile brittle. 'Señor Garcia will be honoured if you would say a few words, and—'

Grainne looks directly at him. 'I'm here to *see* if this man is Colm. If he isn't, we will go home. If he is, maybe then I'll thank you for looking after him. Until that time, the reporters can wait.'

This is interpreted, and Señor Garcia scowls in an affronted silence as the vehicle drives through the vast hall, past a podium that had, maybe, been hastily erected for this event. They scoot past the surprised gathering of reporters, leaving their screaming questions unanswered, and his cold gaze rakes her just once. Some photographers run after them, snapping away, but many simply shrug and watch them leave.

Barcelona airport is huge. She's been here before, but has forgotten the sheer scope of it – the shiny walkways, the ceiling that arcs into a space that looks as if it could house a thousand jumbo jets. A series of images pile into her head. What if gravity disappeared? This heave of humanity would rise and disperse, astonished individuals floating like angelfish in a glass bowl.

Mr Garcia taps the driver on the shoulder to stop, and jumps down. He snaps at his assistant, and even Grainne's minimal Spanish catches the message. 'Ring me when there's a decision. We'll reschedule.'

'I think he's not happy,' Da says.

'He's an idiot. Why on earth would we hold a press conference now, when we don't even know?'

'He wanted his moment of glory, because if it's not my boyeen, there's no point holding a press conference at all,' Da says, with matter-of-fact comprehension.

'He's a self-important fool,' Grainne says derisively.

The interpreter's lips twitch before she ushers them into the back of a waiting car, and hops in the front beside the driver.

'We need to go to the airport hotel, first,' Grainne tells her, indicating Rónán. 'My mother is waiting there, to take the child for a few hours.'

'Is not far,' the interpreter says, and instructs the driver.

Grainne texts her mother to say they are on their way. Both her parents are waiting outside when they get there. It's a long, curved building, faced with glass. It was described as impressive, but to Grainne it's a typical staging post: big, functional, and clinically devoid of character. It suits her present mood. A place to sleep, then leave, with neither regret nor sentiment to cloud the memory.

'Give me your bags, we'll book you in, love,' her father says, with unusual helpfulness, while she passes Rónán to her mother, a complete stranger to him. He looks as if he's about to scream, so Grainne gives him a quick kiss, says, 'Thanks, Mam, Dad. Now, go with nana, love; mummy will be back soon. Wave bye-bye?'

Before Rónán has a chance to voice his irritation, she's back in the car.'

'Okay, we go to Castelldefels, now,' the interpreter says.

Rónán's arm is waving until they are out of sight, no doubt powered by her mother's hand. It's the first time Rónán has been out of her care since he was born. It feels decidedly strange, as though she is abandoning him, and will never see him again. She tells herself to stop being daft.

The city is enormously foreign, with remnants of ancient stone buildings intermingled with more modern efforts, but like any other city, it's noisy, bustling with the blare of horns and unrelenting rush of traffic. Gradually they ease out onto a wide, fast road heading west, she thinks. Grainne is grateful she doesn't have to deal with taxis, directions, or questions. As the crowds are left behind, the interpreter takes on the role of tourist guide, twisting around to face them as she gesticulates expansively.

'On the left is Delta del Llobregat, a very beautiful national park, then beyond is the Balearic sea. On the right here, we grow a lot of fruit that we export to England and Ireland, and in the distance you can see Muntanyes d'Ordal, where you can walk and paraglide. There is much history there.'

The mountains don't look so high from here, but Grainne gets the impression of a vast, fertile plain sweeping towards a distant escarpment of grey rock. Closer, the marching rows of orange groves and olives seem to be clawing themselves out of parched, barren soil. She understands why people come here as tourists, for the sun and sea, but can't imagine why her parents would want to be here permanently. This barrage of heat surely doesn't compensate for the loss of everything familiar.

The air is strangely dry, the sun unrelenting. The houses they pass are impersonal. With their windows shuttered to keep out the heat, they emit a sad air of abandonment, as if the populace just upped and moved out, en masse.

Da stares around silently, stunned or shocked by the sheer vastness of the landscape. It's one thing seeing strange places on the TV, quite another to be there in person.

Grainne has been here before, on holiday, in that

other life, but this is different, surreal. Right now, she doesn't know if she's chasing her past, her future, or some undefined destiny.

Finally, leaving a cloud of dust in their wake, they turn onto a long private drive leading to a unit the interpreter calls a *mental rehabilitation centre*. 'More usually, this place is for people who have had brain injuries,' she explains. 'Here, people learn again to speak, to walk.'

'Does he—' Grainne also finds herself searching for words. She can't refer to this man as Colm. 'The man we're coming to see. Does he speak at all?'

'Oh, sure. He speaks well.'

'So, he can make himself understood? People here speak English?'

'I don't understand? He speaks Spanish fluently.'

Grainne's eyes meet Da's, as she exclaims, 'But if he speaks Spanish, it can't be Colm! How stupid of me. I should have asked that before we came all this way for nothing.'

Da's looking confused. Perhaps she's punctured his dream. But perhaps, all along, he'd known it couldn't possibly be Colm. The circumstances are too bizarre, too unlikely.

Here, a different crowd of reporters have gathered, and there's a bustling and jostling for place as the driver and the interpreter scream at them in a fast patter of Spanish – probably accentuated with ripe language – for them to make space, let the guests through.

As she's shoved towards the door, Grainne is glad that Rónán is not here. As much as she hadn't liked leaving him with her parents, she can't imagine coping with him in this bedlam. The reporters are finally locked outside, despite voluble dissent, and peace descends. This is going to be unpleasant enough, without them snapping images every second.

Inside, they're met by a casually dressed, slim man, who extends a formal hand to both Grainne and Da, accompanied, presumably, by words of welcome. The interpreter says, 'Doctor Diaz asks if you would like refreshment. Coffee, or cold orange juice?'

'No, thank you. We would just like to get this over, and go home.'

'Si, si, sigueme, come,' the man says. He ushers them on down a flagstone corridor. 'Mister Pedro, here.'

They pass a glass door to a large room in which several people are sitting, some in wheelchairs, some twitching involuntarily, some staring blankly at puzzles that they no longer have the ability to interpret.

Dr Diaz stops by another door and opens it with a flourish. It's a room for art therapy, papered with crude images, like an infants' classroom. At the far side, a man is bent over his work, studiously, oblivious to their presence. As she draws near, Grainne's throat closes, and her breath disappears, leaving her light-headed. The man is painting, with a degree of skill, an exquisite scene of a rock on which two seals seem to be watching a brilliant sunset descend into night. But what shocks her more is that the curve of the man's back, the shape of his head, and the very stance of his body are familiar.

'Colm?' she whispers.

The man freezes for a long moment, then he carefully places the brush beside his work and stands and turns, bewilderment transforming irrevocably to knowledge. 'Dad? Grainne?'

Tears trickle down Da's face and, seeing him tremble, Dr Diaz puts a hand under Da's elbow, his own face beaming with the joy of a rare, happy ending amidst his litany of sad stories.

Colm puts both hands on his father's upper arms, and squeezes gently, looking him directly in the eye. He is almost crying, but his lips quiver into that quirky smile Grainne recalls so well. 'It took you a long time to find me, Dad. Didn't you want me to come home?'

Da draws in a shuddering breath. 'Colm, my boy, is it really you?'

'So it would seem,' Colm says, adding, in wonder, 'How can a person forget who they are, and then, just like that, remember everything? It's very strange, so it is.'

Father and son, who had probably not hugged in years, now hold each other with a kind of desperation. Eventually, Colm puts Da aside and reaches for Grainne. She's pulled into his arms, and as his mouth reaches for hers, he ends up kissing her cheek as she turns her head.

He backs away from her rigid body with a wry smile.

'Grainne?'

Her voice is ragged. 'It's been eighteen months, Colm. All that time, I thought you were dead.'

'All that time, I suppose I was. And now?'

'It's like meeting a ghost. You need to give us time—'

He nods, accepting the truth of her statement. 'And the others. What of Aidan and Niall and Eoghan?'

'I'm sorry,' she says. 'The other boats came in, but the *Faery Queen* was lost with all hands. Or so we thought. Niall's body turned up, no others.'

'All of them? Eighteen months gone, and I didn't know?' His face slackens with guilt, and tears spring, as if this is a lack of good manners on his part. 'It was like yesterday we left Bantry, laughing and joking together, talking about old times, and they're all gone? All passed? Just like that? It's hard to take in, so it is.'

'We had a service for everyone. Including you,' Grainne says softly.

'Including me.' He shakes his head, struggling to process the weight of this moment.

'This is strange for everyone. Let's get you home, shall we?'

He's grateful for her understanding. 'Yes, let's get home. Back to the farm. Then we can start over.'

Grainne feels something sink inside her. There's a possibility that they will start over; that suddenly all that love, that emotion will come flooding back. But what if it doesn't? Should she stay with Colm because she once vowed she'd love him until death parted them? At the time she had meant it. But, to be fair, death had already parted them, and some things can't be undone. She plasters a smile on her face and nods. 'Sure. The future will take care of itself, I guess.'

Colm laughs uncertainly, no doubt realising that nothing will ever be the same.

Dr Diaz steps forward, says something, and the interpreter translates. 'Doctor Diaz says not to be sad. This is a happy time. We must have happy pictures for the periodistas, the ah, newspaper people.'

Chapter 12

It doesn't take long for Colm to pack. He has little enough, just a few clothes that have been given to him, and a few of his own paintings. Everything else – books, materials – belong to the unit. It takes even less time, just a couple of phone calls, for the authorities to agree to his leaving Spain for Ireland without a passport. The process is, essentially, deportation. They're informed that flights will be booked, documents filed and stamped and delivered to him at the hotel. He will be escorted from the hotel to the airport by local police, for his own protection, of course, but they will make sure he gets on the plane. They don't much care what happens at the other end when he arrives passport-less. Grainne realises, belatedly, that it never occurred to her to bring his passport. Was that because, deep inside, she had been certain it would not be him?

She has almost forgotten about the reporters, but the news has already filtered outside, and the determined crowd of reporters at the door has multiplied. As the door opens, to a waft of hot air, flashlights sparkle like sun on glass. People are screaming in Spanish and English, each trying to be heard above the others:

'Colm, what do you remember about the storm?'

'Do you remember your ship going down?'

'What is it like to remember who you are, after all this time?'

'Did you know your wife and father when they came in?'

'What will you do with your life now?'

'Are you looking forward to going home?'

She is standing close beside him. His arm is around her, and her fixed smile is forced. Colm holds up his hand, waits until the noise dies down, then responds in fluent Spanish. She doesn't know what he's saying, but the reports are lapping it up eagerly, their microphones pointed like weapons.

A few days ago, he was a lost soul, and now he's the centre of attention, exactly where he loves to be. Grainne realises that for him time stopped, and now it has started again. He was left dreaming while her world spun on without him.

The interpreter whispers to her, 'He is saying he really doesn't remember anything prior to finding himself on the ship that lifted him out of the water. He is grateful for the care he has been given, and will always remember the Spanish people for their generosity.'

Grainne clearly hears Colm's Irish accent underlying the Spanish words. It sounds vaguely amusing. His smile is infectious, his eyes are sparkling with Irish charm. He turns, pulls her close, and kisses her slowly and lovingly. The reporters love it. She tries not to flinch. He sounds and looks like the Colm she used to love, but the man pressing himself against her is a complete stranger.

The reporters then turn their microphones to Grainne and Da, and the interpreter translates their bemused responses No, they really thought he had died. They never expected to find him alive. Yes, they are very pleased, of course.

Grainne is relieved when they are finally able to make their excuses. They are tired. They just want to get Colm home, now. It's been a traumatic experience. Wonderful. Thanks very much for bringing Colm back to his family.

Grainne thinks about what she has said, afterwards. She said she was pleased to find Colm alive. She means it, too. She would be pleased to have found any of the sailors from the *Faery Queen* alive. But she isn't ecstatic. She doesn't experience the spark of excitement that might be expected in the circumstances. But then, neither does Da. The reporters probably put this down to the confusion of the moment, but she and DA both know that this present flash of trauma is going to pale into the shadows of the longer-term trauma of what Colm's return means for his family.

'Are you excited to see your son?' a reporter shouts out as Colm turns to leave. The surprise on his expression is priceless, and the reporters' eyes widen with glee at this moment of revelation.

All eyes track to Grainne as Colm turns slowly to face her, his eyes wide with shock and wonder. 'I have a son? Grainne? I have a son?'

'Yes, Colm you have a son. Rónán is waiting for us, at the hotel, with my mum and dad. We're going there now.'

Colm face is a picture of amazed triumph.

And the cameras flash and flash and flash.

Later, she whispers to Da, 'I didn't know he spoke Spanish.'

'He didn't,' Da says, 'although...' His eyes drift into the past. She waits, sensing intrigue. 'Alyssa, his mother, was beautiful. She had hazel eyes, like Colm's, jet-black hair, and skin the colour of honey. She didn't speak at all when she was first found. She learned some words, but English was always a struggle. Foreign to her tongue. She didn't speak often, as though it was dangerous, somehow. But sometimes when she was by the sea, I'd hear her singing. It was haunting and sad. She never told me where she had come from, what she was running from, but I think she'd become massively homesick.'

'She was running?'

'That's what it seemed like. She came from the sea, with nothing. Off a boat, most likely. As though she'd escaped from someone or something. Why would she bury herself in a small town in Ireland, unless she was afraid? I thought she loved me, to start with, but I think she just chose me for protection. I never told anyone that before. I thought she was contented enough, despite that, but maybe she was homesick. I like to believe she didn't take Colm down to the sea to watch her drown. I think she just started swimming, and didn't stop.'

'Poor Alyssa. To be so unhappy. The locals say she was a selkie.'

'Phut! Katie, I suppose.'

Grainne smiles. 'But you can see why.'

'They like their tales, the daft biddies. Colm was six when she, ah, left. I wonder, now, if she was Spanish? Maybe she talked to Colm when I was busy on the farm, like a secret language between them, and when he lost his memory, after the *Faery Queen* went down, what came back was what he'd heard as a child.'

'Subconscious memories? Subliminal learning? It's how we all learn our first language. But—'

'I know, I know. It doesn't make sense. But what makes sense in what we're seeing today? Yesterday my son was dead. Today he's alive. I'd accepted his death, and now I have the strangest feeling that he shouldn't have come back from the dead at all. It doesn't feel right.'

'Oh, Da, don't say that. He's your son. You love him.'

'I do. But I love you, too, Grainne, girl, and little Rónán, and we've all moved on. I wonder, will you rediscover your love for Colm? Is it possible? I hope so, but I don't know what's going to happen now. The only thing I'm sure of is that nothing will be the same as it was. It can't be.'

They're dropped off at the hotel, fighting to get through yet another barrage of reporters, and Grainne is grateful for the uniformed Guardia who are containing the situation.

Grainne had called from the hospital to tell her mother the news, not wanting her to hear it from some tenacious reporter, ahead of the pack. She asked her to let Aisling know, for the same reason.

Now, she texts her mother to say they're on their way up. She's unsettled by the changes in temperature, from the bludgeoning heat outside, to the air-conditioned internal spaces: the hospital, car, and hotel. She's longing to be back in Ireland, with its natural pervasion of damp air, inside and out.

In the lift, with the aversion one reserves for avoiding contact with strangers, Grainne squeezes herself against the back wall. In another life, another time, she and Colm would have been pressed so hard against each other she would feel his heart beating against her breast, but now they're like three strangers in a box, trying to keep from touching each other.

Colm is silent. She's sorry she can't just take him in her arms as she had once loved to do, to rock him back into the safety of the world he had once known. He said, in the taxi, that for him, it was only yesterday he'd been joking with his friends on the way out in the *Faery Queen*. And she knew what he really meant: that only yesterday he had risen from their last union in the early hours, bidding her a loving goodbye, and today she met him with the coolness of a stranger.

Grainne's mum is waiting at the door to their room, Rónán in her arms. She casts a glance at Grainne, maybe seeing the distance Grainne has placed between herself and her husband.

Colm has eyes for no one except the child.

He treads carefully, in a trance, a smile of wonder on his face. He stops and stares. Rónán stares back, as wide-eyed as Colm, and when Colm holds his arms out, Rónán reaches for him, eagerly, as if he knows.

Da's blinking hard as he puts his arm around Grainne's, and only then does she realise tears are sliding down her cheeks, driven by those in Colm's eyes, which have surely been born of exquisite joy. The doctor was right. This is a happy day for Colm. While her own relationship with him is teetering on the brink of total meltdown, he has Rónán to cling to, like a lifeline.

It's a strange couple of hours, with her parents, and Da, and Colm, and Rónán, all contained in a small hotel room, trying to treat as normal a situation that is anything but. Only time will allow everyone to find new pathways in a life that had veered wildly off course.

Grainne goes down to the foyer with her parents to bid them farewell. She has enough to cope with, and maybe they feel the same way, discovering themselves an intrusion in a situation that is already fraught. Her mum is blinking hard. She hugs Grainne briefly. 'Grainne, love. I hope it's going to work out. It's not what you expected, I know.'

Her father is confused. 'It's good, though, isn't it?'

'I don't know how it's going to work out,' she says honestly. 'I've moved on and Colm, well, he's stuck where he was eighteen months ago. He would happily slip between the sheets as if he'd just been on a fishing trip, but for me, too much water has flowed between us.'

Her mum nods, understanding the full implication of what has not been said. 'But you'll keep Rónán?'

'Whatever happens, Rónán is my child. I carried him, I bore him, I nursed him and loved him by myself, while his father was absent. It's not Colm's fault, but Rónán stays with me, whatever.'

With more insight than Grainne had given her credit for, her mum says, 'Be careful. Colm is possessive towards the boy.'

'But they'll be a family, again,' her father says. 'Soon everything will be back to normal, you'll see.'

Grainne smiles and kisses them both on the cheek. 'Go now, the taxi's waiting. You don't want to miss your Murcia flight. I love you both. Take care.'

They look startled, and she wonders how long it's been since she's uttered those words, if ever.

Then it's just the four of them, Da, Colm Rónán and herself, navigating a long evening, awkward as strangers, save for Rónán in the middle, binding them together.

Rónán had just learned to say *Ma* for mother, and *Da* for Darragh, but he's now sleepily saying 'da, da, da' to Colm, as though he knows this is his father. His tiny hands explore Colm's face, his lips, his ears, his hair, and Colm's eyes drink him in, like a parched sailor presented with trip, a long draught of water, as the child falls asleep in his arms.

There's a single moment of confusion in Colm's expression, followed by sad comprehension, when Da says it's time to turn in, and waits for Colm to join him at the door. 'We're across the hall,' he says to his son, and another bridge is crossed: Colm will not be sleeping in the same bed as his wife, nor in the same room as his son.

Somehow, they get through another traumatic press conference at the airport, where the mayor, not to be sidelined, grandstands his role in returning Colm to the bosom of his family.

'You'd think he'd done it all himself,' Da says in a loud whisper. 'He's got a gob on him, to be sure.'

'Shush,' Grainne says, on the edge of a hysterical laugh.

But, again, it's Colm's natural charm that steals the show, and the way his eyes continually flash down in astonished wonder at the child he's holding in his arms. The press is loving it. He can still talk the blarney, Grainne thinks, even when it's in another language.

Eventually, the Guardia escort them through to a private lounge, where airport security personnel take over then escort them out onto the tarmac. As they climb up the steps into the plane, walk down the aisle, and settle into their seats, other passengers acknowledge them with big grins, as if they're celebrities, which in a way they are. Colm is seated by the window, holding Rónán, who has clearly attached himself to his father, and Da is sitting on the other side of the aisle.

'Why do they keep showing us their phones?' Da asks, leaning over.

'They're taking pictures.'

'On phones? Jaysus. I didn't know they could do that.' He grins at Grainne and sticks his finger up his nose. She frowns, then bursts into hysterical laughter. His dry humour, which rarely surfaces on the farm, is inappropriate; then Grainne realises he's done it for her benefit, no one else's. She's tired, mentally exhausted, and knows this won't be the end of it. They'll be besieged by the press on arrival in Shannon, and again by everyone with a claim to being local when they get back home.

Colm is a stranger to her. It's weird to be sitting so close to him that their arms touch. She's tempted to incline away, but forces herself to be still rather than hurt his feelings any more than she has already. She discovered in the past that she disliked close physical contact with previous partners, the chemistry that had once brought them together later repelling her, like reversed poles of magnetism. A couple of years ago she would have laughed at the idea of feeling that way about Colm, but the sensation is undeniable.

Rónán gives a wail and she turns to Colm with her hands out. 'He needs to settle,' she says.

'I can settle him.'

'Colm, he barely knows you. Please. Pass him over.'

Colm does, with some reluctance, and Grainne is pleased when Rónán snuggles into her shoulder, sucking his thumb, and eventually falls asleep. It's a scant two-and-a-half-hour flight to Shannon, so despite an increasing ache in her shoulder, she grits her teeth and bears it. A tired, grumpy child won't look good on-screen, even in the arms of a man come back miraculously from the dead.

At Shannon, she groans, seeing a TV truck on the concourse, and gratefully relinquishes Rónán to Colm as they wait to exit. The flight attendant comes and asks them to please remain seated until everyone else is off the plane, and despite the irrational urge to tell her to mind her own business, Grainne sighs and complies. When the last of the other passengers have gone, she hauls her baby bag and Da's battered case from the overhead locker. She stands back to let Colm go down the stairs first. He's the man of the hour, and sure enough, as he stands at the top of the stairs, like some visiting dignitary, the cameras whir, the bulbous mics are thrust towards him, and a TV presenter from the local news begins to talk into the camera.

Colm is ushered into place, and Da and Grainne

follow behind as questions are fired, first at Colm, then at her and Da, who is surprisingly polite, saying, of course, he's stunned and thrilled to discover he has a son. It's a miracle, so it is. Grainne thinks carefully before answering the questions thrust at her. People don't want to hear that she's no longer in love with Colm. They want to see her hanging on his arm, praising God for his delivery. They want this to be the ultimate tale, the happily-ever-after ending of all happily-ever-after endings. She conceals her lack of enthusiasm beneath shock and tiredness, and says they all need time to rediscover themselves.

Well, that, at least, isn't a lie.

When they're finally released, the cameras follow them out to the pickup area, where Lén is waiting. He's heard it on the news, of course. Everyone has. It's the news event of the moment, flooding the channels the moment word filtered from Spain.

Lén reaches out to Colm, and the two men hold each other silently. When they step apart, there's a faint smile on Lén's face as he says, 'Welcome home, mate. That was a long blooming fishing trip. What took you so long? We were starting to get worried.' Colm's uncertain smile stretches into a real one, and the moment becomes lighter, as Lén adds, 'So, let's get you home, shall we?'

Chapter 13

Colm descends into a stunned state of lethargy on the way home. He's watching the scenery flash past, with the detachment of someone who knows it too well to exclaim at its beauty. Grainne's not sure how she expected him to react – like someone who'd been away from home for eighteen months, maybe, but for him, this is like the second day after going out fishing on the *Faery Queen*.

He recalls the squall hitting the boat, and the shocking weight of freezing water, but his next memory was a sudden awakening when she spoke to him, a day later, in the rehabilitation unit. The eighteen months or so of amnesiac time had the strangeness of a long, waking dream that was quickly fading. To him, this sense of compressed time also meant that his loving wife had gone into the fairy mound and come out a day later, inexplicably distant, with a child in her arms. Whereas he was still the same person he had been yesterday, when he'd been fishing with the lads, leaving the love of his life stretching in the early dawn in their marriage bed.

She sees the puzzlement in his eyes as the question flashes across his face: *What happened to your love for me? Where did it go?* For him it had disappeared overnight, but for her it had drained over a long eighteen months.

As they drive up towards the old house, the first sign of real time passing is the renovated wreck at the foot of the lane. 'Jaysus,' he says, astonished, as if it had flown up overnight. Which for him, it had.

Grainne explains the situation. 'Old Liam O'Sullivan sold up, left Young Liam with nothing. Da couldn't cope without you, and I'm no farmer. So, Young Liam has the old house and the farmland on lease. We thought you were dead,' she adds, to soften the blow.

'Well, I'm not,' he says curtly.

That's the first sign of irritation he's shown, but it's not surprising. It's his land, his sheep, his inheritance, and it must feel as though they had simply given it all away.

'I don't know how this works out by law,' she adds, 'but don't be mad at Young Liam. I guess the lease is invalid, but I wouldn't want to give solicitors the chance to fight over the issue. You'd both end up with nothing. You should wait, talk to Young Liam, sort it out between you. All his future disappeared with his father selling up. He made a new start, and now you come home, and all that has gone up in smoke, too.'

Colm makes no answer as they carry on up to the

house, and he stands on the threshold for a moment, looking around, as if seeking other changes, but the kitchen is as it always was. Only the little bedroom upstairs has changed.

Then Rusty is there. Feet firmly planted, hackles raised, he protects the doorway, teeth bared.

'It's me, Rusty, old mate,' Colm says, putting his hand out. He snatches it back hastily as Rusty snaps, and Grainne has to hold Rusty's collar to allow Colm into the house. 'Bejaysus,' Colm says, warily. 'The bloody dog doesn't know me.'

'Rusty, lie down!' Grainne commands, and he obeys, reluctantly, his narrowed eyes never leaving Colm. It's weird enough. Rusty was Colm's rescue, always close on his heels, as long as he wasn't in with the scary sheep. But now, Rusty is staring at Colm as if he will leap at any moment and tear his throat out.

Lén follows them in, carrying their bags. Colm seats himself at the kitchen table with Rónán. But Rónán knows where he is again, and yells to be let down, fed, played with, anything but sit still. Colm turns him to face himself, and bounces him up and down, making silly faces, as he had once before, with another child, on a honeymoon that lies in the distant past.

Grainne fills the electric kettle and asks Lén, 'Will you stay and have a cup of tea? It's been a long couple of days.'

'I will, so,' he says, perhaps realising that she needs moral support for these first, strange moments. 'Then I really have to get back. I have work waiting on me.'

When Lén finally pushes his chair away and leaves, with no more than a brief wave, it's as though this is the same as any other day in the past. Everything is back to the strangest sense of normality. Colm's little family is finally as complete as he had once wished, yet is as broken as it possibly could be.

After a long silence, he asks, 'I need to know. Is Rónán truly my child?'

'You know he is,' she replies, trying not to be annoyed. 'But you can ask anyone. They'll tell you. I was already pregnant when you were lost to the sea. Just look at the dates. Look at his eyes. But you knew, really, the moment you picked him up.'

Grainne somehow survives the dreadful welcome-home party in Bantry, escaping early, with Da, to put Rónán to bed. Where Colm slept that night, she didn't ask, but he didn't come back until the next day. It had been surreal, with the fools drinking too hard to cover an uneasy situation no one had thought to ever experience. Had they supposed it would be like a birthday bash? *Surprise!* How could they have ever thought it was a good idea?

The days pass in a strangely disjointed way, with Colm and Da and Grainne tiptoeing around each other, not so much as brushing a sleeve in passing. It's a stressful time for all of them, almost worse than coping with

Colm's death.

Grainne feels as though something will soon break. It's not helped by Rusty's continued antipathy towards Colm, as though Colm is a danger that's been unleashed into his home.

Rónán's cot is moved back into her bedroom, and Colm has the little room, with its brightly painted mural. Da offers to move back into the bungalow in Bantry, but Grainne's instant panic probably alerts him to the fact that it isn't a good idea. He's needed here, in his role as buffer between his son and the girl he has treated as a daughter for the last eighteen months.

Over the weeks, things settle a little. Colm acquires a small car, and during the day he takes Rónán with him on his various visits as he comes to terms with his changed circumstances. Grainne is never quite sure what he does with this time, but he seems in no hurry to get his hands dirty on the farm. He has walked down several times to see Young Liam, and she's hopeful that they will thrash out details for a future, but the previous friendship is strained.

Grainne gets the impression, though Colm never quite comes out and says it, that an unbridgeable gulf has opened between him and his erstwhile friends. They had mourned him, reminisced over tall tales and past follies, and moved on. Yet here he is once more, inserting himself into their closed group. It's as though he's committed some grievous sin by still being alive, when everyone had got used to the fact that he was gone. He's become the uninvited ghost at the wedding.

Grainne's boss, Nigel, learning of the news of Colm's amazing reappearance, phones asking after Grainne's new work, and she's able to assure him that she has more time than before. As Colm is happy to look after Rónán during the day – indeed, she feels Rónán might be the saving of him – she shuts herself in her room to feverishly consolidate the new storyline, prompted a year back by Katie and her gossipy tales. Grainne doesn't believe in selkies, any more than she believes in fairies, but fantasy provides a bold platform for a screenplay, with larger-than-life characters and stunning special effects.

The first series, almost trashed by sceptical financiers before it had aired, had sky-rocketed, attracting a fan base even Nigel, at his most avaricious, could never have predicted, and he's keen to keep the gravy train rolling.

Queen Maeve is a manipulator, both hero and anti-hero in her own stories. She is the earth goddess personified: powerful, charismatic, and utterly selfish. In the last season, she persuaded a fairy clan to steal the crown of eternal youth from the underworld by making promises she had no intention of keeping. Ye gods, the make-up artists and costumers had done her proud! Even she, who had envisaged the scene in her storyboards, had shivered at the fairies' cold, inhuman beauty.

The fae, realising they had been played false, had furiously summoned a storm the like of which had never been seen before, and now the crown lies at the bottom of the sea, along with the bleached bones of innocent sailors. She had tried to get the mermaids to fetch the crown, but the flighty creatures had circled down into the depths and promptly forgotten why they had done so. No, she needs a creature with intelligence, memory, and better still, one who can walk on land. Such a creature comes to mind... the selkie. But they are few, and well hidden from the landlocked. How will she find one, and what could she promise to make the selkie obedient to her wishes?

The story starts to gel, inked out in black on the white paper in a comic strip. She will fill in the detail later, for herself and the potential print run, but for now, she's provided Nigel with the outline.

When the postman delivers an art tube, some three weeks later, Grainne rips it open and curiously draws out the contents. She finds herself holding the painting of seals that Colm had been working on in Spain. Only then does she check the packaging and finds it's addressed to Colm.

Perhaps some fragment of his life had seeped through his amnesia, carrying the scent of the sea and memories of the great grey seals scattered the length of the cold Atlantic coast, bobbing in the foam, or resting on the black rocks. She and Colm had stood on the headland in the evening, holding hands, listening to them calling into the encroaching evening with the eerie sounds that sometimes held the faintest hint of a human word.

Or maybe his image is something older, more traumatic. He knows the legends and gossip surrounding his mother, and maybe, in some corner of his mind, there's a hazy recollection of watching her enter the water, to never return. Perhaps believing her transformed into a seal is easier than believing she'd been so desperately unhappy that she'd drowned herself, leaving her six-year-old screaming on the beach.

Perusing the watercolour more closely, Grainne is stunned at the intricacy of the brush work. How could Colm have had this talent and she, an artist herself, had not known? But then, her own parents had seen her artistic ability as a glitch in the money-making cycle. It's possible that Colm's teachers, in the heart of a practical farming community, had never recognised his talent for what it was, either.

She doesn't tell Colm that the painting has arrived, sent on by Doctor Diaz, who thought he might like it as a keepsake of his time with them. Instead, the next time Da drives her into Bantry for shopping, she takes it in to have it framed.

Da has errands to run in the farming supplies store just outside of Bantry, and once she has completed her chores about town, Grainne strolls to the quay to wait for him. Not the quay Colm left from that fateful night, but the old one behind the supermarket, where there's a small beach running along the estuary, exposed only at low tide. She's leaning on the rails, watching children search for small treasures amidst the tideline flotsam, when far down the strip of beach she spies Colm and Rónán. Colm's fear of water had been something of a standing joke, but had been a real phobia, in fact. Yet there he is, standing in the water with Rónán, his jeans rolled up to his knees, holding Rónán above the waves, teasing, while Rónán splashes both feet into the water, screaming with delight. She can hear their laughter from here, and feels a little left out.

She glances at the time on her phone, and heads back to the supermarket, where Da will be arriving any moment. It's an unspoken arrangement that Da will continue to take Grainne to town for shopping. She can scarcely bear to be in the same room with Colm, never mind be trapped in a car with him. It's not for fear of him – she knows he'd never hurt her – but fear of hurting his feelings. Once or twice, when she relaxed her guard, Colm had taken it as a sign that she was thawing towards him, so she's at pains to avoid being alone with him, or giving him false hope. It's hard, but he's going to have to accept that she's moved on, that he has to find his own way in this new reality.

The problem, of course, is Rónán. She loves him more than anything else in the world. Which is why she hadn't allowed herself to get pregnant by Colm before, though he had desperately wanted her to. A child would be a commitment, a tie, and a potential disaster if their marriage failed. As, indeed it has, albeit through unimaginable circumstances. Perhaps she knew, even then, that the halcyon time with the youthful clown Colm had been wouldn't last.

But the present situation is dire.

She can't ask Colm to leave, as he owns the farm. She can't leave with the child he cares so much for, because Colm is still fragile, recovering from his accident, the deaths of his close friends, and her own apparently unreasonable change of heart. She can't take Rónán from Da, either, because Colm's return doesn't replace the love the old man has discovered for this unexpected grandchild. She wonders if this is the conundrum that Colm's mother had faced all those years ago, when she took her last, lonely swim out into the bay. A problem with no discernible solution growing into a monster of a crisis, and the long silence of death finally presenting itself as the only option.

In the supermarket, she finds Da wandering the aisles, seeking her. His glance betrays deep awareness of her situation. She was never a replacement for Colm, after he was lost, but Da's eyes reflect a love for her that has penetrated his soul, despite himself.'

So, here she is. She looks fair haggard, poor girl. One of these days I'm going to wake up and find her gone, along with the child. Then it will be just Colm and me again, as it was before. Only it can't be the same, can it? We both love her and the wean, and when she goes, she'll leave a hole in our hearts that will never be filled. I thought it was bad when Colm died, but we will never get over this loss. Never.

Grainne slowly pushes the trolley, stewing over what she's just seen, and decides to share. 'I just saw Colm, on the beach with Rónán.'

'Ah. He said the boy likes the sea.'

'Yes, but Da, Colm was in the water himself.'

Da stops and frowns. 'He was?'

'Absolutely. He had his trousers rolled up and was paddling. Maybe something changed in him after he was in the water all that time? An experience like that would change a person, for sure.'

They wander down one aisle and up another. Grainne absently picks biscuits and coffee and tea from the shelves. Da shakes his head, reaching for the chocolate biscuits he fancies above all others. 'I'm bothered about my boy. I know it's going to take time, but he doesn't work the farm any more. It's like he's given up on it. Young Liam is doing all the work, and I don't know what arrangement they've come to, not at all.'

'He doesn't tell me, either. I asked, and he was evasive. I might go and ask Young Liam. It's great that Colm is so taken by Rónán, of course, but it's as if he has nothing else now. Sometimes I want Rónán to stay with me, in the house, as it used to be, but if I insist, Colm stays, too.'

'And that's difficult for you. I know. I don't suppose there's any chance—'

She stops to face him. 'I did love him, once, Da. I loved him so much. Everyone told me I was a fool to marry him, but I didn't listen because I believed I was following my heart, but now I know I was following a dream. I loved what Colm stood for – the freedom to not be burdened by material things, his love for his little patch of Ireland, his tomfoolery, his exuberance for life. And there was me, stuck in that London society, drinking too much, seeking something else, something more, only I didn't know what. He just met me at a time when I needed to escape. Do you hate me for that?'

They begin walking again, slowly, to the tills.

'No, girl. At least you're honest. We all hanker after things we can't have.'

'Is there something you want? You know I have a bit of money saved.'

'I didn't mean that. I meant we hanker after things that aren't meant to be. I was beguiled by Alyssa, by her exotic foreignness, her beauty. People told me she was bad news, that it would all go sour, but I was smitten, and didn't listen. Wherever she came from, I think she was used to money. The way she danced, the way she loved nice clothes, but couldn't cook or sew, or do anything useful.' He smiles in sad recollection. 'I don't think she'd ever had to work, before. I wonder how I ever thought she'd be happy, living the way I did.'

'But she chose you.'

He sighs. 'Maybe that was my misfortune. Maybe she followed a dream, too, and discovered it was a nightmare. I often wondered who she left behind, whether she had parents grieving for her, never knowing what happened to her.'

'Oh, Da. I think she must have loved you a little, too.'

'Maybe. But that's all in the past, sure, and we'll never know. It's the present that bothers me. And the future.'

Chapter 14

When Grainne hears Lén's truck outside, her first panicked thought is that something is wrong. Maybe there's been an accident? He hasn't visited since Colm's return, and although she understands why, there's a little niggle of hurt in the back of her mind. The car door slams, and he knocks and comes in without being told, as he always did. He nods a greeting. 'Da, Grainne. How's things?'

'Difficult,' Da says.

'Ah.'

'Colm's not here,' Grainne informs him. 'He's out with Rónán. He'll be back by five, though, because one thing he can't do is give Rónán his night-time feed.'

A slow smile breaks on Lén's face, and her heart somersaults. It seems that absence has made the heart grow fonder, after all. But not, perhaps, a useful thing to discover at this time. She turns and busies herself with the kettle. His solid presence in their kitchen is comforting, though. She's pleased he hasn't abandoned them.

'It's not Colm I came to see,' he admits. 'The thing is, I'm hearing things. Rumours.'

Grainne is worried that the rumours are about her, which wouldn't surprise her at all. In this community, she's still the outsider, and now Colm is back, any headway she made has taken a backward turn, probably because Colm is around town without her. She raises a brow in question.

'Ay. Well, not rumours exactly. The thing is, Young Liam told me something the other day, and I don't know what to make of it. He was drinking, you know?' He pauses, and blurts out, 'He's after telling everyone that Colm's making the farm over to him.'

Da and Grainne share a startled glance.

'He can't,' Grainne says. 'He'd need my agreement.'

'Well, that's what he's saying. Maybe there's some clause about you and Da keeping this house?'

Da's jaw drops before he finds his voice. 'That's what he's agreed with Young Liam? But the farm has been in our family for generations. It's Rónán's inheritance! Surely he won't sell it out from under his own son, like Old Liam did?'

Grainne knows Da had only suggested selling it when he thought Colm was dead and he thought maybe Grainne needed a home that wasn't in the back of beyond.

'Maybe he's thinking of leaving?' Lén's words drop overloud into the silence.

'Leave?' Da's confusion is complete. 'And go where?'

'He wouldn't leave his son,' Grainne says, shaking her head to dispel the shocking thought that maybe

Colm was thinking of running away with Rónán.'

Da shakes his head, frowning in confusion. 'Colm never wanted to be anywhere other than here. He always joked that even the occasional visit to London or America was because it was such a pleasure to come back home. And if he left, what would he do?'

Grainne shivers. Colm's experiences were enough to change anyone. But she was right: he wouldn't leave Rónán, but would he *take* him? Would he take the child from her? Her mind in a strange place, she absently puts a pot of tea on the table, and eventually Lén gets up, finds mugs and milk, and pours it out. She wraps her hands around the mug. 'What are we going to do?'

'Maybe he needs help?' Lén suggests.

'A psychiatrist?' She shakes her head. 'He won't. He thinks he's fine.'

'He's not, though, is he? He's off on his own, with Rónán. He doesn't visit his friends the way he used to. He doesn't go for a drink with the lads. He's been seen walking the old paths. Around the headlands. Just him and the child. To me, that doesn't sound fine.'

Grainne has seen him herself, on the goat path, watching the seals, or simply staring out to sea from the point where she had once stood, grief-stricken at his loss. She had supposed him to be dwelling on what happened to his shipmates, as she had once dwelled on him, imagining their bones gradually disintegrating, becoming part of the sea bed.

But what if it's something else?

Da voices her fear. 'You don't think he's after thinking about... ending it all? You don't always see it. I didn't know Alyssa was going to drown herself. Surely, he wouldn't—'

'No, he wouldn't leave Rónán.'

Lén says soothingly, 'Darragh, I don't think we should read too much into it. He's come through a trauma, and is just working it through, in his own way. He doesn't seem like a man about to do away with himself. And as Grainne says, he loves that child too much to harm him.'

The breath she'd been holding escapes slowly. Lén's right. Colm's connection with Rónán is a little too needy for comfort, but he wouldn't harm him. Maybe she's been spending too much time at the drawing board, worrying about losing her niche in the volatile field of dreams, when she should have been caring more about her family. She's been stewing over her own needs, her intentions towards Colm and the future, never considering the possibility that he's been busy making plans of his own. But what on earth could they be, if they don't revolve around the farm?

'You got Rónán a passport,' Lén says, voicing one of her internal fears. 'Do you know where it is?'

She rushes to her desk, thankfully finds it, and hands it to Lén. 'Will you keep it for us? Just for a while.'

He tucks it into his shirt pocket with a grimace.

If Colm is thinking of running, at least he couldn't take the child further than England, but she feels guilty, all the same, for suspecting him of planning something so dreadful as to take her child from her. 'I've been neglecting him,' Grainne says. 'I've left him to work it out for himself. I should have understood how hard it was.'

'He hasn't realised how hard it has been for you, either,' Lén says, reasonably. 'Coping with his death, having his child, then having him discovered alive eighteen months later, when you've got used to the fact that he's dead? That was a shock, all right. Colm is only thinking of himself, as always. You're right in saying he needs our help and support, but to be fair, he's pretty much pushed everyone away who's tried. And no one can pick up the pieces of an old relationship, not when they've mourned him as dead and gone. It's not just you, Grainne. Colm has never seen anything but his own needs. Sorry, Da.'

'And I've been keeping him at arm's length,' Grainne admits. 'He needs to talk to someone. I should have tried harder.'

Lén rises. 'I should have paid more attention to what was going on, too. Try to persuade him to see a counsellor. I'd better go, now. I don't want him thinking I've been up here talking behind his back. Next time, I'll come when I know he's here.'

Da brings Colm's seal painting back from Bantry, framed, and stares at it with some surprise. 'My Colm did this? I didn't know he had an ounce of art in him.'

'I'm thinking he didn't know himself,' Grainne says.

'In Spain, not knowing who he was, he had plenty of time to indulge in something he wouldn't have done before. Maybe he didn't know what he could or couldn't do, until he tried. It must have been strange enough for him, to have a blank slate where your past should be.'

Her own art is so much of who she is, but what if she didn't recall she could do it? Would she have looked for something else to fill her days, like gardening or sewing? She didn't think so.

'It's fine enough,' Da says. He's never had time for fripperies such as curtains and paintings. 'Will we hang it here, in the kitchen?'

'I suppose so.' She doesn't like the idea, but maybe it's better to have it where they can talk about it, rather than hide it away in one of the bedrooms.

When they hear Colm's car returning early in the evening, and Grainne is making dinner, Da quickly takes himself off to the sheep shed, with some excuse or other.

Colm's smile is radiant as he comes in with Rónán. She can see why she fell for him. It's the smile he had courted her with. She used to think it was for her alone, but now she realises it's a mask he wears to hide the insecurity inside. Her heart bleeds for the child who grew up without a mother, in the care of a man who didn't know how to express the love that was inside him.

'Ma,' Rónán demands, and reaches his hands towards her. She takes him and perches him on her hip while stirring the gravy. Colm steps towards the door, heading for the living room, where he spends his evenings watching TV.

'So,' she says, halting him in his tracks. 'What did you two do today? Where did you go?'

He glances at the far door as though he'd like to take to his heels through it. 'Um, we went to Castle Townshend, to see Jerry's boat come in. I was teaching Rónán about the trawling, and the different fish.'

Teaching him? He's one year old, she thinks. But there's no harm talking, it's how he will learn the language.

'I didn't tell you, but look.' She points at the picture Da has hung on the wall, with a farmer's expediency of a big iron nail.

He stares. 'Oh. Is that what I did In Spain? Funny, I'd pretty much forgotten about it. You might as well throw it away.'

She's startled. 'Why would I do that? It's stunning. That's why I had it framed.'

'It's childish.' His laugh is a little like it used to be. 'You're the artist. You're the talented one in this house.'

'I do comic strips,' she says with false modesty, adding honestly, 'What you've painted there is something I couldn't do in a hundred years.' She holds Rónán up to the painting and points. 'See the seals, love?'

'Sea, sea,' Rónán says, reaching out to gently touch one seal's face, then the other.

Grainne laughs, startled. He has several words now, mostly related to what he wants, or doesn't want. 'When did he learn that?'

'We've been watching them off the headland,' Colm says in an offhand manner, as though it's of no importance. 'He picked it up almost immediately.'

But Grainne thinks he must have heard the word associated with the creatures many times for it to come so easily to his lips. She instructs Colm, 'Go and tell Da dinner's ready,' she says. 'I think he hasn't realised the time.'

She lays the table properly and he sits with them, somewhat reluctantly. Up to now she's been grateful that he takes the tray into the other room, but she makes an effort to include him.

Da tries to engage Colm in what's happening on the farm, but Colm seems detached from what was once the centre of his life. And when Da asks him something specific, he shrugs. 'Young Liam's handling all that, now. He's well able.'

'So, that's the way it's going to stay?' Da presses for a response. 'Are you going to let Young Liam continue to manage the farm? But what will you be after doing? Have you plans? Will you work at the building, or the welding?'

'Liam can stay for now,' Colm says shortly. 'I don't know what I'm going to do, but I can't just pick up where I left off. Everything's changed, hasn't it?'

There's nothing they can add to that obvious truth, and they eat in silence for a while, but as Colm pushes his chair back to leave, Grainne says gently, 'Don't be off with Rónán tomorrow. I'm going to take him to the mam and toddler group. He needs to spend time with children his own age. Learn how to be sociable.'

'What about your precious storyboard?'

She flushes slightly at the derisive tone. 'It can wait. Rónán's needs must come first. I've been missing him. He's my child, too.'

Katie is delighted when Grainne walks through the door into the little hall where the toddler group is held. She jumps up with an exclamation of surprise, and rushes to make her welcome. Grainne is drawn into the circle of women, and Rónán is placed on the floor with the other children, who he eyes suspiciously.

'Sure, and it's about time you came back into the world, love,' Katie says. 'What happened can't be undone, but look, life has to go on. And how's Colm doing, these days? Is he back into the farming? How is Young Liam coping, with Colm coming back and all?'

Grainne finds herself almost laughing at Katie's unreserved query, while the other mothers keenly listen for titbits to take home. 'Colm is a confused soul,' she explains. 'It will be a while yet before he recovers himself. Da and I, well, we got used to him not being around, but for him, it's just been a few weeks since he recovered his memory. It's all fresh and dreadful, and he's mourning his friends from the *Faery Queen*. But he loves being a father. He's well taken with Rónán.'

Katie nods enthusiastically. 'We've seen him,

Grainne, love, taking the child all over. We wondered why you weren't with him at all? But the child will be the saving of him, don't you think? It's a shame he can't find it in himself to come down here, you know, instead of keeping himself away. But men, eh?'

All the women agree that men are useless when it comes to socialising with babies. It's a women's job, for sure, and did Grainne want a coffee and a couple of biscuits? But as they make further small talk, it becomes obvious that her foundering relationship with Colm is common knowledge, so eventually she admits, 'I don't think we're going to make it, Colm and me.'

'So, will you be after moving back to London?' Katie asks.

'I couldn't hurt Da that way. Or Colm. I don't know what I'm going to do. I did wonder whether to move into Da's bungalow in Bantry, then we'll be near enough for Colm and Da, and we can go from there.'

'It's a good solution, so it is,' Katie agrees. 'The wean will be near his da, and Da.' As everyone laughs, she stops and thinks about what she's said, then, delighted with herself, adds, 'Well, you'll have to be after finding another name for Rónán to call his dad, as Darragh can't be changing his name at his age.'

Chapter 15

Grainne tries to talk to Colm, about the farm, and about his future, and about maybe seeing someone to help him get through the trauma. He insists he's not traumatised, just happy to be back. He's thinking, he says, and when he's decided what to do with his life, he'll let her and Da know. Well, she can't really blame him for being snippy. That solitary cogitation bothers her, but if Colm refuses to see a doctor, there's nothing she *can* do.

Grainne worries that his decision will include kidnapping Rónán, for he knows she won't let Rónán go. But they do come to a slightly better arrangement about sharing Rónán, Colm taking him three days, and Grainne for four. The fact that Colm doesn't quibble about this new arrangement doesn't relieve Grainne's growing sense of unease, but she can't deny Colm access to his own child, not when he has proved to be such a committed parent.

Colm still sleeps in the house with them, but on the days he doesn't have his child, he disappears, making no effort to involve himself with the running of the farm.

He doesn't admit to making any promises to Young Liam, but Grainne asks Da to go and have a quiet word with their solicitor, to confirm that Colm doesn't have the right to simply dispose of the property off his own back, now that he has a wife. It's not for herself that she does this, but more because the decision should be discussed and shared. Da gave the farm over to Colm knowing his son would farm it, not so that he could simply dispose of it.

Grainne makes a point of quizzing Colm very gently about his day, trying to discover what he does with this time, but wise to the expected inquisition, Colm always has an answer on the tip of his tongue, and she's sure it's often not the truth.

His life has taken a strange turn, but hers is torn in two. On the days she has Rónán, she gives him her full attention, and on the days when Colm has him, Grainne devotes herself religiously to her work, trying to fit five days' work into the three, creating storylines strong enough to satisfy Nigel, and keep the accountants off his back.

Maeve has sent her most trusted warriors out to the shores of the five kingdoms, seeking news of a selkie. For a long time, they search, but finally Domhnall the Damned ventures onto a rocky island, where he discovers Rón, a man issued of a selkie mother.

The unsuspecting Rón tells Domhnall that his father, having fallen hopelessly in love with a selkie, hid her sealskin in a cave so she would not be able to return to the sea. His selkie wife was happy with her mortal lover for a few years, then despite her love for her son, began to pine desperately for her home in Suleskerrie, but her husband refused to tell her where he had hidden her sealskin. One day, when Rón was six, he accidentally discovered the sealskin and showed his mother. She quickly donned it and disappeared into the sea. Rón grew up terrified of salt water, but even after his father died, he stayed by the sea, hoping his mother would one day come back to see him. Eventually, he married and had a daughter of his own, but when his new wife learned that he was part Selkie, she ran away, leaving him and the fae child behind.

Hearing this, Domhnall the Damned kidnaps Rón's girl-child, leaving instruction that if he wants her back alive, he must complete a task for Maeve. He has to conquer his fear, and allow himself to become a true selkie. Once he has changed into a seal, he must swim into the deep chasm where Maeve's ship lies and recover the crown of the underworld. If he brings this to Maeve, he will get his daughter back. If he does not do this within one year and one day, his daughter will be slain.

However, neither Rón nor Maeve realise that the selkie who bore Rón was the Queen of Suleskerrie. Hearing of the kidnap of her grandchild, she is furious. Older than Maeve by a few centuries, and one *of the elder fae, she already knows where the crown lies, and is aware of Maeve's treacherous and covetous nature. When Rón finally enters the water, she goes to meet him, and together they plan a way to get the child back and wreak vengeance on Maeve.*

Grainne decides that Rón's child should be a girl, to separate this story yet further from that of Da and Colm. And Maeve will be deceitful, as always. Once she has the crown, she will decide to keep the girl, as currency for some future plan, but Rón is aware of this, and rescues her; at the same time, he tricks Maeve out of the crown.

Grainne's storyline is a mix of the old selkie legends, and the rumours that surround Colm's mother, Alyssa. She is confident the CGI team will create some fantastic underwater scenes, providing a totally different environment to the previous land-based seasons of *Maeve, Queen of the Celts*. Da won't mind her poaching a little of his story. Even if local tales hint of mystery and the supernatural, he knows that Alyssa was not fae, just a beautiful, sad, lost soul, running from something she wouldn't, or couldn't speak of.

Grainne divides her storyline into ten episodes with cliffhanger endings, and from there into individual scenes which she sketches out briefly into action strips. She hasn't quite worked out how the selkie queen will exact her revenge on Maeve, or get the child back, but she knows the storyline will make itself known to her as she works. In the meantime, the storyboards begin to flow and she despatches enough material to Nigel for the film crew to work on, while continuing to build the pages that will eventually become the next graphic book: *Maeve and the Selkie.*

For a few weeks, life continues on an even keel, but there's a growing tension in the farmhouse that's hard to ignore. Eventually, Grainne asks Da to mind Rónán, and asks Colm if he'd walk with her to the headland. He gives her a strange look, as though he's about to argue, then nods. He, too, knows it's time.

It's a chilly, blustery day, with winter hard on the heels of summer. The environment, already closely cropped by Atlantic storms, is bowing under the harsh onslaught of squalls, retreating into itself to wait out the cold. The few stubby trees, clinging determinedly to crevices between the exposed rocks, have shed their leaves and diminished to skeletons against the heaving, grey cloud base. Underfoot, the path is squelchy and treacherous, the moss pillows morphing into new bog, the ferns dying back into their hearts. Grainne finds it amazing that in the spring, fresh fronds will uncurl from the hidden roots, reaching into the sky for another short season.

Colm follows her in silence, his feet treading the old paths with easy familiarity, while she slips and stumbles. More than anything, she hates the winter, when winds howl like hungry wolves, ripping the lime plaster from the stone walls, scouring empty cottages to shells that gradually unravel back into the landscape. The land eventually reclaims these deserted places, just as it has obliterated the traces of the ancient people. All that remains are the overgrown raths, the mysterious *fulachtaí fia*, and the massive stones, dragged into circles, maybe for worshipping for long-forgotten gods, or for some other purpose modern thoughts cannot even conceive.

Finally, she stands on the platform from which she had once wished herself dead, and Colm eases up beside her. There's a long silence as they listen to the sea breaking below, and the mournful cry of seagulls. The seals are absent today, maybe hunting in other waters. The day is chill, overcast, the Atlantic sullenly reflecting her grey thoughts. 'I'm so sorry,' she whispers, her eyes watering in the wind.

Colm takes her hand, and she lets him. He clasps it gently, not reaching for something he can't have, but for the spatter of memories that are fading fast. 'I'm sorry, too. Ah, but it was grand for a while, wasn't it?'

'It was,' she agreed. 'It was a real fairy tale. I did love you, Colm.'

'But your love faded, while my love endured.'

She pulls her hand back, tucks it in her pocket, feeling like a child reprimanded for doing something she hadn't realised was wrong. 'I didn't choose it, Colm. You were dead to us. I grieved for a long time, so did Da, and then Rónán arrived, and we had to move on. It was as though he'd been sent to us to make up for our loss. I was pregnant with a child whose father was drowned. I floundered for a long time, thinking morbid thoughts about you lying dead, rotting under the water. Then I had to make my mind up to live – for Rónán, and for Da.'

She looks up at him and sees her own sadness echoed in the dark set of his mouth. She carries on, finally. 'But for you it was different. You didn't spend eighteen months missing me; you simply forgot. Then when you came back, that time was gone, in an instant, like that.' She snaps her fingers.

Colm whispers, 'We can find it again. Our love. We can be a family. If only you would try.'

It's a cry from the heart, but she has to be hard. 'Colm. You were lost to me when the *Faery Queen* went down. We can't get that back. We both lost all that we were, all that we dreamed of being. And then you came back. I can't simply pick up where we left off. I've moved on, and now you have to move on, too. I can't live like this. It hurts. It's not fair on any of us.'

His irritation breaks through. 'Live like what? I keep out of your hair. I don't moon around pining for what I can't have.'

'No, but you take Rónán, and I don't know where you go, what you do.' Now quiet tears spill, and her voice lowers. 'Every time you take him, I wonder whether that will be the last time I see him, whether you will drive away into the world, and I'll never find him. Don't tell me you haven't thought of that.'

A short silence tells her she is right, then Colm says,

'He's my son, too. I want him to know me. What would you have me do? Simply move away and forget I have a child?'

'I don't want that for Rónán. You're a good father, Colm. But I don't know you any more, and it's scaring me. The farm is your inheritance, and Rónán's, yet you want to give it away. I don't know what you're planning. Whatever you think, you aren't the same person who went away. You've changed. Even Da says so. You have to accept that.'

Halfway between her and the horizon, a small yacht chugs through the swell, its empty mast dipping and weaving. She finds herself wishing it was not there, that the captain had more sense than to risk a day that looks as if it will turn to storm in a second.

'I used to think I loved this place, that I'd chosen to stay,' he admits finally. 'But I didn't. It was a duty. I loved it when I went away, to London, to America. All that space. All those opportunities. Then I met you. I thought bringing you back here would make me complete, fill the old home with warmth and children. Make it bearable. I don't know why I thought that. More children died here than lived. This land sucks the joy out of a man. Why did you stay, after I disappeared?'

'You know. For Da.'

He nods. 'Some don't understand the pressures we put on ourselves because we don't want to hurt the ones we love. You do. I knew that about you, the moment I met you. You didn't belong with that crowd in London.

I had the vaguest feeling that I was rescuing you.' He smiles wistfully.

'I think you did,' she agrees.

'I don't want to hurt Da, but I don't want Rónán to have the farm,' he says finally. 'I don't want him to feel trapped, like I was, like Da was, and his kin before him. I don't want to hurt you or Rónán, either, but if I can't have my family, what's left here for me?'

From the corner of her eye, she catches his profile and glimpses the rogue she'd fallen in love with, behind the new, harder planes of his cheeks. There's no instant attraction now, in fact, quite the opposite. She feels like a woman caught out with a younger woman's husband, unclean, wishing she could undo the years she'd spent under his spell. What she feels right now is self-pity. 'We just have to work it through. Act like adults, because Rónán needs us to.'

He nods. 'You're right, for now.'

'Da and I will work something out. But Colm, don't sell the farm. Lease it out. Rónán might want to work the farm. Did you think of that? He might love it here, as Da does, as I think you once did.'

His lips purse in a scowl. 'If he's that way inclined, he can buy another farm, one day. D'you think I don't know about the money you have, tucked away in a bank somewhere? You've been playing at being the farmer's wife. It was never a necessity. You always had options. And that gives Rónán options I never had. He can be so much more than a small farmer, clawing a living out of a patch of land that gives up nothing willingly. I don't want Rónán to be hedged in by tradition and expectations. Young Liam belongs here. He hasn't any other ambition, he's the salt of this earth, and it would kill him to leave it.'

Grainne recalls the dissatisfaction that has settled on Young Liam's face since Colm's return, and knows that Colm is right. 'So,' she says finally. 'What will we do?'

'Let Young Liam buy the farm.'

'He can't raise that kind of money.'

'Let Young Liam have it for whatever he can raise. It will provide for Da, for the rest of his life.'

'And you?'

'Me, I'll take a share. Old Tom is up for selling me the *Lively Lad*.'

'After what you went through? Colm, you can't! You hate the sea! And you don't have the experience to run your own boat!'

'I'll learn. Like everything else I've done. I can turn my hand to anything, you know.'

'And what about Da? He's lost you to the sea once. It will kill him to see you going out, day after day.'

'Da will have to finally accept that I've grown up.'

'But—'

He turns her to face him, placing his hands on her shoulders. His dark eyes soften. 'I still love you, Grainne, and if things could be as they were...' He sighs. 'But they're not. I thought, when I came back, that maybe you were thinking of marrying Young Liam, but

I see that's not how it is.'

She smiled. 'Young Liam fancied his chances because it was a way of getting the farm. I don't blame him for trying, but no.'

'Then what will you do? Maybe you'd best move back to London. Your Nigel would love that.'

She snorts a laugh at the sly look on his face. His sense of humour hasn't entirely deserted him. 'You know I won't take Rónán from you. Besides, this is Rónán's home, his people. When he's a teenager, and has a clue what he wants to be, then maybe things will change. As you say, I can support him through college.'

'When Rónán decides what he wants to be,' Colm echoes, and pulls her close, hugging her. Startled, she makes herself accept his embrace. It's comforting, in a way. It's tempting to relax, put her arms around him. She misses being held, being loved. His chin moves, hard on her shoulder when he speaks. 'Soon enough Rónán will find out what he is, you're right. Maybe I'll find some sense of purpose, too. But you, you've got your art, your purpose. I envy you that.'

'You have a talent for art, too, Colm. You just didn't realise it before. That picture hanging in the kitchen is quite beautiful.'

He gives a quirky grin. 'Art isn't for me, my sweet. I don't have the patience. That is my one and only piece, and maybe Da will have it to remember me by in years to come. You know who it is, don't you?'

'Who?' she says, confused.

'My mother and me. While I was in the water, she was holding me up, keeping me safe. She stopped me from being afraid. Let's get back. The wind's picking up, it's getting cold.'

He puts her aside, missing her shocked realisation that he is not, in fact, coming to terms with his changed circumstances, but hiding a deep psychosis.

He turns and holds his hand out, to help her down onto the slippery path. He's right about the weather. The sky has lowered even more while they've been talking. The lone yachtsman has gone beyond the headland, to safe harbour, she hopes. As they're descending, Colm smiles back over his shoulder. 'I'm glad we had this talk. Now we can all move on. Liam can have the farm. You and Da and Rónán can move into the bungalow. It will be warmer for Da's old bones, and he's not needed at the farm. I'll stay here, at the old house for now, and help Young Liam out for a bit. I'll bring Rónán there on my days. It won't seem so strange for him, and will save us traipsing over the Sheep's Head in all weathers. Then we'll see.'

Colm turns and skips down the slope before her, neat as a goat, leaving her to follow gingerly in his wake. By the time she reaches the old house, the tail of his car is disappearing down the rutted track.

She tries to explain to Da what Colm said about the farm, but it's hard for him to grasp that Colm doesn't want the farm, never really wanted it, and doesn't want it for Rónán, either.

'What if Rónán wants it?' Da asks, bewildered.

'As Colm said, Rónán can buy a new farm, one day, if that's what he wants. Maybe somewhere inland, where the weather isn't so harsh. I kind of agree with Colm. I see where he's coming from. Why saddle Rónán with the knowledge that this inheritance is one he must hang on to at all costs? That's how it is, here. That's why Young Liam can't leave. This land is in his blood. It's not in Colm's, well, not any longer, and maybe it's not in Rónán's, either. Colm's right. We will give Rónán the freedom to choose.'

'Colm had the choice, too.'

'Da, he didn't. Don't you see? There's loyalty in the sons who stay, knowing it's a life choice they might regret forever. Colm stayed because he was the only son. It was kind of an unspoken obligation. The ones who leave, even those chasing fool's gold, are the ones who have chosen to not be bound by history, not obligated by the needs of their forebears. Colm is giving Rónán the choice he didn't really have.'

Da blinks back tears and his voice cracks as he whispers, 'So, Colm never wanted the farm?'

Da's voice is sad enough for a tragedy, and Grainne hugs an arm around him. 'Da, he stayed through loyalty, but what happened changed him. It changed all of us. We can't make him stay where he's unhappy. It's good that he's come to terms with that himself. He's young enough and smart enough to start over, and he'll have some money to invest in whatever he chooses to do. It's a good decision.'

'I'll sleep on it,' Da says.

Grainne doesn't tell Da what Colm said about believing that his mother saved him. She needs to think about that, maybe talk to Lén, ask his advice. She doesn't tell him about Old Tom and the boat, either. That can wait, and maybe in the meantime Colm will find some sense.

But over the next few days, Grainne sees Da looking at the old place with new eyes, assessing every piece of home-made furniture, every rough shelf, every stone corner, as though committing it all to memory.

Chapter 16

The move to the bungalow isn't as traumatic as Grainne feared it might be. They take very little with them. Da already has his room, which has been waiting for him since the tragedy. Grainne won't hear of him giving it up. For herself, she squeezes a single bed in beside her drawing table, and makes do. Rónán has the tiny box room to sleep in, but the whole of the living area becomes his personal playroom.

Rusty comes, too, as Colm is wary, wondering every moment if the dog will attack him. He's worried for Rónán, but he needn't be. Rusty is as placid as ever, with the small nucleus of Grainne, Rónán, and Da. If he recalls Colm at all, it's not with the affection Colm is due.

Grainne watches from a distance as the man she once loved communes with his child with an intensity she has seen in no other father. He has time for Rónán. He has patience with the games and toys, and throws convention to the wind when decorating Rónán's bedroom in the bungalow. Colm's hidden talent for art shines through as he and Rónán paint it with streaks of blues and greens, and lines of light which could be the sun fingering the earth, or reaching down into the depths of the sea. The splashes of abstract colour could be shoals of fish or birds in flight. The whole room becomes a vibrant space, ripe for dreams. They buy a child's bed, and fill the room with things Rónán knows: his stuffed toys, plastic bricks, and picture books.

The cot made by Lén stays up at the old home, although Rónán has pretty much grown out of it. They have taken the side out, and wedged the rocking mechanism, but soon it will have to be replaced with a real bed, but for now, they try to make his life, split as it is into two separate pages, as normal as is possible under the circumstances.

The final touch to the bungalow is when Colm bangs a nail in the wall, hanging his seal painting where Rónán can see it as he's drifting off to sleep, or stare at in those moments where dreams are gradually replaced by the strangeness of waking. Somehow, the painting becomes the focal point of the room, and when Grainne quietly suggests, later, that it would be nice to have it in the living room where everyone can admire it, Rónán screams, red in the face, tears running down his cheeks, yelling, 'My sea my sea.'

At twenty months, the move is just something Rónán accepts, the way he accepted a dad appearing out of nowhere. It's explained that he will go back and live with his dad at the old house for some days, and be with his mam at other times, and he's too young to query the necessity. He still recalls the time before Colm blasted suddenly into his world, and is fine living with Grainne and Da in the bungalow, but, equally, looks forward to his days at the old house, too.

Grainne worries about him being cold up there, and lonely, but he comes back talking about sheep and walks on the headland, and *Liam said this*, and *Daddy said that*... So, she has to accept this reality and work with it. She gains a measure of comfort in the fact that Colm hasn't mentioned his mother again, and as the winter hardens, he spends more time on the farm than striding the headland paths.

Once Rónán starts preschool, though, Grainne feels it would probably be better if he spends weekdays at the bungalow and weekends at the farm. She mentions this to Colm, who shrugs an okay, but wears an enigmatic look that is becoming familiar, one that says *when the time comes, we'll see*.

Grainne wonders when Rónán will start to put it all together, that his mum and dad aren't living together like other children's mums and dads. But then, so many families are like that these days, maybe it isn't an issue, after all. For now, she explains, it's warmer in the bungalow for her and Da's old bones, and that Colm has to be up at the old house to work the farm with Young Liam. Rónán's young enough to accept the lie.

For a while life settles into a routine that lends a sense of peace, of gradual acceptance and coming to terms with Colm's strange return from the dead.

Somewhere in the back of Grainne's mind lurks the unspeakable knowledge that Colm was dead, and it would have been better for everyone if he'd stayed that way. There are times she wishes her mam had never made that life-changing phone call. If he had never seen her or Da, would his memory have stayed locked away? If so, Colm would have discovered a new life, eventually, in Spain, assuming he was Spanish, and they would have continued mourning the man he was, rather than worrying about the man he had become. Whenever that faint thought fleetingly surfaces, hard on its heels comes the knowledge that it's an intensely selfish thought, and it's quickly buried.

People talk of how lucky they all are, the luckiest of all being Colm. In truth, the lucky are having a hard time coming to terms with this new reality, Colm having the hardest time of all.

Beyond the warmth of Da's centrally heated bungalow, winter is now in full blast. Weather rips in from the Atlantic, and the forecast becomes a daily talking point of the close community. Will the boats go out, or should they not risk it? Will the slates hold for another year? Will the electricity fail again as ageing trees topple onto ageing lines, usually in the early evening when folk are cooking dinner? Will the sea defences hold, or will the road along the estuary, undermined by the continual wash, finally slip into the water? Will the rains never stop, and will the old roads become impassable as the run-off turns them into streambeds, throwing up new potholes, only discovered when the tyres hit them?

Sometimes Grainne pauses in her labours over the inked-in work, thinking about those brief years up at the farm. The deep enjoyment she and Colm had shared becomes more unreal with the passing of the days, like old photographs fading further with each exposure.

And there's no doubt Colm is finally growing up. In the light of his newly discovered sense of parental responsibility, and his caginess about the future, it's hard now to recall his previously ebullient nature, his gung-ho attitudes, and his careless enjoyment of life. No, not careless – driving optimism, for a future that never materialised. Without it, he's simply a young man who holds no magical attraction for her, and it's difficult to recall quite how she had fallen under his spell.

It's also hard to recall why she had been so determined not to have a child. Rónán is the delight of her life, and whatever strange chance made it happen when it did, it fulfilled a desire she hadn't been aware of. And for that, Colm is fully responsible. If she hadn't met him, she would never have conceived, never experienced the deep and abiding joy she has discovered in motherhood.

Sometimes the mornings are bright and sunny and cold, and lift the spirits. But more often the skies hang low, casting a pall over the land and the mood of the people huddled beneath it. And with the pall comes a call from Aisling: she's coming to visit. Knowing there's little room at the bungalow, she's booked herself into the West Lodge Hotel, a five-minute walk along the seafront from Da's bungalow. Grainne feels guilty for not paying her sister more attention, but in truth, she's had a lot to cope with. It's only now that she recalls her sister's comment about being unhappy, just before the surreal trip to Spain, and feels bad for forgetting. Now, she wonders what her sister had been wanting to unload. It couldn't be very serious if she was only now making the effort.

As she's pondering, she hears Lén's truck pull up outside, and a small lurch hits her breast. He's pretty much avoided her since Colm's return, though he knows her marriage is beyond rescue. She suspects, or hopes, it's out of respect for Colm rather than a cooling interest towards her. She misses his solid company, his pragmatism and common sense. She also admits to herself that she had been anticipating a gradual blossoming of their tentative interest in each other. At first it had been gratitude for company in a place that had become a foreign shore, but when the shock of Colm's death had dulled to acceptance, her interest had solidified into the truth that she felt easy with him, that she could contemplate a future with him.

At first, she hadn't been sure he felt the same way, but the odd glance, the rare shared smile were not invented, surely? Just because he had never married, never had a serious relationship with any girl, doesn't mean he hadn't wanted one. It just meant the right girl hadn't come along.

But what might have transpired between her and Lén is on the back burner, slowly cooling. Colm's return brick-walled that budding possibility, because old loyalties are preciously guarded in a small community, which is why she's now surprised when he pulls up outside the bungalow, his dented truck rattling with a sound she recognises long before it's truly penetrated consciousness. As Lén comes to the door, she has it already open, and within minutes the news of his visit will be setting out on its journey down the Bantry grapevine.

'I can't stay long,' he says, echoing her own fears. 'So, how are you? And how's the boyeen?'

He stands at the door, smiling, and her heart flips. She smiles a welcome as she would to any other person who came asking how she's doing, keeping clear distance between them. 'Rónán's with Colm today. And Da's out at Leary's, no doubt dispensing advice about the fields he's breaking.'

'Ah, no doubt. And telling them how it was when they had to do it by the graft of their own hands.'

He hovers, and she senses he has something to offload. 'Do you want to come in for a cup?'

'I will, that,' he agrees.

He fills the kitchen with the scent of motor oil and the sweat of honest labour. She's never known a man like him before. Big, somewhat hairy, his hands engrained with the marks of his profession. In another life, that life back in London, she wouldn't have given him a second glance. Where Colm had charmed her off her feet, this quiet, gentle giant would have stood back and watched, an enigmatic smile on his face, and then faded away out of a life that wasn't his, rather than grasping what he desired with both hands and taking it with him.

Experience, of course, is now hers to contemplate, and hindsight reveals her infatuation with Colm the way almost everyone else must have seen it: an unlikely relationship inevitably bound for disaster. But no one would have imagined for a moment the actual disaster that had scrunched her dreams underfoot, or the burgeoning emotional disaster the future is promising. She bustles about the business of filling the electric kettle and fetching mugs and milk and sugar to the small table, all the while, aware of Lén's eyes on her.

Ah, Grainne, girl, we're in for a tough time of it, the two of us. With Colm walking a strange path, and you not knowing which way to turn. I wouldn't have blamed you for taking the child and running, but you wouldn't do that to Colm or Da, would you? And your own life put behind you as though it has no other purpose. When Colm brought you here, I wondered what he was playing at, and, like everyone else, thought you'd run back to the smoke the moment the bubble burst. But he knew more than the rest of us, I guess. There's a strength sitting behind you. And it's just as well, because everyone is saying Colm has finally grown up, that he's accepting the situation, trying to decide what to do with his life, but there's something in his eyes that tells me they're wrong. He has accepted nothing. I've tried to talk him into seeing someone; a counsellor, a psychiatrist, but he just closes me out. Maybe he sees that I have an interest in you, Grainne, girl. Maybe not. But whatever I feel, I can't do anything until Colm has his boat on an even keel, and I know you feel the same. He loves Rónán like there's nothing else in the world, so I can't imagine what he's going to do. I just know you and Da are going to be caught in the backlash, and I hope you're strong enough to weather it.

'This isn't a social call, it is?' Grainne says finally, leaning back against the sink, clutching a mug to her chest with both hands. She knows Lén that well, even if she can't read minds.

'No,' he says slowly. 'I don't want to be speaking out of turn, but you need to know. Colm has been after going out fishing with Old Tom, on the *Lively Lad*.'

'He told me he's up for buying the boat.'

'Ah. So, you know. I wasn't sure if you'd heard. It's not exactly the path I would have chosen for Colm. And not one I'd have suspected he'd choose for himself.'

'No, it's weird. I'm scared, Lén. He told me himself, and also—' She breaks off, then takes a deep breath. 'He also told me that it was Alyssa who saved him. He said his mother held him up, stopped him from drowning.'

'Does he believe that?'

'I'm afraid he does. I thought I'd be pleased he's not scared of the water any more, but it's gone beyond that. Almost as though he's turned to the sea as his rescuer, the reason he's still alive, not the reason he nearly died.'

He nods. 'It bothers me, too. But Colm's closed himself off, won't talk to me. People say he's getting over it, but you don't get over something like that, you just learn to live with it, and I'm not sure that's happening.' Lén takes his time, stirring in sugar, staring into the tea as if the future is there to read.

'I did think, when he came back, that he'd work the farm,' she says. 'I was surprised when he turned his back on it. I thought he loved the farm, loved the life. It turns out he never loved it.'

'It was all an act,' Lén agrees. 'He just couldn't leave Da.'

'You knew that?'

'His whole life was an act. Like he was doing a comedy routine on stage. I saw glimpses of it sometimes, when he was depressed. I hoped, when you came bursting into his life—'

She smiles. 'When he came bursting into mine, you mean?'

'Ah, he was a livewire, all right. But now you're seeing the real Colm. He loved you, Grainne. That was no act. He still does.'

'He loved an idea, not me. I was the older one, the mature one. I should have known it wasn't real. I was stupid. I fell for a dream, too.'

'You're human.'

She flushes, realising he's agreeing, and explains. 'No one had ever been like that with me before. Telling me I was wonderful. Making me feel so good about myself – as a wife, a life's companion, not as an artist, a money-spinner, or a quick lay.'

Lén's voice is soft. 'Just as well he got you out of those circles, though?'

'It was magic while it lasted,' she admits, tears stinging the backs of her eyes. 'But what will happen now? What will he do? I get that he doesn't want the farm. Even Da's come to terms with that. End of an era, he said to me the other day.'

'Darragh said that?'

'Yes. He actually said, "that harsh patch of God's earth isn't so much an inheritance as a ball and chain. I should have sold it years back". He said he'd felt its weight, sometimes, after Alyssa left, when he was alone with his little boy.'

'Damn me, I didn't know he felt that way.'

'Maybe even he didn't know?'

After all, it's not until someone gives you permission to speak that these things bubble to the surface, she thinks. Are any of us ever truly honest? We all want to shake off the shackles of our past at times, to have the freedom to choose where to go, and not be bound by convention or self-imposed commitments.

Lén knocks back his tea and stands. 'Okay, so. I'll be off,' he says.

She's pleased he came around, but he's right. The gossipmongers will already have noted his truck on the drive.

'I'll tell herself in the shop that I came to see Da but he wasn't here. Now I'd better think of a reason for wanting to see him, I guess.'

Grainne loves his quiet humour, the way he sees things as they are, but doesn't judge. But then, she's still the outsider, and he's looking after Colm's interests, not hers.

When he's gone, the unfairness of it all hits her. Somehow, in all of this, she has to pay the price and watch Lén slide quietly out of her life. But who could have foreseen that Colm would come back? They'd all been telling her to move on, and she had. Then they'd expected her to simply pick up where she'd left off, pretend everything was as it once was? That would have been no recipe for future happiness, for sure.

They'll come around, she thinks cynically, and if they don't, well, she has her art, and Rónán. She thinks, again about leaving, making a fresh start. She sighs. Rónán is the only thing tethering Colm to his sanity. She can't leave. Not yet, anyway.

And what about Da?

Chapter 17

It's late in the morning when Aisling arrives, carrying Siobhan, her third daughter, who is just a few months younger than Rónán. She enters the house, staring around with interest as she hangs her coat. They hug and kiss. Aisling looks haggard, and Grainne can feel her bones through her clothes. She's lost a lot of weight.

'I brought buns,' she says, parking Siobhan in the waiting high chair. 'Where's Rónán?'

'He's with his father, up at the old place. He'll be back with me tomorrow.'

'That's good.'

Grainne wonders what's good. That Rónán is with his father, or up at the old place, or not here? But her sister's eyes are somewhere else. Grainne bustles around, again, making coffee, putting the buns on plates, then sits down. Aisling bursts into tears. 'Spit it out, Ash,' she says quietly.

Siobhan is still, watching her mother warily, so Aisling collects herself and hands the child a bun, which she carefully separates into piles of crumbs and currants.

'It's Brendan,' Aisling says, finally. 'I don't know what I'm going to do without him.'

'Oh, Ash,' she says. She had thought maybe Aisling was unhappy with Brendan, was maybe thinking of leaving him. It hadn't occurred to her that it would be staid, fatherly Brendan who'd do the dirty. She reaches a hand over the table and closes it around Aisling's wrist.

Aisling snatches her hand back. 'He's not leaving me,' she snaps. There's a brief pause over Grainne's confusion, then she says, 'He's got cancer.' She takes a deep breath. 'I couldn't tell you, could I? What with Colm dying. I mean, well, he didn't die, but we didn't know that, then, did we?'

'You should have told me,' Grainne says, slightly annoyed. 'You should have. I'm your sister.'

Aisling's voice holds a sneer. 'Yes, you would have coped with it, the same way you cope with everything else. Always the strong one. You stood up to Dad when I couldn't. You moved to London, went to college, lived the life, despite him cutting you off financially. Then you barged into a fairy-tale romance...'

She pauses, and her voice drops to that of a confused child. 'I was so jealous. Brendan was seeing me for two years before he proposed? He used to come around for Sunday dinners. He'd bring a bottle of wine and a box of chocolates every time. He courted Mam and Dad, not me. And between them, they decided it was a suitable match, and before I knew it, they were planning my wedding. We never had sex before we got married. And when we did, on the honeymoon, it wasn't romantic. It was just messy. And no matter how much I showered, I smelled of him, for the whole two weeks.'

Grainne recalls Aisling's wedding, in snatches, like photographs. In them, Brendan looks immensely pleased with himself, but that's nothing new. And Aisling was a beautiful bride, bubbling with happiness, having the best day of her life... or so it had seemed. 'But I thought you loved him?'

'He offered me a big house and stability and children. I thought that was enough. And I was afraid if I didn't marry him, no one else would want me. You thought I was so confident, but I wasn't. Not really. So, I pretty much scuppered my own future. It's not Brendan's fault. He's just who he is, and never pretended to be anything else.'

Grainne sighs. 'Damn it, Aisling. Why didn't you tell me you were so unhappy?'

'You were wrapped up in your own life.'

'Was I that selfish? Truly?'

'Not selfish. Just living. I didn't want to mess up your happiness. And I was grateful to Brendan, in a way.'

Grateful? To Brendan, for marrying her?

She recalls all the trips Aisling had made abroad with the first two children, as Brendan was too busy to leave work. It smacked of their own childhood, those holidays, staying in posh hotels with their mother, being paraded around as though they were twins. She had realised a long time ago that her mother had been making up for a shortfall in her own life, but had no idea Aisling had fallen into the same hole.

Aisling pushes the bun aside, barely touched. Grainne waits, wondering what's coming next.

'I wasn't living, Grainne. I was existing. Brendan has given me a lovely home, three lovely daughters, everything I wanted. I didn't have to work. It should have been a fairy tale, but it wasn't enough. I was buried under all that *stuff*. I was bored and lonely. And once Siobhan came along, it made going out on my own so difficult. He's kind. He hired an au pair so I could get out and about, but I was so lonely, I even considered having an affair.'

'Goodness! Did you meet someone?'

'No. It was just the *thought* of doing it, to add some kind of spice into my life. I was checking out the men I bumped into for a while, wondering which one to choose, but I'm too conventional; I couldn't do it.'

Thank goodness for small mercies, Grainne thinks, echoing her mother's oft-quoted words. She gives a small snort of laughter. 'You checked out men, like what, shopping for the right hair colour, the right body shape, the right age?'

Aisling looks peeved. 'See, you think that's funny.'

'Well, really, it is. But I'm glad you didn't do it. I have a nasty feeling you would have confessed all to Brendan, and that truly would have been a bad move.'

She gives Grainne a straight look. 'I told him I was thinking about it, in the end.'

'Oh,' Grainne says weakly. 'And how did he react?'

'He was upset. He thought he'd made me happy. He got a bit moody, then a few weeks later he told me he had cancer. I tried to be there for him, all the way, but he didn't believe I cared any more. I've lost him, Grainne. And it's not just the cancer.'

Grainne is confused. 'I thought you didn't love him?'

'But I do! I just didn't realise it until I knew he was going to die.'

'But he might not, you know, chemotherapy, operations. It's amazing what can be done these days.'

'It's in his brain,' she says dully. 'They did chemo, shrank it down a bit, but it's inoperable. There are days when he's fully lucid, but it's getting worse. He's starting to lose his memory, become temperamental. He never used to shout at me or the girls. He's losing his motor abilities. He's had to leave work. Soon he'll be hospitalised, and he'll never come out.' She glances at Siobhan. 'Aoife and Roisin know, of course.'

'Oh, hell, Ash,' Grainne says, stumped for a way to express solidarity with her sister's trauma.

'Hell,' Siobhan says, experimenting.

Grainne claps a hand over her mouth, and Aisling gives a small smile. 'She's a quick learner, I told you.' She pauses, then gets back to Brendan. 'I do love him, you know. Only now it's too late. He thinks I really did have an affair, and doesn't believe me when I said I didn't. I've always been a good wife, haven't I?'

'The perfect wife, love. I expect Brendan knows that, really. He'll come around, in the end.'

'There's no time. He's feeling enormously sorry for himself: that his planned retirement isn't going to happen, that we're not going to drift into old age together, that he's not going to see his grandchildren. He says he's too young to die. He begged them to operate, but they can't. They won't. He's angry, and on top of that, I've let him down.'

'Do Mam and Dad know?'

'Yes. I told them not to tell you. You had so much to cope with, what with Colm being found. I didn't want to destroy your happiness.'

'Only I wasn't happy, was I?' Grainne says.

Grainne had explained, though not in great detail, why she and Da had moved down to the bungalow. She grimaces a little, then says, 'It's a strange old life. You being so sure I had the fairy-tale romance, when I was living a life that was a sham, and me being sure you were content, when you weren't. I thought we knew each other better than that. But no one really knows anyone else, do they? There are always things that churn around inside that you can't tell people, because once it's said, it can't be taken back. What will you do now?'

'Nurse him. Until the end.'

Grainne is shocked by the finality of her words. 'We're both floating,' she says. 'We simply don't have any control over our lives, do we? I got used to the idea that Colm was dead, only he isn't, and I don't love him. But I can't steal Rónán away from Da and Colm, so I feel as trapped here as you did in your outwardly perfect marriage. And now Brendan's going to die, and you have to convince him that you love him, and always have. You'll do it for the children, and for Brendan. I know you will. And then you'll have to replan your life without him. You're stronger than you think.'

Grainne reaches across the table with both hands, and Aisling grips them, hard. 'I'm glad you told me. A problem shared doesn't make it go away, but at least you can phone up and talk to me now, whenever you need to. No more secrets, eh?'

'Mam always said every black cloud has a silver lining,' Aisling offers unexpectedly.

'Mam was always quoting rubbish.'

'No, but listen. If you'd carried on living with Colm, and Brendan hadn't got cancer, we would have carried on going our separate ways. There were times I thought we'd never be sisters again.'

'What a way to find out, eh? What a nightmare.'

Aisling stays for a couple of days and makes herself and Siobhan known to Rónán, who takes these new people into his life along with a couple of new words. When Aisling hugs them both and disappears on the long road back to Dublin, Rónán asks, 'Where's She an' Aunt Ash?'

'They've gone home, love,' Grainne says. 'We'll go on a train, soon, and visit. That will be fun, won't it? You have two more cousins to meet.'

'An Da an' Daddy?'

'No, love, just us two. Daddy and Da will be here waiting for us when we get back.'

'Okay,' he agrees solemnly.

Chapter 18

In the end, Grainne goes to Dublin with Rónán for Christmas. Da and Colm both agree it's something she has to do; family is family, after all.

Christmas in Dublin is strange for Grainne, exciting for Rónán. But Grainne feels homeless, drifting from one strange situation to another. Not so long ago she had thought they were all happy, her with Colm, Aisling with her perfect family, and now look at them. Their safe lives exploded into fragments and shards, the future hanging in some strange place.

Aisling buys a Christmas tree, and Grainne and the two girls decorate it, but a sense of impending doom hangs over the home. Christmas seems like some kind of medieval pageant in bad taste, but they go through the motions, for the children.

Brendan had been moved from the hospital to the hospice two weeks earlier, but his moments of lucidity are long gone. When Grainne visits to say goodbye, she doesn't recognise the ancient, shrunken, and misshapen face, with its closed eyes and bruised skin. But she kisses him and says the right words, for Aisling's sake, if not Brendan's. She tells him that Aisling loves him, and has always been faithful, and he must take that knowledge with him on his journey.

One morning, as Aisling is sleeping in the chair beside him, he quietly breathes his last, and exits the world without a fuss. The girls, at eight and ten, are traumatised by their father's death. Aisling is grief-stricken, and Grainne does her best to support her. It's role reversal time, and she recalls how Aisling tried to comfort her when she was grieving for Colm and how she had pushed her sister away. She feels guilty for that now. 'He knew you were there for him,' she says. 'That's the most anyone can expect at a time like this. He wasn't alone. He had someone there who loved him. What you have to do now is treasure the good times.'

'As you do?'

Aisling's bitter snap is justified. But even now, there are moments of their life together that rise, unbidden, bringing a smile to her lips.

Their parents turn up, and with typical bull-headed dominance, their mother takes possession of the funeral details, nearly coming to blows with Aisling at times. But they're grieving, too, having brought Brendan into their lives like the son they never had. And that was the point, Grainne realises. They did think of him as a son, and Aisling as his wife. She had always wondered why her father had seemed so distant while they were young, and realises, belatedly, that her father's desire for a male child had distanced him from his daughters. She wonders if that's why Aisling had conceived again, so late after the two girls, in the hope of satisfying her husband's desire for a boy. If so, he had been disappointed. It seems the women in her family were good at producing girls. Apart from herself, the black sheep of the family, who had achieved that prize through no desire or fault of her own.

As Grainne muses on the historic bias towards male heirs, a twist to Maeve's storyline springs into her mind. If an ancient matriarchal society dictates that the man takes the woman's name on marriage, would men still desire a male child?

Grainne had always been a little jealous of the way her parents had doted on the *good daughter*, but now realises how stifling that possessive love must have been for Aisling. When she finally kisses everyone goodbye and catches the train back to Cork, she feels the weight of her childhood lift from her shoulders a little more with each mile. But she also knows that something has happened between her and her sister, bridging the gulf of childhood traumas towards a new, adult relationship that might pass the test of time.

Lén picks them up from Cork in the truck. She said she was quite happy to get the bus, but he had insisted, and Rónán likes the truck. With his child seat high between them, he can see where he's going. She's glad Colm didn't insist. Two hours stuck in a car with him would have been difficult. How sad it is that she feels that way, when a couple of years back nothing would have made her happier.

Rónán holds his arms out to Lén, who grabs him, swings him around and then smacks a kiss on his cheek.

'Scratchy,' Rónán says, rubbing at his face, then chortles as he realises he's made them both laugh.

As Lén pushes south, taking her back to a situation that is not so much intolerable as suspended in time, Grainne's mood deteriorates. He glances over and says, 'Spit it out.'

'It was awful. Brendan looked about two hundred years old, and the cancer had pushed his face all to one side.' She shudders. 'It was a relief to everyone when he finally let go. I never got on too well with Brendan when he was alive, but there was no harm in him. Poor Aisling, to have to see him go that way.'

'Not that. Sad as it is. I mean, what's putting that look on your face now?'

She's silent for a moment, then admits, 'I don't want to go back. There was a time I loved driving down this road, out into the wild. The rocky escarpments, the rutted roads with grass in the middle, and when I saw the sea beyond the old house, I knew I was home. But now? The isolation feels like a prison. I feel as though I was let out to attend a funeral, and now have to go back to my cell.'

'Bantry's that bad, eh?'

She smiles, but it doesn't reach her eyes. 'Not Bantry. Just the situation. The farm. Colm. And I still feel like an outsider. It's not much better for Colm. He said he feels like a leper. Everyone gives him space when he walks in to a room; before, he used to be the centre of attention, the life and soul.'

'Yes, his old mates are wary of him. It's difficult all around. He was dead, and now he's not. No one knows how to handle that. Sure, *I* don't know how to handle that.'

'Do you think he's suicidal? Going out with Old Tom, wanting to buy the boat, after what happened? It would make more sense if he wanted to move inland, as far from the sea as he could get.'

'You'd a thought it, all right.' He grimaces, then adds, 'There's something going on in his mind, but I don't know what. Him wanting that boat is crazy.'

'Sea,' Rónán says.

'Yes, love, I can see the sea,' Grainne says absently. 'We're nearly home.'

'Sea, sea, *seas*,' he yells.

Then she gets it. 'Seals?'

Rónán nods, making clumsy swimming actions with his hands, as he's obviously been taught. 'Sea, sea.'

'He wants the boat to see the seals?'

For some reason that scares her. For Rónán to be able to communicate something so abstract means that for him it isn't abstract at all. It's something Colm has been talking about so much, it's real. She sinks into silence as they drive the last half-hour, and finally wind into the small road where Da's bungalow nestles. All the lights are on, and Da has made an effort to make it still seem like Christmas, with lights and candles, despite the fact that the New Year is upon them. And there he is, at the door, a beaming smile on his face as he holds out his arms for his grandson, and she knows she can't leave him alone. Then she realises that she has totally discounted Colm in that single thought. As though he truly had died out on the *Faery Queen*, and his soul is, even now, rocking fathoms deep beneath the sea.

Thoughts of Maeve surface, as they always do when storylines present themselves. What if the Colm she had loved really had died out there, in that freak Atlantic squall? What if something not quite human had come back, wearing Colm's body like a coat?

She and Lén go back out for her bags. She snags Lén's hand as he lifts one out. 'Colm thinks he's a selkie,' she says in a low voice. 'And if he really believes it was his mother out there, that night, then he must think Rónán is a selkie, too.'

Lén is shaking his head as they walk to the door. Not because he doesn't believe her, she realises, but because he does, and the thought is almost too bizarre to contemplate. 'But he wouldn't harm Rónán,' he says doubtfully. 'He loves that boy. You've seen how he is with him. Rónán is the only thing tying him to reality.'

'But the boat? Why would he want the boat?'

Lén has no answer.

'I can't let Colm take Rónán out on any boat,' Grainne says.

'I can't see how you can stop him.'

'I can stop him having Rónán altogether.'

'If you try, and he takes it to court, it would become a media circus. He's become a kind of folk-hero figure since coming home. People are coming to Bantry just to meet him, to commune with him, to touch his hand and see if his good fortune rubs off on them. Oh, and they want to make a film of what happened.'

She's shocked by the fact that she didn't know this, that the information was coming from an outside source. 'How do you know that? Who's they?'

He shrugs. 'I don't know. There was some crew or other down here while you were away, doing a test of some sort. Apparently, Colm has *screen magnetism*.'

'God forbid,' she says. 'I didn't know that. He used to joke about my series, about the media attention.'

'Maybe he was a little jealous?'

'He shouldn't be. I wish Nigel had never told anyone who I was, so that I could keep creating the stories in peace. I should have used a pseudonym.'

'Your Nige would have leaked it anyway.'

'You've got that right. And he's not *my Nige*.' She mutters a very unflattering epithet under her breath, making Lén grin, albeit briefly.

'I thought you knew about it,' he says. 'I got the feeling that whoever is doing it had spoken to you first.'

Realisation hits her. 'It's Nigel! Damn it. He knows how I feel about the media sticking their noses into my personal life. I thought we'd got past all that months back, when it became old news.'

'You'll never get past it,' Lén says, with insight. 'A real-life tragedy turned romance? A soap opera for the masses? They won't want to know you're living anywhere but on the farm with him. It seems he was quite annoyed to come down here and discover you'd gone up to Dublin.'

'He probably arranged it that way!'

'Well, it makes good TV. Everyone has a right to know, after all.'

She opens her mouth to snap, then shakes her head, smiling.

'That's better.' They hear footsteps coming down the stairs, and he touches her hand, almost a caress. 'It sounds as though Da has got Rónán to sleep. I'll just say goodbye, and be off.'

'You don't have to run off,' Da says. 'Colm knows. Everyone knows.'

'Knows what?' Lén asks, baffled.

'About you two. Colm's okay with it. He told me.'

Grainne's cheeks burn, and one of Lén's brows rises nearly to his hairline.

'Ah,' he says.

Surprisingly, Da seems to be happy that she and Lén are getting on all right, though neither she nor Lén have given the least indication there is anything between them. Or so they thought. It seems that everyone knew something she and Lén hadn't quite worked out for themselves. She glances sideways at Lén, and wonders. And if something should develop between them, where would that leave Colm?

Grainne absently answers her mobile the next day and is irritated to hear Nigel's overt bonhomie. If she'd checked the screen, she wouldn't have taken the call; not in light of Lén's dramatic exposé of the previous evening.

'Grainney, darling,' Nigel enthuses, 'I absolutely adore those last storyboards. The first few episodes are in the can, and out with the CGI for the underwater scenes. Laura is delighted with her dialogue. She loves it when she gets scenes she can get her teeth into. Keep it going, keep up the good work, eh?'

Yes, Laura probably does love Maeve's latest lines. The scenes where Maeve is at her bitchiest work so well because Laura's not acting. But Grainne decides not to voice that opinion. 'What do you want, Nige?'

'Well, now. Someone at the studio had the

marvellous idea of doing a piece on you at your home, to accompany the launch of the new series.'

He sounds too loud, too happy, which means he's nervous about her reaction. Not that that would stop him from pushing for whatever it was he wanted. 'I heard,' she says dryly.

'Oh, Colm has spoken to you, has he?'

'No. Someone else mentioned it. So, what's the story?'

'Well, you know, a docufilm. Colm going out fishing, the tragedy, the boat going under, and finishing up with you finding him still alive and bringing him home. We thought we'd do a bit of interview here and there, a bit of CGI for the underwater scenes. It'll be a blast. A really great way to springboard the new Maeve series.'

'You know Colm and I aren't together any longer?'

'Yes, yes, well, we can just gloss over that bit, do the whole romance of the thing, and end before you leave the farm.'

'So, you've spoken to Colm?'

'Yeah! Wow, that guy is one helluva presence. You should see the raw footage. My God, he's going to break hearts! I didn't know why you wanted to go off into the sunset with an Irish spud basher, but now I get it.'

Spud basher? Has Nigel forgotten that she's Irish, too? And does he realise that the area where they live is littered with innumerable mass famine graves? Whole families whose decaying houses still stand testament to the *spuds* that had blackened and rotted in the ground while they starved? He's unbelievable. Her voice chills. 'And you think I can work with Colm, pretend everything is okay between us so you can produce a phoney documentary?'

His voice hardens, too. 'He's prepared to do it, darling, so maybe you should get over yourself. Help him find his way. This could be a career move for him.'

'Is that what you've promised?'

'We've suggested it's a possibility. But he won't do it with an actress standing in for you. It has to be you.'

'You know Colm can't swim. He's terrified of the water.'

'Oh? Well, it didn't sound like it. Anyway, we assured him we'll have the works. Rescue team on hand, divers, lifebelts. All we need is a bit of a choppy sea, the rest we can add afterwards. Even do his bit in the swimming pool, if he's that bad.'

'No,' Grainne says.

'No what?'

'No, I won't do it.'

She hangs up and returns to her work. He'll want the final scenes before he decides to let her go. And in a way, she'll be glad. There's plenty of work out there for someone with her credits. What a cheap, low-down snake he is. She realises, in hindsight, he'd probably *timed* his meeting with Colm to coincide with her visit to Dublin, so she didn't make a scene, send him packing with his tail between his legs. Except that snakes don't have legs. She draws a cartoon of him with his head up Maeve's backside, and feels much better for expressing herself in art.

She's half expecting Nigel to call back, but he doesn't.

Chapter 19

Two days later, Colm arrives to collect Rónán, who hugs his arms around his father's neck, cooing, 'Daddy, Daddy.'

'Ah, you missed me, my little pup,' Colm whispers.

'Well, I missed you, too.'

Grainne watches, heart in her mouth. Is it going to be this bad every time Colm comes? Will she always wonder whether one day they'll walk away and simply not return? She bites the words back that are on the tip of her tongue. Lén was right. She can't withhold Rónán from his father. She has nothing except her own fears to use as leverage, and they would make her sound nuttier than Colm actually is.

He doesn't look at her as he says, 'Your Nige called me the other day.'

'He didn't just call,' she says flatly. 'He sent a scouting team. When were you going to tell me?'

'You weren't here,' he says reasonably. 'I'm telling you now.'

'It's a bad idea.'

'I think it's a great idea. They want to make a documentary about the squall. About the *Faery Queen*. They've contacted Niall's Family, and Aidan's, and Eoghan's, and they've all agreed. They're going to set up a fund to buy a new lifeboat for Bantry.'

Well, that's clever. Nigel doesn't miss a trick.

'And all the people who were on the quay that day, when the *Faery* didn't come in, they'll be there and they'll be interviewed and everything. It'll be a real boost to the economy, here. Everyone's really excited about it.'

Are they? she wonders. Oh, the power of a producer! She has no doubt, now, that it wasn't Colm who said he'd only do it if she did, it was Nigel. Colm had been provided with a chance to bring himself back into the fold, to become a hero to his erstwhile mates, and would be happy to make the film with an actress. He'd probably been told if he couldn't persuade her to take part, then it wouldn't happen. And if she said no, once again she'd be the black sheep, the party pooper, the outsider who stamped on the possibility of a small town enjoying its moment of fame.

Damn Nigel to hell.

After letting Nigel stew for a week or so, she sends him an email agreeing to do it, and if he doesn't get that she's presently angry enough to take her skills elsewhere, he's an even bigger fool than she took him for, which is nearly impossible.

After some deliberation, it's decided that the

documentary will be made in May, a time of variable weather conditions that will hopefully provide some stormy, overcast days with grey, choppy seas, and also a few days of brilliant sunshine, when the actual interviews could be held outside, against the backdrop of the fishing vessels.

The props team scour Ireland and eventually discover a small vessel similar to the *Faery Queen*, and hire it. It's stripped back and painted with the *Faery*'s colours, and her name is printed on the hull. It's finally motored down to Bantry, a couple of months later.

This nearly scuppers the project.

To fisherfolk, who brave the sea on a daily basis, superstition is more binding than law: sailors don't swim; never sail on a Friday; never whistle on board; don't say *rabbit*; don't bring flowers on board; don't kill the albatross; women are bad luck; cats are good luck; and most immutable of all, never rename a boat.

It's bad luck of the very worst kind. And using the name of a boat that had not only perished in adverse conditions but had taken the lives of three fishermen, adds a chilled note to the community's fanfare of excitement. There's much grumbling about bad omens, and it's not just fisherfolk who are filled with a sense of impending disaster. The air is thick with it. The film has the community divided; not just those who lost family in the original disaster, but in the breasts of every individual, the currencies of emotion versus common sense are wrangling for supremacy. The community is still grieving, and that should be respected, but in a coastal community, the promise of a new lifeboat weighs heavily towards acceptance.

Not that it would have saved anyone from the *Faery Queen*, Grainne thinks, torn by the same internal arguments. But there is the future to consider. What if Rónán grows up to be a fisherman, even a reluctant one, as Colm had been? Wouldn't she be pleased there was a new lifeboat to hand? And was there really anything in the superstitious nonsense about renaming a boat? She has always thought of herself as pragmatic, but living within a small community has softened the sharp edges of that hardened stance. She'd been amused the first time she saw Da throw salt over his shoulder, then after a while it had simply been something Da did. Like not stepping on the cracks in pavements, like saying *bless you* after a sneeze.

Grainne feels that the impending film has lent an air of stability to Colm, which is its one redeeming factor. It's caught his interest, tickled his imagination. His plan to buy the *Lively Lad* has been put on hold by this new challenge, which is easier for Da, at least, to cope with. Colm is no longer in immediate danger of throwing himself at the mercy of an environment he truly knows too little about.

And in the midst of it all is the ghost of the *Faery Queen*, bobbing at the quayside in Bantry. Grainne shudders every time she sees it, as she does now, pushing Rónán before her in the stroller. Rónán is excited, as always, at the sight of the boats, or the sea, or both. Grainne is not sure quite what Colm has been teaching him. 'Boat. Boat. Boat.' He says the word clearly, over and over, pointing at each and every vessel to emphasise it.

His internal vocabulary astounds her; she sees him catch words in their conversations, latch onto them, tasting, sensing, learning. He can string a couple of words together now, but soon enough, she knows, he will produce whole sentences. His development is not so much incremental, but expressed in leaps and bounds. One moment he was lying safely on his mat, the next he was hauling himself around the furniture. Now he's everywhere, wobbling like a drunk as he turns, grabbing at everything that isn't screwed down.

She's pleased he still hasn't got the dexterity to undo the clips on the pushchair's restraints. She's sure he'd be out and running down the quay. Living so close to the water scares her, and she's determined that Rónán will learn to swim. She discovered a mother and toddler swimming session on Thursdays, and that's where she's going now.

Rónán hasn't got Colm's fear of the water. It's warm enough, and after the first shocked minute his whole body is going, arms and legs splashing so hard she can barely retain her hold. His glee is infectious and she laughs out loud. Then the instructor is beside her. 'Duck under,' she says. 'Let him know it's safe and that you'll be back up again. Make a game of it.'

She does, and Rónán gives a belly laugh whenever she pops up, as he had when playing *Boo!* with Da.

Then the instructor holds out her hands for Rónán and says to Grainne, 'Do you trust me?'

Grainne nods doubtfully.

'Sit on the bottom. Hold it for a minute. Can you do that?'

She does, and through the shards of light sees Rónán staring solemnly down at her. She bursts up, and the instructor says, 'Again.'

Grainne sinks again and looks up to see Rónán's head under the water, watching. His lips are pressed together, small bubbles escaping. She stops herself from panicking, and smiles and waves. Rónán echoes her actions before being hauled upwards.

'It's natural,' the instructor says. 'If you get them young enough, they know to hold their breath under water. Now he can do that, he'll swim. Watch.'

She holds Rónán tummy down on the water. His arms and legs begin to paddle, almost automatically. She puts a hand under his tummy and allows him to sink a little. His face lifts out of the water, and there's a lot of splashing and blowing, as if Rónán is fighting for his life. Grainne's instinct is to grab him, but the instructor holds a hand, palm out. 'Wait.'

When she lifts Rónán, a moment later, he isn't crying, or upset. His face has gone thoughtful, and he says, 'Sea, sea.'

'It's not the sea, sweetheart,' the instructor corrects. 'It's a swimming pool, and you're learning how to swim. And you're doing really well. Good boy!'

But Grainne's heart freezes. Rónán isn't saying sea, he's saying seal, pointing a chubby finger towards himself.

The instructor blithely gives instructions for her to keep up the good work, stressing that the most important aspect is for Rónán to not learn fear of water, that she has to be brave herself, and she's doing the right thing by starting him young. Children are like any other baby mammal, she says – if you start them young enough, water is a natural element. She moves on to another parent, and Grainne is filled with a driving need to get out of there, but she hides her fear, as instructed. The session is only twenty minutes, but feels an awful lot longer. And Rónán enjoys every second.

As she walks home, she's not sure she wants to go for another session the following week, but something deep inside tells her she must. The instructor is right. Rónán must not be afraid. He must learn to swim.

Chapter 20

With May, the film crew arrive, on the back of a cold sun. There's a chill in the air, still, but the light is perfect for filming. Grainne has to give one of the first interviews alone, without Colm. He will also do one on his own. She wants to be there when he does his solo bit, hear what he says before they're obliged to stand together, holding hands. If they want to make a fairy tale of it, well, she doesn't blame them – the real story is far too complex.

Rónán is heading for his second birthday, and has quite clearly learned the difference between the words Da and Daddy, and is stringing together words, like *Daddy come*. He squeals with delight when Colm comes to take him to Goulalough farm.

But he likes his swimming days even more. He's a live wire all the time, but almost manic in the water. He's swimming now, not like the seal he's named after, but like a puppy, with his head lifted, his arms cycling madly. He has no fear of the water, and despite his age, is happy to plummet to the bottom of the little pool, and jump up again, screeching with laughter. Grainne had bought some swim aids, as advised by one of the other mothers, but the instructor had been adamant he shouldn't wear them until he could swim, that he has to learn to trust his own body. But the swim aids would be useful, later, to take the strain when he tired.

Back at home after their swimming lesson, Rónán is dried and packed, waiting for Colm. There's a knock at the door and Grainne opens it expectantly, only to find Nigel's narrow face beaming as if he's the prize she's been waiting for. He's dapper in his too-tight jeans, overlarge jacket, and a lurid orange shirt, largely unbuttoned. He hasn't dressed down for his foray into the wilds of Ireland.

'Grainney, love,' he says, stepping in without invite. He catches her up in a hug and kisses her cheek before she can protest. It's the overt kind of social statement she's grown unused to. It intrudes on her personal space.

'Nige,' she says flatly.

He's too self-involved to notice the tone. 'Damn it, it's been a bloody age since we've caught up. Any chance of a cuppa? Then we can discuss your interview, and I can update you on the itinerary.'

She indicates the kitchen, and follows him in. They are alone, save for Rónán, who is staring at the stranger as if he's come from another planet, which is almost the truth, and Rusty, who isn't sure whether to bite the stranger or lick his hand. Da is up in the town somewhere, taking a message, undertaking some chore or other he doesn't feel the need to explain.

Grainne isn't much interested in the itinerary, except learning where and when to avoid the whole film crew. But she's seen shoots before, and knows that will be impossible. They will simply barge in, do what they have to do, and leave once they have what they came for. It will be bedlam. The locals will be alternately annoyed and charmed, putting up with the disruption for the kudos and influx of income into the small town.

Nigel tells her little that she hasn't already worked out for herself. There must be no hint of the romance going sour. She must smile, and behave as if she still thinks Colm is the best thing since sliced bread.

She dresses carefully for the interview. She has to seem both sophisticated and native. A challenge. She thinks she's achieved it, with the kind of outdoor wear the horsey set choose: a Barbour coat, brogues – plain but expensive. A little make-up, but not too much. And, of course, Rónán. He's her trump card, really. All eyes will be on the magic child who had turned up unexpectedly after Colm's perceived demise.

When she arrives, the crew is already there, setting up alongside the quay. They're lucky. It's a mild day, and the sun ices the water with a layer of glycerine smoothness. She is ready to charm, disguise her true character, which is not so much vindictive as outraged. Nigel struts over the cobbles with precise little steps, dragging a polished presenter in his wake. 'Grainney, darling, this is Caroline. She's going to go through a few questions with you before we start.'

Grainne shakes hands with Caroline, no more deceived by her gloss of friendliness than she is by the sea's present tranquillity. Beneath the surface lurks a monster who simply wants to feed. The questions Caroline rips speedily through are exactly those she had asked herself, so she'll have no trouble answering honestly and openly.

Amidst what seems like absolute pandemonium, order gradually surfaces. The stage is set. A growing audience is pressing as close as they can, wanting to be here, in the making of history, wanting a moment of glory beaming with smiles that are too wide, too desperate. *Did you see me on TV last night? That was me, there, on the left, look, with the blue coat on.*

Grainne is calm now. This isn't new to her, but Rónán is wide-eyed, solemnly drinking in the strangeness. A cameraman is filming background takes, snippets of which might be included in the final airing. She's very careful to keep a neutral expression plastered on her face at all times, knowing all too well that fleeting expressions can be coupled with inappropriate commentary, creating lies from truths.

The press is here, too, the reporters not even trying to hide in the crowds, but she's not sure what angle they are seeking. Their presence is overt, pushy, as they capture the crew filming the rushes – the unedited, raw visual and sound footage from the day's shooting.

Big fish eat little fish, she thinks sourly, and out there in the depths of the Atlantic is something so big it swallows great white sharks for breakfast. She wishes it would rise out of the water and swallow the press in a single bite. This is worse than the media horde that had besieged her when Colm had been discovered. Then, everyone had sought sentimentality, a sugar-coated, happy-ever-after story to offset the continual blast of media negativity. Now, they're seeking the chink in the armour, looking for something that's been hinted at, but not verified, that this isn't a love story, after all.

She's pleased when Nigel finally calls for action, and she feels distanced from her own responses, as though she's standing on the outside, looking in, untouched by emotion. She holds Rónán in her arms for a while, then puts him down to stand at her side, his hand in hers.

She isn't sure at what point Colm turned up, but suddenly notices him watching. His eyes catch hers and he gives a little thumbs-up. Rónán sees him at the same time, pulls free and runs to Colm, yelling, 'Daddy, daddy.' The cameras swivel, en masse, to follow. Smiles break out behind emotional tears, as Caroline says, 'I was told you'd rather Colm had died?'

It was the back-hander she'd been expecting. If Caroline had been trying to prompt a careless remark, she was to be disappointed.

'That's a rather stupid accusation,' Grainne says

pointedly. 'Whoever invented that untruth should have the courage to tell me to my face so that I can put them straight about my love for Colm, and his for me.'

Her gaze roves the crowds, but as far as she can see, no eyes shift from her direct challenge. She guesses it was Marie. Over the last year, rumours had trickled through the community about Marie's Deirdre, who had apparently considered herself jilted when Colm had come back from London with some socialite in tow. She'd thought they had an understanding.

Colm thought otherwise.

Devastated by Colm's seeming betrayal, Deirdre had gone to Galway and got herself pregnant from some drunken langer, and was there now, stuck in a doomed relationship, with a baby to mind and little enough to live on. It's easy to blame others for the failings of your own precious offspring, Grainne thinks, but Marie should know it wasn't Grainne's fault.

In hindsight, she wouldn't be surprised to learn that Colm had had a fling with Deirdre at some stage. He'd never suggested he'd been celibate, but Grainne was the first one he'd wanted to marry.

That she believes.

When she's finished, it's Colm's turn. He's good, she thinks. He acts the fool for the camera, but there's something in his dark gaze that teases the wishful minds of the watching women. He has screen presence, sex appeal, as Lén had suggested, but his absolute lack of fear of cameras or the media takes her by surprise. She had seen it a little when the media had hounded them from Spain, but now he's in his element. He fields shouted questions as if he's been doing it all his life, with clever repartee and profound insight. It helps, of course, that he's carrying Rónán the whole time, and that Rónán is clutching him around the neck, nuzzling him.

'And what about going to sea again?' Caroline asks. 'When they start to film, and you set out on the *Faery Queen* once more, how will you handle that, do you think?'

'It's not the *Faery Queen*,' Colm says, neatly avoiding the question. 'It's a prop. The *Faery* is at the bottom of the sea with my mates.'

'Sea,' Rónán says, pointing behind him.

Colm smiles and kisses him. 'No seals today, pup.'

But Rónán insists. 'Sea, sea, sea!'

Colm turns. Only a few yards from the quay, a large grey seal is floating on his back, curiously eyeing the assembled, mismatched crowd. All attention refocuses on the water. Cameras swivel on their stands, and the director is yelling, 'Get closeups and get that bloody idiot out of the shot!'

The seal watches them for a long breath, then gives a single bark, rolls over, and slides silently under the surface.

Grainne thinks she sees him rise, much further out, but the sun breaks the surface of the water into mirrored shards, distorting reality.

'Clever boy,' Colm says, lifting a giggling Rónán

above his head, then smacking a kiss on his cheek. 'You were right, after all. It was a seal.'

And the camera crew got that, too.

When Grainne is invited back to finish the interview with Colm, he puts his arm around her and gives her a fleeting kiss. 'For the cameras,' he whispers. 'Don't worry. We'll get through this. It's going to be fine; you'll see.'

Grainne isn't sure what's going to be fine, but it's nice to see Colm being a bit more like his previous self. She wonders if he really is coming to terms with everything, after all. But Lén's words rise from some half-forgotten conversation: *You never see the real Colm; he's always acting up for the audience.* And maybe, this time, he still is; acting up for the biggest audience of his life: world TV.

Chapter 21

A few weeks after the excitement of those first interviews dies down, filming begins in earnest. Anyone who's never seen a film being made must be marvelling at the quantity of cameras, electronic equipment, satellite dishes, leads, vans, and people required to make an hour and a half of film. They bring an influx of caffeine-fuelled city-speak to the previously sleepy market town, and a few of the local establishments, whose yearly trade is largely supported by, at best, two months of tourism in the summer, benefit massively. Everyone else seems to be walking around in a daze, wondering if they're living in an alternative universe.

The weather dictates the atmosphere at any given moment, so the crew chases all over the Sheep's Head peninsula seeking those fleeting magic moments, filming hours of rushes that will be snipped to seconds.

This time is strangely disconnected from Grainne's present reality, but, somehow, she manages to be the person she's required to be. Her placid acceptance of each moment is a veneer stretched thin over her emotions, and other than Da, she's not sure if anyone is even aware. Nigel certainly isn't. His rhino-skin of self-importance is glued firmly in place, and maybe, for now, the community wants to believe that the romance of Colm and Grainne is intact. Everyone needs a fairy tale sometimes.

Grainne plays her part when asked: one moment standing on the rocks in the rain, mourning Colm's death, the next dancing with him at the wedding where they had met and fallen instantly, amazingly in love. Another time she's back at the memorial gathering, a year after the tragedy, another woman's baby in her arms. The community, as a whole, is largely excited, tickled to be part of the project, despite its origins.

The few who object do so by discretely opting out. It seems to be a trait specific to West Cork, to be so conscious of the feelings of others. Whatever might be murmured in the privacy of the home, outwardly everything is nice, wonderful, good, talented; even when it's not. She's learned to listen to praise with a grain of scepticism. She recalls Katie saying, '*Oh, do you mind Caitlin's Eilis, who's opened the art shop? Such a brilliant artist, you know. You should go and introduce yourself, you'd get on, for sure...*'

So, Grainne had gone, but hadn't introduced herself. The girl had a reputation that exceeded her talent, the work barely competent. Beyond this parochial community, she doubted people would be so mindful of the artist's feelings. But Grainne wouldn't be the one to tell her.

In a way, Grainne likes this community spirit, with its overt tolerance and kindness; it's rare enough, and she wonders, in fact, if it hasn't made her a better person.

Though she goes along with it, she finds the filming unsettling and bizarre, but Colm is in his element. If ever there's a film star in the making, it's him. He does whatever is demanded of him, and everything he does adds something stunningly brilliant, stealing each scene. His childlike joy, which had entranced her when she met him, is back in force, charming everyone, especially Nigel, who's making the picture of his life, and knows it. He's dreaming of Oscars and wealth and fame. He's dreaming of Hollywood and houses with swimming pools under a hot sun.

She wonders if Colm is dreaming of these things, too.

Despite his present facade of a man having the time of his life, living the dream, there's a part of him that now remains hidden: the part he discovered in an adventure that was a nightmare made real. Grainne knows, even if no one else can see it, that the experience changed him forever. She recognises that enigmatic response to a question, that hint of something left unsaid and concealed.

Perhaps she should be worried, but as Lén said, when she voiced her concern, let's wait until the film crews have gone, and Bantry sinks back to being the sleepy town it normally is, and see what transpires. Let Colm have his moment of glory; after all, whatever is going on in Colm's confused mind, he'd never hurt Rónán.

She believes that. His love for his son is genuine, if a little too consuming. Colm's outward attention to his son is generally perceived as a wonderful gift for Rónán – what a rare thing, to have a father so caring, so involved with his child! – but to Grainne it's scarily obsessive. She's hoping that the whole filming thing will distance him slightly from his infatuation with his son.

Meanwhile, Lén has made himself useful to the film crew as a mister fix-it, with his wide skillset and knowledge of local artisans and those skilled in necessary trades. Grainne sees him often enough, and they exchange a casual word in passing, with a caution reserved not for the Bantry grapevine, but for the endless round of reporters on the lookout for scandal or a new twist to the old story.

There's an overwhelming belief, or hope, within the community that the love story in the film will become fact, but Grainne knows this is false hope, driven by the dream machine, and wonders if Colm's overt acting up to the camera is a bubble that will dramatically burst when the film crew pack their bags and head off to some other location.

Maybe, just maybe, Colm will go with them.

That inexplicable charisma that works so well in person becomes magnetic on film. It would not be unreasonable to suppose that his screen debut will result in other commissions. It might turn out to be a blessing in disguise. She could stay with Rónán in Bantry, and Colm could come and be father whenever he wanted. He couldn't be a film star and a full-time father at the same time.

But, here and now, the filming is drawing to a close, the crew waiting only to shoot the moment when the *Faery Queen* founders. Those final, dramatic moments will be cobbled together in a mix of live action, archived storm footage, and CGI. Actors have arrived to play the parts of Aidan, Niall, and Eoghan. Colm will play himself. Grainne wonders at his ability to laugh and joke with these men who are pretending to be the friends, now dead, who had set out with him on that fateful morning. It seems as if he's put the emotions of his experiences in a mental box, and firmly battened down the hatch. He talks of the event as if it had been no worse than a fishing trip with his friends that got rained-out: a horrible experience, at the time, but something to joke about after everyone was dry and a little merry with relief.

Chapter 22

As the filming draws to a close, every moment is squandered money, as the film crews and actors are on standby, the directors viewing the unseasonably good weather with irritation.

A few days later, an oppressive wall of cloud heralds a massive low front driving in from the Atlantic, conveying a rare buzz of delight. As the sea heaves, scaled with an ominous battleship grey, Nigel screams orders ineffectually into a rising wind. The *Callybird* and the *Lively Lad* are standing by, and it seems as if the whole of Bantry is out to watch.

Grainne watches the camera crew don life jackets and take to the sea, an ungainly lifeboat bobbing heavily in their wake. The small cavalcade motors past the graveyard, past Whiddy Island and Bere Island, towards the Atlantic. Up to now there has been an upbeat mood around the docufilm – time has passed, and surely it isn't wrong to let the world experience the full extent of the tragedy? But now, lines of figures straggle the walkways on the Sheep's Head peninsula, buffeted by a strong onshore wind, and silence hangs over the packed quays and waterfronts. Hoods are drawn up as a faint spit hits the air, and the temperature plummets. No one says as much, but Grainne doesn't think she's the only one sensing doom in the air, as if the re-enactment is about to go horribly, tragically wrong: are they tempting fate, going out in the face of a storm-force warning, simply to make a film?

At the least, it seems irresponsible.

The wind registers force five, rising through six at the moment, but the boats aren't planning to go too far from shore. Just beyond the shelter of Bantry Bay, where a large swell will be heaving, three or four metres in height, the tops cresting with knife-thrusts of blown spume as if the petulant sea is contemplating a full-on tantrum but can't quite make up her mind. It could turn to nine or upwards in a second.

Grainne's selkie hero comes to mind, unbidden, and a new storyline writes itself in her head; even as she's watching the boats wallow in a heavy rolling gait, she's weaving a sub-plot into the episode. It's what her story needed to give it depth: Manannán mac Lir, a spurned sea god whose frustration lashes the sea into a frenzy...

The boats are lost to sight as gloom descends further.

It would be usual for a crowd like this to evaporate in the face of the approaching storm, but no one moves. The crowd waits, holding its collective breath. Grainne is pleased Da is looking after Rónán. She wants to stay, too, as the afternoon darkens beneath the rolling clouds.

She hopes Da will understand.

When the boats are spotted battling back into the bay just an hour later, tension is released in a spontaneous sigh. As if thwarted of the joy of the hunt, the wind falls away, and a heavy rain sends the crowd running for cars, for home, the uneventful outing being, though no one would admit to it, something of a let-down.

As the boats tie up against the quay, camera crew and actors battle to swiftly pack equipment into the waiting vans. Nigel sees her and emits a beaming smile. So, they got their shots, then. CGI is all very well, but nothing beats actual footage of the boats dipping and weaving in and out of the deep troughs. She knows how it works. They'll add more spume, more wet, more clouds, and when the final film is out, viewers will be perched on the edges of their seats, hoping the fishermen make it back against a force that's almost unbelievable. It won't seem like a remake; it will seem absolutely real, in the moment. They'll be there, out in the cold, the wet, living the experience, while safe in the knowledge that they're sitting in their own living rooms.

'Where's Colm?' she asks. 'Is he okay?'

Nigel puts a companionable arm around her. 'Your husband's a bloody star,' he enthuses. 'Bloody amazing. I've got a few contacts around. I'm going to get him some deals, you wait and see. He's got presence, but there's something else, too...' He pauses, the words eluding him.

She gets it, though. Colm has got something

indefinable, something almost other-worldly. It's what attracted her to him in the first place. And Nigel is going to worm his way into being Colm's agent. She almost laughs at the transparency. If this film doesn't do it, Nigel will ride to Hollywood on Colm's back.

'Where is he?' She scans the bay for him, then follows Nigel's of sight to watch the lifeboat tie up at the quay. As she would have expected, the volunteers had waited until the trawlers were in safely. Then she sees Colm, wrapped in blankets, being hustled off the lifeboat and into a car.

'What happened?' she yells, pushing Nigel's arm away. She takes a few panicked steps, but the car drives off quickly, without waiting for her. From her peripheral vision, she sees cameras turn to follow her. They couldn't have failed to catch her anxiety.

'He jumped in,' Nigel says, beaming. 'You should have seen it. It was amazing. The best footage ever.'

'You bastard,' Grainne whispered. 'You know he's afraid of the water? He can't swim?'

Nigel is taken aback. 'Of course he can. Anyway, he had a life jacket on.'

Anger laces her clipped words. 'You should not have asked that of him. Not after what he went through.'

'I didn't. We discussed it, and the experts said no, it was too dangerous. We were taking shots of him at the stern, and he just jumped over. Jesus, that sea was scary. He's a nutjob. A freaking *glorious* nutjob. We got real footage of him in the water, on a line, with the waves breaking all over him.'

'He could have drowned!'

Nigel shrugged. 'Tell him that, not me. Anyway, the lifeboat guys managed to snag the safety line and pull him in. Nothing lost, eh, Grainney, love? Shall we get out of this rain?'

She's torn between punching Nigel, and running after Colm to make sure he's all right, but suddenly it doesn't matter. It's done. 'Where have they taken him?'

He pointed with his chin. 'The hotel. Hot bath, fresh clothes, a couple of whiskeys; he'll be as right as rain. Look, don't you worry about lover boy, Grainney girl, he's got a hot career off the back of this. He'll never have to shear another sheep.'

'He didn't shear them,' she says inconsequentially. 'Frank does that.'

'Oh, well, whatever. You know, I really didn't get why you'd fly off to a dump like this, but having met the guy, I get it. What a freaking fantastic character. You're one lucky lady.'

A car pulls up and the driver taps the horn. Nigel clumps her on the arm. 'Climb in, Grainney, love. We're going to have a hell of a wrap party. Starting early. The hotel's done some grub.'

'I've got to get back to Rónán. And I've got a storyboard to finish.'

For the first time ever, Nigel seems uninterested in her storyboard. She wonders if he sees himself finishing this next series, or even starting it. With his new protégé to tout, he's got his eyes firmly on a different kind of future. 'You'll be off tomorrow, then?' she adds.

'No, a day or so. The lads with the truck have to be off in the morning to get the ferry, but we need to get a chat in before I leave. Me and you and Colm. Go over the contractual details. I'll be getting the flight from Cork, after.'

Grainne walks back down the narrow concrete path to the bungalow, watching the sea lash against the wall. It's not high tide yet, so it's likely the walkway will be impassable later. But she doesn't mind. She's not intending to go out tonight, party or no party, storm or no storm. In fact, with Colm revelling in his newly discovered stardom, and Nigel holding court, that's the last place she wants to be.

She opens the door to her home, and her child.

'Mammy!' Rónán yells, leaping at her. 'Where Daddy?'

'Daddy had to see the men about the film, darling,' she says. 'They will be going tomorrow. Most of them, anyway.' She looks over at Da with some relief, and shifts Rónán off her leg in order to peel off her wet gear.

'So, is it finished?' Da asks.

'Nigel and a couple of guys will be here for a day or so. He wants to go through some contractual stuff with Colm.'

'And yourself, Grainne.'

She smiles. 'It's Colm Nigel's interested in. He wants

to make a film star out of him. I'm just the sideshow, the obligatory foil.'

Da shakes his head, smiling. 'You're no one's sideshow, love. But I'm pleased for Colm.'

'Me too. It offers him a future, I guess. Not the one he had planned.'

'I don't think he had anything planned, girl. Well, we'll see, won't we? I got fish and chips for tea.'

She kisses him on the cheek. 'Thanks, Da. I didn't feel like cooking.'

As they sit in companionable silence, Da's away in his own space, and Rónán is consuming and consumed by the unexpected treat. A profound sense of relief settles on Grainne's shoulders.

Maybe it's nearly finished.

She's pleased that Colm's traumas have unexpectedly opened a future that suits his personality in a way farming never did. He'll still be part of their lives, but he can also become himself, the man he was meant to be.

He revelled in being the centre of attention during the filming, and she recalls, to a lesser extent, that he's always been like that: at the wedding where they met, on their honeymoon, and in the pub. It's suddenly, blindingly obvious. If anyone was born to be a film star, it's Colm.

There are decisions to be made, and she knows that life has a way of making sure you never get complacent, but, finally, she can see the way to a future, for all of them.

Chapter 23

Two days after Colm filmed his unexpected grand finale, the storm has blown through and the sun is visible between the trailing remnants of cloud. Bantry is shunting back to normality, waiting for the first straggle of tourists, and Grainne is feeling positive about the future for the first time in ages. She has no doubt that the film, when it airs next year, will bring a flurry of interest to the area, but after, as always, West Cork will settle back into its own unhurried routine.

When she receives the invitation for a farewell blast from Nigel and the remaining film crew, she's half inclined to refuse it. Nigel never does anything unless it directly benefits himself, but what else could he want from this community, from her? Surely there's nothing left to say? But Da says Colm will be there, too, so they ought to go. She knows Da is suggesting that this might be Colm's farewell, and she needs to support him, if that is the case.

Nigel has rented the whale-watching boat for the event.

In the normal course of events, there's more chance of seeing basking sharks and dolphins, and of course, the ubiquitous seals that populate the fringes of the rugged coast, than of seeing any whales. But the boat is there to catch the imagination of bored tourists. Expecting to be enthralled by the bleak romance of their ancestors, they sometimes discover an alien environment with a dreary past, and not a shopping mall or amusement park in sight. Whale-watching at least holds the promise of something different in a land that isn't quite as romantic as the brochures make out, especially when it's cold and wet.

Lén turns up to walk Grainne and Da to the boat. His appearance is unexpected, but she can't keep the pleasure from her face; they see little enough of each other. 'You're coming out on the water?' she teases. 'That's brave!'

He glances up at the sky, with its few indolent, fluffy clouds. 'I'm taking a chance, sure. But I suppose it had to happen, eventually. I'll carry Rónán down the way, then you won't have to worry about what to do with a pushchair.'

She hesitates. 'What about Colm?'

'It was him who told me to bring you. He said he'd feel happier if I was there to help. He made a point of asking me, so I can only suppose he's come to terms with it.'

'It?'

'Us, I suppose.'

'There's an us, then?'

'I'd like there to be.'

Something lurches in her middle, but she nods and smiles as if this is an everyday occurrence. 'Okay, so.'

His hand brushes hers in promise.

When they arrived at the quay, Colm is already there.

'Daddy!' Rónán screams, reaching out.

Colm laughs, takes him from Lén, and hoists him up into the air, eyes locked on his face. He hugs him, while Rónán nuzzles into his neck. Grainne is glad, in the end, that she fell pregnant, after being so determined that motherhood wasn't such a good idea. Rónán might well have saved them all.

Colm's seeming lack of jealousy at seeing Lén by her side suggests that he has accepted the inevitable; not just with good grace, but maybe with some relief, knowing that his son will be loved and cared for while he's away doing other things. And yet, again, Grainne feels a slight shiver of disquiet. Is it really so easy to believe that Colm would be happy for another man to play father to his precious child while he bombs off to London, and possibly America, to pursue a film career?

But his is not the demeanour of a man who's going places, leaving his son behind. She wonders, again, if Colm is intending to snatch Rónán, and decides that until Colm leaves, Rónán will not leave her side.

'Want to go for a boat ride?' Colm says, pointing at the vessel.

Rónán screams with delight, yelling, 'Sea boat, sea

boat!' as Colm carries him on board. He's the only child there, and the skipper asks if Rónán needs a life jacket, but Colm shakes his head, laughing. 'I think he'd just throw a wobbly, and it's dead calm. I'll have a care to him. He's not going in the water without me!'

Grainne casts an anxious glance at Lén, and the moment of happiness is shattered.

'He didn't mean that literally,' Lén whispers as they are hustled on board by Nigel, who is in his element. He's providing a final fling for the locals who had taken part in the re-enactment; being master of ceremonies and his own jester at the same time. He's wearing tight jeans, loafers, a leather waistcoat over a bright yellow shirt, and a designer jacket, topped ludicrously with an Irish tweed flat cap. She doesn't know a single farmer who wouldn't have thrown it to the ground and hammered it with his boots to make it look less obviously new.

Grainne guesses he's already downed a couple of whiskeys, getting in the right mood for his farewell performance. Not that anyone is as interested in him as he believes. It's a free trip around the bay, with drinks and party food thrown in. Who was going to refuse?

This time, there are no crowds waiting to see them off, and they're accompanied by just one camera on the slumped shoulders of a young man who obviously wishes he'd been sent home with his mates.

The sea is a grey mirror when the *Lazy Lizzie* finally pushes off the quay with around thirty people on board.

Some are out on deck, but most have squeezed into the basic seating area, behind salt-encrusted windows. As they motor casually into the bay, Nigel distributes champagne in plastic flutes. 'I won't bore you all with a speech,' he says, to an understated cheer. 'So, straight to the point: to the Son of the Selkie, Colm, the star of his own story.'

'To Colm,' everyone echoes.

Grainne casts a startled look at Lén. 'I didn't know they were going to call it that.'

'Me neither.'

With irritation, she realises that Nigel is focusing on the selkie legend rather than the very real tragedy that had ensued on the back of the horrific squall No doubt he'll bring her latest series into the equation, too. She suspects he deliberately hadn't mentioned any of this to her, because she would have argued against it. This was supposed to be a docufilm, and he was going to emphasise the mythology to boost the ratings of his ongoing series.

Her smile fixes to her face like a grimace.

Lén glances sideways. 'This was never going to end well.'

She sighs, pleased that she doesn't have to explain her thoughts. 'No. We have no say in what happens now.'

For the next half-hour she listens to the noise around her, the bubbling, alcohol-fuelled effervescence of duty discharged, of a job well done. She doubts that any of those present, who have played their parts with dedication to accuracy, have any idea how their words will be manipulated to suit Nigel's needs. It will become less a documentary than a fairy tale. But should she mind? A fairy tale with a happy ending is a good thing, isn't it?

Food is distributed, and Grainne weaves between a forest of knees to take Rónán from Colm, but he stalls her, saying quietly, 'Let me have this time with my son?'

She nods wordlessly, wondering if he's decided to leave, after all.

Rónán reaches for the champagne, and Colm pulls it away, laughing. 'Water for you, my boy! And a sandwich. What do you want? Tuna, cheese, or egg?'

Once Rónán is engrossed in the sandwich, Colm surprises Grainne with a soft glance. 'Tell me you'll always have a little love for me, when we finally part ways?'

'I did love you,' she admits quietly. 'I loved you so much, it was brittle, like glass. It shattered when you left me, and I can't put the pieces back together. I tried. I'm so sorry.'

He leans forward, kisses her forehead. 'You know I'll always love you, don't you?'

She gives an embarrassed laugh. 'Colm, you're young, handsome, and about to become a film star. You'll have so many beautiful women chasing you, you won't even recall my face.'

'I'm not going to be an actor,' he says quietly.

'But Nigel said...'

'Nigel never listens to anyone but himself. That's his

dream, not mine.'

'What's your dream?'

He shrugs, making a comical moue of his mouth. 'That's always been the problem, hasn't it? What's been happening these last few weeks would have been the height of my dreams, once. Becoming famous, being someone special. But it's not me, really. I'm not that person, after all. I like the farm, the silence, the space. I like the sea.'

He waves his arm to loosely encompass the open water around them, the mainland to the right, and the islands, flattened into the horizon by perspective.

'You like the sea? I was surprised, shocked, when someone told me you'd thrown yourself in the water. I thought it was just bravado.'

He grins. 'There was a bit of that, sure. But they needed it for the film. The thing is, I'm not scared any longer,' he says simply. 'You helped me with that. Your stories, you know. I couldn't help seeing that latest one, it was on the desk. In it, your guy says, *If we want to do something enough, we find the courage.*'

'Colm, that's fiction!'

'But it's a kind of truth, you know? I jumped in. I wasn't scared I would drown, because I chose to live.'

It makes sense, in a way, but not for a man who never learned to swim. She didn't know he'd seen her latest storyboards. He'd never shown any interest in them before, and had only watched one of the Maeve series to please her. And he certainly wasn't supposed to read anything into them. They aren't just fiction, but a mixture of fairy tale, fantasy and myth, never meant to be more than light entertainment.

She's confused about where this is leading. 'So, does that mean you aren't going to leave with Nigel?'

'He thinks I'm going to. He's made me all sorts of promises. But I don't really think he has any idea how we would go about things. I mean, this is a sudden decision for him, and films take a long time to produce.'

'Give him time. If there's a profit in it, he'll work it out.'

'Maybe.'

His lopsided smile tells her he knows it's not an answer. 'So, what will you do?'

There's a cry at the back of the boat. 'Dolphins! Look!'

Through the salt-splattered window, Grainne sees a dark bullet shape fly past the window, and is relieved to leave meaningful discussion for another day. She laughs, and pulls Colm's hand. 'Come on, bring Rónán outside, he's never seen dolphins.'

They push their way to the side rail and lean over.

There's a whole pod of dolphins barrelling and weaving alongside them. They fly and dive, and cross suicidally through the bow spray, resurfacing with a speed and power that exceeds the imagination. She can almost see the gleeful smiles on their dolphin faces as their joie de vivre affects everyone, bringing out a flood of smiles and mobiles.

Grainne holds her breath as Colm and Rónán lean precariously out over the water, but Colm has a firm hold, and they're both laughing. She feels a momentary pang of something lost, and wonders what life would have been like if Colm hadn't gone on that fateful fishing trip. Would she still love him? Would they be sharing this moment? She glances behind, at Lén, and his eyes meet hers, questioningly. If she chooses to go back to Colm, he will accept it, understand, and not question her decision; but she's flooded with love for the quiet giant. A love more powerful and lasting than the whimsical and impulsive passion that Colm ignited in her. It's the same deep love she has for Rónán, so inexplicably part of her psyche, she can't begin to unravel the words to explain it.

Then there's another cry. 'Seals! Look at all the seals! Wow!'

The boat slows, the engine dies. The dolphins fly on, engrossed in their own games, and the boat drifts serenely on the still water. Grainne gasps. All around the boat, seals have risen through the mirrored sheen of the ocean.

They lift their doglike, whiskered muzzles, and their large, luminous eyes survey the occupants of the boat with echoing curiosity.

Then a large, dark male barks an order, a command, and one by one the faces slide beneath the surface leaving expanding circular waves, which gradually reach out, join, and flatten.

The silence is broken by a babble of exclamations, of wonder. Champagne, dolphins, seals. The exodus of the film crew had levelled a cloud of uncertainty over Bantry, as though everything that could happen had happened, leaving the locals waking up to reality with a pounding headache after experiencing the party of a lifetime. But this is like a rainbow on a dull day, the curtain closing on an encore, that silver lining in the black cloud that Aisling and Grainne's mother had been so fond of quoting. It brings a sense of completion.

The skipper is standing by Grainne. 'Have you ever seen anything like that?' he says in amazement.

Then Grainne hears Rónán's voice over the silent heads. 'Sea gone, daddy?'

'They're not gone, love,' he says. 'They're waiting, under the water. Let's go and play, shall we?'

She watches in horror as Colm steps up onto the gunwale, Rónán tight in his arms. His eyes meet hers, and with a faint smile of regret, he tips backwards and they're gone.

Grainne screams, 'No!'

Then she isn't the only one screaming. There's pandemonium as the skipper tries to get one of the lifeboats out. He shoves people aside, yelling for them to go back inside, but they hang over the edge, gesticulating and shouting. Grainne punches her way to the rail and would have thrown herself in, but hands grab her arms her clothes, stopping her. She growls, fighting, her brain a red haze of fury.

Then there's an enormous splash, accompanied by more screaming and shouting. 'There he is, that way, that way!'

Grainne follows the pointing fingers. Lén is swimming towards a head bobbing in the water. At first it looks like a seal, then her eyes focus, to discover Rónán, doggy-paddling, his face lifted clear, as he'd learned to do in the swimming pool. She gives a faint sob as Lén reaches him, grabs him, and rolls over with the child on his chest. He sculls on his back, with Rónán clinging around his neck, gasping with shock.

The lifeboat is now on the water, and a deckhand reaches out and pulls Rónán into the boat. Lén doesn't try to climb in, he hangs onto the side of the boat as it's rowed back to the *Lazy Lizzie*. Rónán is pulled up, and without realising how it comes about, Grainne is clutching his blanketed form to her chest, her breath coming in tiny sobs. Water is dripping from his hair, and his mouth is open in a shocked 'O'.

Grainne's ears start to ring, and blood rushes from her head. She's hustled down into the cabin and finds herself towelling Rónán's head, saying, 'It's okay, love, you're safe now, Mammy's got you. You're safe.'

Someone touches her arm. She looks up. Lén is soaking wet, shivering, and someone is wrapping a tarpaulin around him. Her words seem incongruous. 'I thought you couldn't swim?'

'I don't like swimming. I never said I couldn't.'

'Colm?' she asks quietly.

'They're still looking. The lifeboat's on its way, and so is the rescue helicopter. They have the coordinates. They'll keep looking. The skipper's leaving the *Lizzie*'s lifeboat out here with two people, a crew member, and a volunteer. He's been advised to take everyone else back, and return with just crew and a few volunteers.'

She remembers Da, and looks around, but he must be on deck, searching for his son, or perhaps staying behind in the lifeboat. Now tears flow, for Colm, for Da, for herself, for Rónán.

She recalls the bit in her story that Colm had quoted back at her. It's the part where Rón realises he has to put aside his fear, accept his selkie legacy, and turn into a seal... if we want something badly enough, we find the courage, he had said. *I am a selkie. I am! And if I truly believe that, in the water I will become a seal. I will!*

It seems that Colm had believed that, too.

Epilogue

Rónán is three when the docufilm is finally aired. Grainne and Lén and Da watch, dismayed, as it plays through scenes coloured with mystical utterances, lowering skies, and an overwhelmingly enchanted landscape. It seems that everyone played a part in filming a legend come to life, and Colm, for all he said he didn't want to be a film star, becomes one anyway.

The film is the best Nigel has ever made, partially because the mix of truth and legend can never quite be disentangled. Grainne admits to herself that Nigel did a good job. He might be detestable, but he has talent.

Rónán doesn't recall much about the event, and his memory of his father is fast disappearing. Grainne's sure in a couple of years it will fade entirely. He'll just remember what she tells him: that his father loved him but died in an accident at sea.

He'll learn the truth one day, or what now passes for truth, because Colm has also become a legend. His body never turned up, and everyone on board that day talked of a large, dark seal that followed them all the way back into Bantry.

Colm's unfortunate mother probably had a sad story to tell, but had been too afraid to tell it, and Colm, not surprisingly, given the circumstances, had eventually lost touch with reality. In the back of her mind, Grainne carries the fear that as Rónán grows, his fae legacy will haunt him, as it had Colm, and she cannot absolve herself completely of blame. Why had she named her child Rónán? Katie had been right to gasp and cross herself, but it's too late to change her mind.

Darragh refuses to move from Bantry, where memories of his wife and son hover over the dark Atlantic waters. He lives in the bungalow, and takes a daily walk to the bar to meet up with the auld ones and share gossip over a pint. Colm is never mentioned.

Grainne and Rónán move back to the old farmhouse at Goulalough, and after a suitable while, Lén joins them.

Young Liam continues to manage the land, and is gradually buying it, as he'd agreed with Colm. Grainne is pleased when he finally brings a local girl home to share the renovated house.

Despite the isolation, it's difficult to keep tourists from trying to take pictures of them with Rónán, the living legend, the son of the selkie. The legend will never fade, propagated as it is both by Nigel's film and local gossip, the embellished fable gaining life as it's whispered over log fires in old stone houses.

And here, in the remotest rocky peninsulas of West

Cork, squalls from the wild Atlantic continue to roar, while the seals cling to their rocky perches, calling in guttural barks as the night descends.

Author's Note

This novel started as an exercise at UCC (University College, Cork) while I was taking the Creative Writing Masters. After completing the Masters, I carried on and took the story to its conclusion. I have always loved the magical selkie tales, but instead of writing a fantasy, I chose to underpin this drama with a hint of Irish superstition.

Acknowledgements

Firstly, thanks to my wonderful husband, Robin, my first critic and staunch supporter. Thanks to my mother who instilled in me a love of fiction. Thanks, especially, to Angela Snowdon, whose editing skills continue to impress. Lastly, thank you to my readers, without whom my work would be pointless.

Review This Novel Online

I hope you enjoyed reading this work as much as I enjoyed writing it. If you did, an online review will let me know my writing is appreciated.

If you find typos, errors, or storyline glitches, don't judge my creative spirit on them. Let me know so that I can put things right. Your generosity will help me bring the published work up to a tight, professional standard.

When reviewing any work, I'd urge you to reflect on your emotional responses rather than divulging the story content. Let other readers know how the work made you feel.

Writing as Daisy O'Shea

Women's Fiction Published by Bookouture

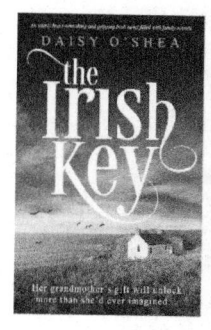

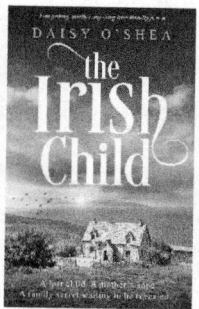

Free short story

Writing as Chris Lewando

'Suffer the Little Children' series
The Silence of Children
The Price of Children
The Loyalty of Children
The Recovery of Children

Saving a child wasn't on Deirdre's bucket list. But it might be the only thing if the bad guys get their way. No Jessica Jones, plunged into an adventure she didn't ask for, Dee discovers an inner strength even she hadn't known about.

> 'The writer's talent is undeniable as it weaves a plausible, visceral tale that effortlessly injects a dose of self-reflection alongside the soaring and plummeting of the plot points. It leaves you wondering if you, too, would rise to the occasion if you had the opportunity to sacrifice yourself to save the innocent.'

'The interweaving of mythical figures provides depth and excitement. This is a very distinctive work which is well worth a read.'

When a rift is torn in the fabric of time, immortals break into the world – but the Wild Hunt cares nothing for life, because their world doesn't know death. The immortals ride flaming horses through the night sky and hunt anything that moves. And when every living thing is gone, they will grieve – because there's nothing left to kill.
A tale in the spirit of Alan Garner or Susan Cooper, and all the legends where good battles against the evil of human greed.

'This Young Adult story is a fascinating study in character development. Liam's personal journey is portrayed in a way which is real and never descends into being cloying or maudlin.'

'The countryside in the area was like a character itself, I really want to see it in person now. The story was very well written, and had some very surprising twists and turns. I'm hoping there's a sequel. I would read anything by this author.'

https://www.chrislewando.com
https://www.daisyoshead.com

westcorkwriter@gmail.com

Printed in Great Britain
by Amazon